Breaking Into The Light

Breaking Into The Light

Dark Fey Book III

Cynthia A. Morgan

For those who Bear the Integration.

Prologue

Cowering childfey scattered at the uproar, screeching in terror and running in all directions. Two Fey of the Light followed after them, attempting to guide them back into one group. As they rushed in chaotic directions, a single crimson arrow shot out of the fissure into the center of the cavern, skittering across the floor near the feet of a fair shefey who shook her head vehemently; then stooped to collect a glowing lamp before she ran towards one of the clusters of childfey. Several other arrows shot out of the dark corridor and the shriek of a youngling pierced the darkness when one of the blood-stained arrows found a victim. The heart-breaking cry was echoed by sadistic Dlalth laughter, but peering from the shadows, crimson gazes narrowed with anger and regret.

"Shields!"

One of the fighting Fey of the Light shouted in a commanding tone to his comrades who gathered on either side of the narrow aperture from which the crimson arrows flew and, holding their broad shields at the edges, these malefey managed to cover a large portion of the crevice, thwarting the rain of crimson death, but, while this ploy effectively blocked the Reviled's ability to kill from a distance, it also enraged them. Mutters of vulgar Dlalth filled the darkness; then viperous laughter, as one of the subordinates was hurled through the obstructed opening.

This commotion caused the one named Gairynzvl to turn his head and he watched a the Fey of the Light drew his sword to severe the Legionnaire's head from his body after he tumbled through their barricade of shields. Curses in Dlalth rebuked this vengeful act and, with terrifying growls and hisses, the Legionnaires rushed one after the other into the cavern. They were greeted by the keen edges of Fey Guard blades and the skirl of metal upon metal rang throughout the shadows. Bright Celebrae turned fierce in anger and obscenities in Dlalth echoed round the chamber, muffling the whispers that discussed the unanticipated battle.

The one named Gairynzvl turned back to stare at the Great Gate rearing up to a height of a dozen feet or more before him. It was fashioned in one immense piece of ironwork; its bars twisting, curling and forged with razor-sharp blades protruding from any accessible handhold. It did not have a lock upon it, which could be undone by magic. It was constructed to stand as an impenetrable barrier between the realm of the Reviled Fey of the Uunglarda and the free lands under the sovereignty of the Fey of the Light. Behind him, weaponry clashed and screams reverberated; arrows tainted by the blood of former victims shot through the darkness, and childfey shrieked in terror as Dark Ones harassed those who had broken from the huddled mass protected behind the expansive wings of one of the malefey. The glimmering light from the lamp the Fey of the Light carried with them blazed outward, illuminating all; including a peculiar ripple of reflected blue-white light that dropped fleetingly from the ceiling or snaked behind Legionnaires. Unobserved by any of the struggling Fey, this blurred reflection of light latched onto Dark Ones unexpectedly, leaving broken bones and slashed throats in its wake. Then one of the fey warriors shouted in Celebrae.

"Cruciavaeryn!"

The Demonfey at whom he directed this spell howled in agony and crumbled to the ground, scrabbling in excruciating pain. The spell-casting Fey Guard then snatched another by the collar of his coat, yanked him backward brutally and repeated the incantation another time, his cerulean eyes glowing fiercely in the strange light of the lamp.

The dark gazes that watched locked in astonishment at this unpredicted development, but those waiting in the deep shadows did not intervene. The one called Gairynzvl glared viciously at the Demonfey causing calamity all around the chamber before raising his hands to take hold of the iron bars of the gate, in spite of the painful razor-sharp blades pressing into his flesh. Growling in rage, he shook the gate mightily.

Dlalth whispers went unheard amidst the turmoil echoing round the Gallery of the Great Gate; but, although they debated the results of the battle, no endeavors were taken to assist either side, even as the heavy gate rattled loudly; even as cries pealed from every direction. Those watching awaited the outcome while Gairynzvl leaned backwards, beating his wings prodigiously and pulling harder than before; utilizing all his body weight in a fearsome hauling, reverse motion as he shook the gate with every measure of strength he possessed. Unifying the forceful thrashing of his wings with the powerful wrenching of his body, his actions intensified in an increasingly wrathful frenzy. Screaming against the pain of the blades burying themselves in his hands, he shook and hauled upon the Great Gate until a thunderous sound pierced the mayhem resounding through the cavern.

Once again, the watchful gazes locked with astounded curiosity.

The sound they heard was both hollow and heavy, and its echo caused Gairynzvl to stop and gaze upward, watching the top of the gate as it leaned perilously inward while the heavy wrought-iron groaned with a tremendous noise. Releasing the torturously inlaid ironwork, he scrabbled backward; beating his wings to speed his escape as the gate pitched forward under the force of its own inertia, unhinging the bolts connecting it to the walls on either side as it fell. The cacophonous din it created when iron met black stone rang through the cavern with a deafening intensity and the horrendous crash caused many of the Dlalth to howl in alarm and race away into the shadowy fissure from which they had issued while those that lingered were dispatched by the Fey of the Light with startling efficiency.

The three Demonfey inflicted by the spell-caster's incantation screamed in unrelenting distress, but the fair Fey of the Light would not allow any of the others to mercifully execute them and his pitiless attitude caused several of the Watchers to gape in disbelief. Fey of the Light were purported to be patient and compassionate, filled with mercy that they were eager to extend, but the ruthless ferocity of these warrior Fey of the Light was entirely unforeseen.

"Freedom awaits!" The one named Gairynzvl called ....

Chapter One

Sparkling snow drifted downward quietly through the vast, reaching arms of the forest giants stretching overhead. The elder tree-spirits listened in the ethereal hush to the sounds of playing childfey as if such sounds had not been heard for countless spans of time. Like the contemplative evergreens, many of the Fey who had gathered in the clearing near the base of the mountain stood equally enthralled by the sounds. The wintry chill of the bright morning did little to impede the youngling's enthusiasm as they tumbled and sprawled in the powdery snow and as they scooped up great handfuls to enjoy the fresh, clean taste or to toss piles of its downy opalescence into the air and watch it with beaming smiles as it fell, sparkling, downward. As they squealed and giggled with infectious exuberance, some of the adult Fey watching their antics reached to dry unanticipated tears or hugged each other with swelling emotion at the blissful sight while others rolled and played in the snow right beside the little ones. Yet, when a fierce Fey Guard adorned with blood-spattered, golden armor alighted beside the Liberator whose hands bled from some nameless, horrifying injury, the jollity that made the bright clearing smile noticeably diminished.

"What defense can we offer against a legion of Dark Ones?" Mardan asked after he heard Bryth's announcement that the Reviled were coming and turned aside from watching a group of younglings to stride purposefully back to the place where three of his fellow Liberators stood. The malefey considered their options. They could protect the childlings by concealing them in the nearby woodland village that was ensconced deep in the embrace of towering evergreens. They could guard the aperture from which they had just emerged. Its narrow dimensions were easily defendable and could be blocked until reinforcements of Fey Guards arrived. If they were fortunate, some of the resident malefey might consider joining their ranks to offer some measure of resistance against the threat of attacking Dark Fey, but the grim reality of their situation overshadowed even their best attempts at optimism.

They had all sustained injuries during their battle before the gate. Not one of them had escaped unscathed, but Gairynzvl was beyond offering any form of opposition should a battle ensue. His strength had been depleted in his efforts to gain their freedom, in spite of the Quiroth that had briefly aided him, and the severity of the injuries to his hands left him incapable of even holding a weapon, let alone wielding one in battle.

"We must see to the safety of the childfey and the villagers, and someone must go to the Temple to alert the Elders and the Fey Guard," Bryth recommended in Gairynzvl's conspicuous silence, adding with an equally assertive tone when he saw him waver with noticeable fatigue, "And you, Fierce One, must allow the Healer to tend your injuries."

Mardan nodded, turning to call to their ministering comrade who had finished aiding Reydan and was now stooping to gaze with unmistakable concern at the small shefey held in Rehstaed's strong arms. His examination, however, was cut short when, summoned by Mardan's urgent appeal, the golden-haired Healer turned from the pair and approached Gairynzvl. He visually inspected his condition even as he crossed the short distance between them.

Their Leader stood with alarming unsteadiness, trembling from head to toe to wing-tip and staring out over the bright clearing with an increasingly vacant expression. The snow he absently held had turned deep crimson and dripped through his weakened grasp to stain the snow at his feet. His nebulous wings pitched downward in an obvious indication of exhaustion and his typically sharp gaze had become glazed and unfocused.

Hurrying his pace, Evondair gestured for Mardan to steady their friend even as he wiped away the snow he held in order to inspect his wounds more closely. The revelation of the deep lacerations crisscrossing his hands caused all three malefey to grimace in dismay. Mardan and Bryth exchanged a profoundly concerned gaze as the Healer looked up into the pale glimmer of their friend's glassy stare. As he assessed his condition, Ayla returned from the midst of a group of shefey who had gathered around a few of the childlings, her anxiety more than apparent. At her approach Mardan turned abruptly towards her and stretched out his wings to obstruct her view before she could see the full degree of Gairynzvl's wounds.

"You cannot help him presently, Ayla." Mardan's soft tone did not diminish the firmness with which he spoke. She stared up at him defiantly, preparing to rebuke his protective actions, despite the fact that they spoke volumes about the seriousness of the situation. Glancing around his broad wings repeatedly, she pointed out that she might be able to lend him strength, but when the Celebrant-turned-warrior insisted that she return to the childfey and organize their retreat to the woodland village, she decided not to argue with him in front of so many others.

"See to the childlings and their safety. Please, Ayla, we must get them as far from danger as possible." His tone was milder and although mute amber locked fleetingly with unyielding cerulean, she nodded in spite of her intense desire to be of some assistance and turned back. She glanced over her shoulder more than a few times as the malefey gathered once more around the former Dark One and spoke with lowered voices.

"I need not say it; I am certain you realize I cannot tend his injuries here. He must be returned to the Temple Healing Wards where the surgeons can properly cleanse and close these lacerations before their effects are lasting," Evondair clarified what they had already guessed and, as if to confirm his assertion, Gairynzvl's eyes closed unexpectedly. His wings fell lax, his head tilted backward slowly, and his entire body would have followed that motion had Mardan not been holding onto him. Bryth lent further aid and the two malefey managed to keep him upright while the Healer drew a bottle of Quiroth from his medical pack and attempted to administer it, despite his patient having lapsed into unconsciousness. As he struggled to get some of the liquid into Gairynzvl's mouth, he spoke in an urgent tone to the malefey gathered round them. "He is going into shock from the loss of so much blood. We must hope the Quiroth will fortify his strength while we bind his hands tightly to stop the bleeding. Then we must hasten him to the Temple."

Listening keenly to the conversation of the malefey from her place amidst the gathering of shefey she had temporarily rejoined, Ayla turned back with determination. Undeterred by Mardan's imposing presence because he now stood holding up their leader, she returned with palpable resolve. Reaching out with her hands even as she came closer, not only to negate any verbal opposition they might attempt to interpose, but to reach for Gairynzvl's hands, she ignored their protest.

"Ayla, you must see to the safety of the childfey," Mardan insisted as firmly as he could manage to sound, but she shook her head with resolve.

"I can attend to them once this is accomplished. I have been given this gift in order to help others, not only when it is convenient and safe to do so, but whenever such assistance is needed." Her single-mindedness silenced any supplementary arguments any of them might have thought to make, but she continued unwaveringly. "I have spent too many years being afraid and living in protected isolation; it is time I play a part!"

Stepping back from her, Evondair smiled at her tenacious declaration and stooped to collect clean bandages as well as a small vessel of salve from his pack while she gently took hold of Gairynzvl's hands. She could not keep from shuddering at the sight of so much blood and the deep wounds left by the razor-protected bars of the gate, but she held onto him tenderly and began to center her thoughts towards him.

In the chaos of the battle and closing herself off from her empathic abilities, she had been only minimally aware of how much he had done to save them; of how much he had sacrificed. Now, at seeing the visual evidence of his actions, she could not hide the predictable response such evidence prompted. Although she clenched her teeth against the rush of poignant emotion that sought to overtake her when she opened herself to him, she could not contain the sob and gasp of dismay that touching his pain produced. An intense wave washed over her, filling her with panic and dread, as well as a strangely euphoric sensation brought on by his unconscious state, but she did not relinquish her hold upon his hands or disengage herself from his essence. Mardan hissed under his breath at her intercessorial actions, but could not deny his concern for the well-being of their friend and, as a result, tempered his reaction in spite of her apparent distress.

"Playing a part does not mean sacrificing yourself to the cause. We need you to help move the childfey to a safer location, so, please Ay, do not over-extend yourself," he cautioned and, at hearing the others agree with his admonition, she nodded before closing her eyes. She could still hear them as they spoke quietly about how they would transport him to the Temple and about the impending battle with the Reviled, but their voices became muffled as she slipped beyond the present moment into the realm of Gairynzvl's being.

The rapid beating of his heart resounded through her, as did the shallow echo of his breaths, but the closeness of his consciousness reassured her in spite of the fact that he was drifting incoherently. After her initial assessment, she opened herself more fully to the unrelenting waves of severing pain that radiated from his hands upward through his arms, across his chest, tightening like a manacle over the nape of his neck and piercing into his mind again and again like a blade. At connecting with his inescapable pain, she could not restrain the cry that slipped past her clenched teeth any more than she could keep tears from running down her cheeks. Her body instantly began to shake and her own heart pounded under the distress of the trauma he suffered. Little wonder his mind had detached itself and released him from such torment! Baring her teeth against the shocking sensations, Ayla felt his hands move in her own and she realized that Evondair had begun his ministrations.

He applied the salve first as evenly as he was able and the perception of the cooling balm made her sigh, giving her a moment to collect her mental acuity in order to direct it back to Gairynzvl. She was briefly able to bolster his strength, but when the Healer laid the first length of cloth across his deep lacerations and encircled it around his hand tightly, the intense stinging it produced nearly caused her to fall in a swoon.

Sounds of retreat filled the quiet grove and the rush of feathers and footsteps drew her attention. It was a welcome distraction from the onslaught of his unremitting pain. Opening her eyes, she watched through tears as childfey were scooped up and carried away into the sheltering eaves of the forest; as malefey clustered in groups discussing the prospect of lending aid in the imminent battle, and as the remaining Liberators collected their scattered weaponry. Fighting to ignore the jagged, stabbing ache permeating every fiber of her being, she closed her eyes once again, drew a substantial breath and then concentrated with all the strength of mind she possessed in order to quell the trauma they were both experiencing.

Perhaps it was the Quiroth Evondair had forced Gairynzvl to drink, rather than her own skill, but as the bandages grew tighter and the hurt should have grown more unbearable, she found it, somehow, easier to ward away. Breathing deeply, slowly, restfully, she pushed aside the pain and centered her thoughts on the lush calm that surrounded him and in that place of serenity where peace seemed to flow over them like tranquil waters and delicate birdsong echoed, she was finally able to ease their mutual distress.

"While the rest of you were idling, I scouted the area." Ilys's sharp tone broke through the hush into which she had fallen and Ayla opened her eyes to find herself lying on the snow beside Gairynzvl at the feet of the other Liberators. Uncertain how long she had slipped into the unconscious quietness surrounding him, she blinked woozily and struggled to right herself as she listened to the conversation going on above her.

"Healing injuries and determining our safest course of action hardly falls under the term 'idling.'" Evondair rebuked her accusation with startling aggression and they glared at each other while the others watched in amazement, but Ilys laughed impishly, shrugged, and continued.

"I discovered the Temple is only a league or two from here, although getting him to it might be a challenge as the surrounding area is heavily forested and deep in snow. This also seems to be the only village for miles, so, my question is: who shall take Gairynzvl to the Temple and who shall remain to fight?" Redirecting the course of their conversation in order to escape the piercing stare the Healer had fixed upon her, Ilys listened to them debate for a moment, then turned aside as a distant peal of discordant horns echoed from beneath the mountain.

"The fastest alternative would be to fly, of course, but two malefey would be required to carry him and we cannot spare anyone," Bryth stated the obvious, unsure about the best course of action to take and he looked to Mardan for his input. The Celebrant-warrior shook his head as his gaze moved beyond them to the mountainside when the sound of horn calls rang into the bright clearing.

"No we cannot spare any malefey. What we require is a cart," he paused, listening keenly to the horn calls before continued. "Do you hear those horns as well? We might be forced to wait until after the battle to take him to the Temple." He mused aloud as he gazed fixedly at the base of the mountain, but in the silence that met his words, while the others listened as well, Evondair rebuked his suggestion with an insistent edge to his characteristically gentle voice.

"That would be unwise. His condition is perilous; I would not recommend delay. If needs be, I shall take him on my own, however difficult it may prove."

Several shaking heads answered his objection, including Rehstaed's, who had given the care of the little shefey over to several of the retreating villagers in order to take his place at the side of his comrades. "We canno' spare you, 'ealer; regardless o' the Fierce One's condition," he retorted with determination as he girded his weapons round his hips and across his shoulders. "If we are t' defeat those comin', we'll be needin' each one o' us 'ere t' repel them; an' perhaps more."

The others agreed, though Evondair continued to shake his head resolutely. They debated several moments longer until their indecisiveness made Ilys flex her dragonhide wings sharply and hiss at them with exasperation. "Oh, for the wit of the Ancients! You dither like oldsters! None of this will help. Make up your minds you pack of squabbling ravens!"

Turning with a harsh stare none of them could interpret, Evondair moved to stand within inches of her and glared down into her upturned face while he spoke with a low and alarmingly menacing tone. "Nor shall your belligerence, sheDemon. If you desire to continually sow discord, then return to the Uunglarda where such a demeanor is appreciated." He hissed at her with atypical hostility and they glared at each other once again, their wings arched in defensive postures. Ilys leaned closer to him, her bright blue eyes narrowing in a challenge yet, before either could rebuke the other a young, beautiful shefey stepped closer to the group and spoke unobtrusively.

"Forgive my intrusion, but if your friend requires the attention of the Temple Healers, perhaps you will allow me to transport him there?"

Chapter Two

She stood an average height for a shefey, several inches over five feet tall, and her lissome frame was delicate and graceful with an uncommon double pair of diaphanous wings that spread wide in opposing directions like a butterfly's. Translucent lavender in hue, they took on an icy sheen near their tips, while the deep, forest green near their base seemed to be reflected in the snowy- jade of her eyes. She smiled at them amiably, her cheeks and nose blushing pink from the whispering chill of the winter breeze in spite of the fact that she wore a woolen cloak over her warm winter dress and similarly woolen leggings, as well as boots that came up over her knees. A muffler of soft wool was twisted stylishly round her neck to ward away the winter wind and mittens of the same delicately knitted threads protected her small hands. Her most striking feature, however, was not her twin wings or the lovely wrappings of skillfully worked wool she wore, but her uncommonly short, tousled, bright blonde hair.

Evondair turned away from his confrontation with Ilys slowly, forcing himself to quell the antagonistic emotions she stirred within him as he took in the aspects of the unexpected stranger. His viridian gaze became a surging sea of indistinguishable emotion. The youthful shefey returned his stare ingenuously, waiting for some manner of response from the group who had, just a moment before, been arguing amongst themselves vociferously; however, when none of them spoke and when Ilys hissed sharply and trudged off, muttering in Dlalth as she went, the young stranger tried again. "The village owns a domesticated Hasparii, trained to pull a cart. If your friend needs the care of the Temple Healers and none of you are able to take him, I will be happy to transport him there."

Smiling at her unanticipated generosity, those standing around Gairynzvl nodded, gladly accepting her offer as a solution to their predicament. Thanking her hurriedly, they continued their preparations for battle; cleaning blades in the snow before sheathing them; tucking bandages into clothing; girding themselves with weaponry, and moving back towards the place beneath the mountain from which they had emerged. That dark yawning portal now echoed with the raucous calls of enraged Dlalth and the harsh noise spewed into the bright, clear Jyndari daytide.

As they departed, Ayla got to her feet and brushed the snow from her clothes while speaking quietly with the youthful stranger, who, in turn, asked if she was feeling better. Ayla gazed at her curiously. "I am. I suppose I touched his unconsciousness too closely, although it has never happened before that I, too, would slip into that state."

The stranger smiled, but shook her head and offered an ambiguous explanation by saying that it was she who had helped ease them both into a more restful place. Before Ayla could inquire further, however, Evondair stepped forward to thank her more directly. "It is very kind to offer your assistance to us." His rich, smooth-as-honey, tenor voice drew the shefey's attention away from Ayla, as did his genuine smile and guileless viridian gaze. Turning toward him, she smiled modestly and continued inquisitively while he stood gazing at her.

"Did...did you really rescue these younglings from the Child Wraiths?"

He nodded. "We did, following him." His gaze dropped to take in Gairynzvl's condition briefly, unable to disguise his concern. "It is imperative that he is seen by the Temple Healers. I cannot help him any further here."

Responding to the honest apprehension she could plainly distinguish in his tone, Ayla stooped and laid her palm against Gairynzvl's cheek as she closed her eyes once more in order to sense his condition. From the distance, another round of threatening horn calls assaulted the bright morning, the sound sending a noticeable shiver through the shefey who gazed after the retreating band of warriors who trudged through the deep snow towards the mountain from which they had come. Her evident fear compelled Evondair to step closer to her as he spoke in a softer, more reassuring tone. "Do not worry. The Reviled cannot cross over into the Light. We are safe for the moment and shall assemble our defense in order to protect the childfey, as well as the village, by the time the sun falls behind the forest fringe."

She returned his encouraging smile and nodded before she gazed down at Gairynzvl who lay unmoving at their feet. His unique, nebulous wings were nearly invisible against the brilliant sheen of the snow, but the wrappings Evondair had secured round his hands were already stained with scarlet hues. Realizing they had little time to enjoy polite conversation, she stepped back and prepared to set off. "He is sorely injured. Will the Temple Healers really be able to help him?"

Evondair agreed they would, but did not mention the fact that, he too, was a Temple Healer. Instead, he inclined his head subtly and offered their appreciation. "We are grateful for your aid, but how shall I thank you?"

Again, she smiled and the tips of her wings curled downward diffidently. "I am Kaylyya Synnowyn and am happy to help." Answering his query genially, she smiled and glanced downward demurely when he introduced himself.

"I am Evondair and am very pleased to have met you, Kaylyya Synnowyn." Unsure how to respond to his unspoken, yet evident overture, she continued by saying she would return with the cart quickly so they could get underway. She then turned to step lightly through the snow before springing into the air amid the graceful flutter of her wings as she headed towards a large complex of barns and fenced in pens set under the eaves of the forest several hundred yards away. He stood watching after her, his thoughts twisting into an unforeseen haze, but his trance was broken when Reydan nudged him. Nonchalantly handing the Healer his sword and shield with a wry grin, he indicated that he would await the shefey's return in order to help lift Gairynzvl into the cart.

Behind them, where the portal exposed by the Great Gate's falling melded two opposing realms into one, the shadows beneath the mountain heaved and hissed with the threatening vocalizations of the Reviled. Crimson stained arrows shot from the darkness, seeking any who might be unfortunate enough to find themselves in their trajectory, yet these tactics could be little more than intimidation; a warning of the conflict to come when the light diminished. The Liberators knew this and stood on either side of the yawning portal, making their presence known by creating a game out of knocking aside with their swords as many arrows as they could and by returning the insidious calls from the presently thwarted Demonfey. Tauntingly, they issued brash invitations for the Cursed Ones to come forth; fully cognizant of the fact that they could not bear the brilliant light filling the clearing, yet jeering at their cowardice.

"It is a treacherous game we play," Evondair noted as he stood beside Reydan, both malefey wordlessly observing the derisive bantering going on while standing over their fallen comrade in the silently descending flurries that had begun falling. Turning to glance behind him with a combination of impatience and curiosity, Evondair's questing gaze came to rest upon a sight he had never seen before and he could not keep from turning his head to one side in wonder while simultaneously jostling his friend to look as well.

Coming towards them through the powdery snow was a deep chestnut-colored deer, which stood easily six feet high at the shoulder. He was harnessed with light leather tack to an elegantly designed cart constructed of wood, which was carved with intricate designs and fashioned with runners, instead of wheels, to negotiate the deep snow of Jyndari winters. The massive Hasparii tossed his head exuberantly in the newly falling snow, displaying his breathtaking rack of exquisitely twisting antlers that stretched to a breadth of nearly four feet from tip to tip. The two malefey who stood watching in awe-struck silence could not contain their smiles at his demonstration and, as he pranced towards them with a high-spirited gait, they stepped aside to make way for the monarch of the forest with observable reverence.

Kaylyya brought the cart to a halt beside Gairynzvl and the enormous beast stood towering over them, blowing into the brisk air with anticipation to be underway. Wasting little time, the malefey lifted their friend carefully and laid him on the bed of the cart upon a pile of recently sheared sheep's wool she had placed there to ward away the winter's chill. Covering him with the supplementary blankets she had collected to keep him warm on their journey, Evondair found himself distracted by the lovely stranger and more than a few times had to refocus his attention to the matter at hand. When they finished bundling Gairynzvl against the cold, the Healer stepped back to consider his condition and bent over him to listen to the sound of his breathing and assess the rhythmic beat of his heart.

It was weakening. Shaking his head with dissatisfaction, he turned to fix an intense gaze upon those gathered near the base of the mountain before he looked back at Kaylyya. "It is unlikely he will awaken before you arrive at the Temple; however, he has lost a great deal of blood and, *if* he wakens, he will be confused and could become combative. Is there anyone who could travel with you to guard you against such a danger? Perhaps someone with knowledge of the healing arts?"

She thought briefly, but shook her head. "Many of the malefey are gathering what weaponry we have to aid you in your attempt to repel the Child Wraiths. Others will be protecting those who cannot fight and the younglings you brought with you out of the Uunglarda. There is only one shefey in the village with healing skills, but she may be needed here after the battle."

Evondair nodded with understanding, but frowned and turned to address his concerns to Reydan. "Gairynzvl's condition requires the attention of a Healer far more than you, here, need my dubious skill with a blade. Besides, the battle will not commence until the light fails, by which time we should return with reinforcements."

Comprehending the course of his argument, Reydan nodded; then glanced over his shoulder at the other Liberators waiting for them. "Agreed," he said simply, holding out his hand. "I would not see you go unarmed, but your shield and sword may prove more useful here, in the hands of one of the villagers, than lying in the bed of the cart unused."

Evondair concurred, taking his armaments from the back of the cart where he had laid them, but as the Healer willingly turned over his weaponry, Kaylyya reached down for something at her feet. The Healer shook his head and spoke with a resolved tone, "The others may not understand, but I cannot abandon one so gravely in need of my skills, no matter the cause."

Nodding, Reydan took his weaponry in one hand and reached to lay his free hand upon his friend's broad shoulder. "Go quickly and safely. We will await your return with the Fey Guard."

They bid each other safety and good-fortune and Ayla leaned into the cart to place a gentle kiss upon Gairynzvl's pale cheek and whisper softly to him. Unsure if he would perceive her thoughts in the depths of unconsciousness, she concentrated to make the communication as potent as her limited telepathic skill permitted, but his lack of any manner of response brought the sting of tears to her eyes. Forcing her predictable emotion aside, she embraced him as she was able, pressed her forehead to his and whispered her love for him before drawing back.

Kaylyya watched them quietly, but when Evondair turned to look up at her in a silent indication of his readiness to depart, she held up a sheathed dagger and extended it towards him. "We do not go unarmed. It is the only weapon I own, but, should we need it, you will certainly be able to wield it far more effectively than I."

The malefey exchanged an approving glance before Evondair moved to the side of the cart, took the offered weapon and secured it between the several belts he wore. Spreading his wings wide then, he utilized a single wing beat to intensify the upward motion of his leap into the cart, landing beside his unconscious friend even as he folded his expansive wings once more behind him. Settling down on the bed of the cart and drawing his cloak around himself, he was unaware of the admiring smile Kaylyya could not quite conceal as she snapped the reigns lightly over the massive Hasparii's withers and whistled a sweet, clear note to encourage him to set off.

The shushing sound of runners through snow swept away into the depths of the forest as they moved off into the distance and Reydan turned to join his friends. Those malefey of the village who intended to add their strength in the defense of their woodland home followed behind him, while the remainder directed shefey and toddlefey towards the many warm and inviting homes beneath the eaves of the forest waiting to receive them. Flurrying snow fluttered down on the grove from a crystalline sky and, for the briefest moment, the only sounds to be heard were the scrunch of snow underfoot and the twitterings of winter birds from the trees.

Then the unmistakable clangor of combat rang out from the shadows of the mountain; the skirl of blade upon shield, as well as the distinctive 'thun' of arrows flying from bows, although none of these missiles came shooting out of the portal into the sunshine. The Liberators gazed at each other with confusion as Dlath curses emanated from under the mountain and those closest to the open portal leaned precariously closer in an attempt to see beyond the swirling blackness of the void into the realm beyond where a battle was being waged.

"Ready yourselves!" Bryth called from his vantage point closest to the chasm while he watched through the haze as vague shadows and indistinct figures lurched against each other, backing towards the opening as if they were being driven out of their own domain.

"Raach!" A fierce Dlath curse echoed from the wavering maw of the portal; then a dozen or so Legionnaires tumbled out in what seemed a reverse crossing, though they flailed their weapons wildly at whatever drove them. With the first touch of Light, they scrambled to find shadows in which to protect themselves and Bryth stepped back in astonishment, realizing the Reviled were not issuing forth in full attack, but rather, in defense of themselves.

Once on the Jyndari side of the portal, they could not escape the bright, winter sunlight and instantly began to howl under its searing effect, but, regardless of their mishap, Mardan growled vengefully and rushed forward with his blade raised aggressively. Rehstaed followed closely, his own blade swinging in a precisely controlled arc to dispatch as many of the yowling Underlings as he could. Discordant peals of Dlalth horns pierced the shadows of the portal and rang out into the bright clearing another time. It was a bizarre overture to even more Legionnaires stumbling backward through the crossing, their weapons raised against whoever or whatever forced them to cross rather than in any sort of offensive posture against the Fey of the Light. As they stepped into the Light, several subordinates clamored off into the closest dusk created by the overhanging forest, but these were pursued by villagers armed with shovels, hayforks and scythes and their fates were soon after betrayed by the echo of screams.

The Fey of the Light defended their side of the portal against this peculiar act of crossing until the sounds of combat no longer issued from the opposite side. Every one of the Legionnaires who crossed over was eliminated; save one, who was disarmed and restrained for questioning. With Reydan holding one arm and Rehstaed the other, they dragged the scrabbling Reviled One into the full shimmer of the noonday sun. Mardan stepped in front of the panting demon-spawn, grasped his collar tightly and raised his free hand over his head in a threatening posture. "Tell us why you crossed into the Light or I will cast the Spell of Inflicted Pain upon you and leave you to die in agony!"

Cerulean fire pierced the deep crimson of the Dark One's eyes, but he spluttered in Dlalth as if he had no comprehension of the common tongue. Tightening his grip, Mardan arched his wings in a daunting display of bristling feathers. "Tell us, you filthy blaylscith!" he growled menacingly, but, again, the Dark One only babbled incomprehensibly. Drawing a deep breath, Mardan shook his head and prepared to cast his spell, but Bryth stepped behind him to grab his hand firmly, distracting him long enough to keep him from delivering the lethal incantation.

"Wait."

Mardan glared over his shoulder at the Fey Guard captain and hissed in reply. "Why?"

"Look at him, Mardan. He is barely older than the childfey we just rescued."

Mardan turned back to stare at the thrashing Demonfey with loathing, his brilliant blue gaze filled with revulsion as he looked upon the pallid-skinned, blood-eyed, filth-covered Fey before them who writhed under the radiance of clear, bright light and spewed out Dlalth curses in a frenzy of speech that left him frothing.

"Perhaps he does not remember our language," Bryth suggested. Then with an astonishingly compassionate tone that caused the others to stare at him in surprise, he continued more thoughtfully. "If what Gairynzvl told us is true, only the Ancients know what must have happened to him."

Mardan considered as he watched the gray-mud splattered Demonfey hiss and flail unceasingly. "What, then, do you suggest we do with him?" he ground out, clearly unwilling to offer mercy, but uncertain enough to debate the issue.

Bryth stared at the young Legionnaire as well, his gaze taking in the length of the spines protruding from his wings, which he could easily use as weapons despite the fact that they had taken his sword from him. "I am not certain," he paused, speculatively; then he and Mardan locked gazes. "But do not cast your spell."

Glaring at the Dark One another time with evident disgust, Mardan released his grasp upon his grime-smeared collar and dropped his free hand to his side. Then, seeing the layer of filth left on his skin from the Reviled One's encrusted clothing, he bent down. "We cannot let him go. He would only attack one of us at the first opportunity," he advised while he brushed his hands through the snow to cleanse them. Agreeing, Bryth turned in one direction and then the other, searching the clearing with a sudden purpose of action. "Where is Ilys?"

Chapter Three

"It's time to act. We must go now!"
  "How do you know we can trust them?"
  "Trust has nothing to do with it."

* * *

The shimmering light of morning dissipated beneath the shade of overhanging evergreen boughs, creating a perpetual twilight that enveloped them with a deep hush as the Hasparii drawn cart slipped into the depths of the forest. Familiar with the barely visible trail, Kaylyya set the elegant deer to a surprising pace, turning the cart round indistinct bends and slowing to negotiate barely perceptible knolls with relative ease in spite of the fact that Evondair could not distinguish any variance between the track they followed and the snow-covered forest floor stretching away on both sides.

The heavy stillness of the woods surrounded them like a mantle, muffling sound and decreasing perception. The unfamiliar ambiance caused Evondair to turn his head to one side and then the other repeatedly, finding the thick hush peculiar and beguiling. The Healing Wards of the Temple were tranquil and calm, serene and restful, but the Temple complex in which he made his home was vast and filled with the echoing intonations of chanting and the constant sound of running water from the many fountains throughout its halls and chambers. Now, surrounded by the deafening silence of snow laden woods, he felt strangely ill at ease and as time went on this uneasiness turned nearly into panic. Shifting uncomfortably, he shook his head more than once in a vain attempt to clear his senses and, although he checked Gairynzvl's condition often to try to distract himself from the disquieting sensations hemming in on him, his uneasiness became increasingly apparent.

Without forewarning, Kaylyya began to sing. The sweet tone of her voice was light and effortless, lilting gently upon the heavy quietness like ethereal birdsong and Evondair found it impossible to keep himself from staring up at her, enraptured. The sensation of being trapped that had been building within him eased and, although he had not even been aware that his grasp upon the sideboard of the cart had turned into a white-knuckled clench, his grip relaxed. Smiling with unexpected contentment, his eyes closed involuntarily as he listened to her wordless song. As her voice rose and fell, grew bolder, then diminished like a gentle breeze, he could not stop himself from sighing in the pleasing calm that wrapped round him. Her melodious tune allayed the tension that had been mounting within him ever since he stepped through the portal in the Room of Transition and crossed into the Uunglarda, but, through the magic of her softly lilting voice, he felt the placidity he had always known as a Healer of the Temple return at last.

After several moments of blissful relaxation, he realized she had stopped singing. His viridian eyes snapped open and he fixed an astonished and wholly curious gaze upon her only to find her glancing over her shoulder at him while smiling with shy satisfaction behind the tip of her lovely wing. The logical side of his nature burgeoned with fascination over the wonder of her gift. It was one he had never encountered before and a dozen questions filled his thoughts even as his own gift of Discernment reached out to seek a better understanding. Shifting from his seated place beside his unconscious friend, he moved to crouch behind the raised bench upon which she sat and stared up at her intently. "That is an extraordinary talent," he said with genuine appreciation and her smile broadened.

"Do you feel better?" she inquired as if she already knew the answer to her question, but posed it for his sake. Turning his head slightly to one side, he inquired further without answering.

"Do you mean to say you sang for my benefit?"

Her smile brightened further. "If you are feeling more at ease."

He smiled as well, enjoying her ambiguity while finding himself all the more intrigued by it. "I am, very much so," he admitted and the reward for his honesty was the beauty of her smile as it blossomed like a radiant flower, turning her lips and wrinkling her nose when she giggled self-assuredly.

"Then yes, I did." They shared a moment of hesitant delight with each other, but the pleasure of their conversation abruptly vanished.

Dropping into the cart from the overhanging branches of a nearby tree with an unexpected thud, a solitary Legionnaire hissed ferociously at them like a monstrous viper, his dragonhide wings spread wide to exhibit the many spines they boasted and his curved Dlalth blade held high. Shrieking in terror, Kaylyya shrank away from the threat he posed, leaning over the front of the cart precariously while the startled Hasparii bellowed at the menacing intruder and doubled his pace in an attempt to escape. Galloping away through deep snow and the shaggy undergrowth, the deer veered from their course, zigzagging in his harness instinctively with the light cart careening wildly after him.

Glaring down at the startled Fey of the Light at his feet, the Legionnaire lashed out with the back of his free hand, the metal studded gloves he wore sending Evondair sprawling and leaving bleeding scratches across his cheek. Momentarily stunned, the Healer reached blindly for Kaylyya's blade secured between the several belts he wore, but before he could successfully unsheathe the dagger the Dark One attacked again. Swinging his sword at the fair malefey viciously, the Legionnaire left Evondair only a second to duck beneath the arc of the blade to avoid losing his head. The blade, however, skimmed over his exposed shoulder and the curve of one wing, ripping a broad hole in his cloak as the sharp edge sent feathers flying.

Sweeping one leg forward forcefully the Healer knocked the Legionnaire off balance, causing him to stumble backward as the cart jostled over an unforeseen obstruction buried in the snow. Evondair unfurled his wings, using a deliberate wing beat to help gain his footing while Kaylyya hauled upon the reins in an attempt to control the stampeding Hasparii. Leaning backward and beating her wings in a reverse motion, she tried to slow his progress, but he surged onward.

"Drachalych!" the enraged Legionnaire snarled in guttural Dlalth, staggering unsteadily and tripping backward over Gairynzvl who lay motionless at his feet. Taking advantage of the Dark One's instability, Evondair flexed his powerful wings to produce momentum and lunged at his foe, forcing him into a backward tumble. Perusing him with the blade of his dagger seeking the flesh of the Legionnaire's exposed throat, the Healer sought the quickest means of ensuring death, but as they fell the Dark One curled his wing between himself and his attacker. They crashed together onto the bed of the cart and grappled with each other. The blade of Evondair's dagger sought its mark, but the Legionnaire twisted sharply, pressing the spine of the wing he had managed to get between them sharply into the Fey of the Light's side.

Evondair gasped harshly in pain at the unanticipated attack and pushed away with an abrupt backward wing beat, glancing downward to discover if the Dark One's wing-spine had pierced his flesh deeply. Although his warm woolen vest had been torn and he was bleeding, the puncture wound he had sustained was not deep. His opponent scrabbled in the opposite direction, but his retreat was hampered by Gairynzvl's body, who he clambered against violently. Cursing at the hindrance he presented, the Dark One lurched to his feet as the cart swerved sharply to one side. Flapping his dragonhide wings in an ungainly action, he attempted to keep his balance in the careening conveyance. As he struggled to maintain his footing, his boot came down upon one of Gairynzvl's hands and the scream it brought forth from the unconscious Fey shocked both combatants into motionless astonishment.

Gairynzvl's eyes opened in a wide, unfocused stare as he hissed a disjointed sentence consisting of all the languages he knew at the same time and the Legionnaire looked down at him. His distinctly stunned expression twisted into an evil leer while he hastily assessed the situation. The wounded Fey of the Light had not fully regained consciousness, but was alert on only the most instinctual level. His panicked stare and use of Dlalth, Celebrae and the Common Tongue together in one sentence betrayed his incoherent, survival-driven condition. At discovering this, the Legionnaire smiled viciously and stamped the heel of his boot down another time onto his bound and bleeding hand.

Gairynzvl thrashed his head violently as waves of excruciating pain overwhelmed him. The Legionnaire hissed with sadistic laughter, digging his heel deeper into the blood-soaked bandages betraying the Fey of the Light's injury while glaring at his rival as if daring him to come nearer. Evondair stared back, immobilized by the sound of Gairynzvl's scream as it pierced the surrounding woodland and then distorted into a livid growl. This alteration made the Dark One look down again, suddenly uncertain, and the stares of the two Fey locked, furious icy-lavender piercing blood-crimson as the wounded Fey of the Light opened his wings against the bed of the cart. With them splayed wide and his arms pressed to the floor of the cart, he forced a single wing beat against the opposing wood beneath him and, in an unanticipated motion propelled by the strength of his wings and his own powerful physique, he drew his feet upward abruptly, together, aiming for the Legionnaires face.

The swiftness of this conjoined action of wing and body strength sent the unsuspecting Dark One staggering backward, flailing wildly as he tumbled over the edge of the cart. Hissing with fury, Evondair launched himself after the Legionnaire knocked senseless by the impact of Gairynzvl's boots. Tumbling together through the deep snow, enraged Celebrae blended with viperous Dlalth. Feathers and wing spines entangled as one Fey sought death and the other thrashed frantically to escape it, but the glittering dagger, which had until that moment rarely left it's sheathe, was sharp as severed flint and found its mark.

The Legionnaire arched in an instinctual posture of trauma, his wings stretching wide though he was held by Evondair's hand clenching the collar of his coat. Withdrawing the blade from the Reviled One's throat, the Healer stared down at his victim, frozen in a state of horror as his adversary's crimson eyes opened wide with pain and astonishment and began filling with tears. Turning his head to gaze up at the fair Fey who had taken his life, the Legionnaire drew a final, shuddering breath. Their gazes locked and his lips curved upward in a broad smile as his blood rushed from the gaping wound in his neck to cover the Healer's hand. His wings shook in a final, unmistakable indication of death and his eyes slowly glazed.

Unable to release him or even to draw breath, Evondair stared down at the lifeless body, his emotions twisting in a wrathful storm of terror, relief, and utter dread at what he had done. Standing immobilized, he did not notice the cart finally come to a stop, nor did he see Kaylyya when she dismounted and came quietly to his side. He did not hear her when she spoke softly to him and barely sensed when she placed her hand upon his, which still grasped the dagger in an iron-like clasp. Her words swam in a dizzying haze that combined with the pounding of his heart and a sudden rushing noise that loomed up out of nothingness. He would have been entirely engulfed in horror if not for the softest sound he had ever heard.

It started very quietly; just a whisper; a hint of something inexpressibly beautiful touching the essence of his being. A delicate sound unlike any he had ever heard before, it muffled the chaos threatening to devour him and soothed the pounding revulsion circling him like madness. His eyes blinked unhurriedly; his senses melded into a sweet union of sound and tranquility, and the shuddering that had overtaken him, stilled. His vice-like grasp upon the Legionnaire's collar relaxed, but as his lifeless body slumped to the ground in a heap, Evondair's gaze was focused on the snowy-jade of Kaylyya's staring back at him.

Reflexively, he drew a deep breath as the soothing sound of her voice, singing in a language unknown to him, seemed to blend with birdsong and an underlying tone of ethereal serenity. He was surrounded by verdant, lush forest. He floated in a realm of intoxicating beauty and delicious calm. He could even feel the warm kiss of radiant sunlight as it streamed down through the emeraldine canopy in pearlescent ribbons that caressed and eased. There was only the sound of her voice and the luxuriant hush it created; there was nothing else.

Stillness.

Lush and deep.

The sweet balm wrapped around him, as soothing as a warm blanket on a bitterly cold day, and his only thought was peace.

Then his viridian gaze widened in surprise.

Forcefully shaking himself from the blissful reverie into which he had fallen, Evondair refocused his gaze upon her, utterly astonished by the magical enchantment she cast with the sound of her voice. As the winter's chill breeze tousled the waves and layers of his golden hair and nipped his bleeding cheek, he looked down at the Legionnaire lying dead at his feet and could not keep from gasping heavily with dismay.

"You did what was necessary," she told him gently. He gazed back at her, unable to express the emotions raging within him. "You protected us." Her reassurances did not quell the mortifying sensation of duality emerging within him as Healer and Warrior struggled for dominance.

Staring back at her, he did not reach to hide the tears in his eyes as they rimmed and slid down his cheeks. He answered her with a deep, wavering tone that required no clarification. "I am not a warrior."

Chapter Four

The scintillating light of early afternoon sparkled and glimmered through the swirling shadows of the open portal, reflecting off the black stone floor of the cavern and twisting like glistening smoke as the crossing slowly wavered and warped. Those standing before it waiting uncertainly winced at the touch of the crystalline light and ducked out of its way as it snaked through the gateway, but they did not run from it. Neither did they draw their weapons in a show of bravado against those lingering on the opposite side, whose voices echoed through the turning vortex as if they travelled a vast distance. As they listened to the Fey of the Light discussing what had just occurred, those watching argued amongst themselves.

"We must go. Now!"

"There's no guarantee they won't kill us, just as they killed those we forced to cross over."

"You're wrong. There is a way to guarantee our safety." Crimson gazes locked, but the one who led them brandished his weapon audaciously, then sheathed the curved sword and unfastened the baldric holding it in place. Thrusting the armament out at arm's length before him, he spoke to the others with grim determination. "We must cross unarmed." Dropping his weapon with dramatic flair, he glared at the others staring back at him with disbelief, challenging them to disagree. They did, vociferously.

"You're insane. They'll slaughter us all."

"Go unarmed? Why not just cross over and lie down at their feet, offering our necks for their blades?"

"Haven't you ever heard of the Prison of Daylight? We'll die horrible, painful deaths at their hands!" They spat their dissention back at their leader, but he laughed derisively before hissing at them with harsh anger, silencing their protests.

"You pack of whining shefey! These aren't Legionnaires of the Realm we are talking about; they're Fey of the Light! They won't kill one who is unarmed. Their sense of justice and mercy would never allow it."

"You saw how they fought before the gate. You'd risk all our lives on hearsay?" A subordinate retorted sharply, but the leader leaned closer to him and glared at him threateningly.

"Cowering Blaylscith! You've studied the writings as well as me. If we didn't all believe them, we wouldn't be here, would we?"

The others glared uncertainly at each other, hesitant to relinquish the only protection they had, but, at last, one of the young Legionnaire's cursed sharply, unclasped his sword belt and hurled the weapon it supported onto the ground while he stared at the others defiantly.

"Senzuur is right. We didn't come this far to turn back out of cowardice." The leader grinned fiercely at him as the others haltingly disarmed themselves. When they stood entirely unarmed, he drew a bottle from a leather halter hanging from his belt and raised it high.

"Trach klynnoch vla sladdin!" he shouted in fluent Dlalth and he was answered by all.

"To the courage of fools!"

* * *

The Fey of the Light had retreated into the shade of an overhanging evergreen heavy with new fallen snow in order to prevent their captive from suffering any further discomfort in the glow of the afternoon sun. Having bound his hands behind him using a belt from one of the fallen Legionnaires, they stood guard on either side of him with their weapons sheathed while Bryth and Ilys attempted to communicate with him, but their questions went unanswered.

"He is a half-wit!" Ilys hissed with frustration after several attempts to explain to him using multiple dialects of Dlalth that they would not harm him, but her attempts were pointless. He babbled inanely.

"He is speaking Dlalth, is he not? Why not translate what he is saying and allow us to decide?" Bryth questioned with less exasperation. He was fully aware from having interrogated other Reviled captives, that they would use any number of ruses to escape questioning.

"What he is saying makes no sense."

"Perhaps you should tell us anyway and let us decide." Mardan repeated Bryth's suggestion with mounting ire, his frustration with the entire situation palpable.

Ilys glared at him with an unreadable expression before responding insolently. "He is saying they were forced to cross over by a band of Legionnaires, but that is ludicrous."

Mardan's brilliant gaze narrowed at her acerbic reply and he moved closer to glare down at her confrontationally. "Well something forced them across and I certainly do not know of any other Fey of the Light currently residing in that reeking cesspit." Their cerulean stares melded and even Bryth found himself holding his breath in anticipation of the outcome of their mute challenge. Ilys hissed sharply with her wings arched high in defiance, but after a tense moment she turned aside. Familiar enough with both their personalities to know it would be unwise to allow the situation to swell out of proportion, Reydan interjected with a diplomatic tone in an attempt to redirect their hostility.

"Why would another band of Legionnaires force them to cross over knowing we were waiting on the other side? What would they hope to gain?"

Continuing to glare at Ilys petulantly, Mardan shook his head, but Bryth nodded and turned to face her once again. "I agree, it makes little sense. Do you wish to inquire further or shall I ask in a far less personable manner?" He illustrated his suggestion by clenching one fist before him and covering it with his other hand, his stare piercing the young Legionnaire with evident, malicious intent. The unspoken threat caused the Dark One to hiss viperously at him before he doubled his efforts to escape.

"I just told him you would not harm him!" Ilys rebuked his threat harshly, but when Bryth turned his piercing gaze to her and the intimidation he had directed at the Legionnaire still gleamed in the depths of his cobalt-hued eyes, she silenced her protest abruptly. Surrounded by powerful, aggressive malefey, she felt suddenly vulnerable. It was a sensation she had experienced on many occasions in the Uunglarda and one she had hoped to never suffer again after leaving that dark realm. Try as she might, however, she could not trust the Fey of the Light in the same way she trusted Gairynzvl. Without him close by to ensure that none of them turned on her, she felt unnerved by their imposing size and assertiveness in the same way she had felt threatened by the Legionnaires of the Realm.

No matter how hard she tried to convince herself otherwise, she could not force herself to believe they would not unleash their hatred of the Reviled upon her. Standing among them while attempting to disguise her sudden uneasiness, a dark recollection of the days of her Integration sprang forward from the recesses of her memory where she continually struggled to keep it sequestered and she could not stop herself from squeezing her eyes closed against the horrors it renewed in her mind.

The painful memory pressed in on her like a flood of icy water. She shuddered at its bitter touch as echoes of harsh threats and numbing fear pierced into the heart of her, in spite of the many years that had passed since such traumas had actually taken place. Regardless of her tireless efforts to guard against any sign of weakness, which would have been immediately exploited in the Uunglarda, the memory filled her thoughts and spawned undisguisable fear within her. Blurred images twisted in her mind like daggers. The harrowing memory of Legionnaires crowding around her with hands grasping and pulling, forced tears from her tightly closed eyes. The memory of brutal kisses and ruthless bites, of callous laughter that mocked her pleas for mercy and of lascivious demands made while her innocence was savagely plundered shook her to the core.

Shaking her head in an instinctive effort to dispel the barbaric images, she could not quell the terror rising from within as she relived the vicious Initiation she had suffered as a young shefey shortly after her abduction. The images raced and spun through her mind like a whirlwind of razors and it was all she could do to keep from screaming as tears wet her cheeks.

A touch upon her shoulder shook her from the waking nightmare and her tear-filled eyes snapped open as she recoiled in dismay, expecting to see Legionnaires surrounding her once again. Instead, she found Mardan gazing down at her. Hs cerulean stare, which had only moments before been wrathful and alarming, was now softened by confused concern, but before he could question her as to the cause of her unanticipated emotion she backed away from them with a defensive hiss. The malefey around her exchanged bewildered glances as she shook herself with visible effort to try to clear her thoughts and spun about to address the young Legionnaire. He had paused from his violent, fear-instilled thrashing to stare at her as well, the depths of his crimson eyes filled with an unanticipated measure of compassion, as if he recognized the pain she sought to elude. Taking advantage of his silence and ignoring the puzzled stares of the malefey, she hastily dried her eyes and attempted to continue as if nothing had happened.

Speaking in a dialect of Dlalth she rarely utilized, she queried once again and he stared back at her, considering what she had said before he said something in response. They conversed a moment, then she stepped back from him, waving her hand in front of her face in an undisguised gesture of disgust at the fetid stench surrounding him. Shaking her head, she turned to face Bryth once more, although she stared at the ground at his feet and would not meet his piercing stare. "I am not sure I understand him. He is using a form of Dlalth I have rarely heard, but he seems to be saying the ones who forced them to cross are The Watchers. The Waiting Ones."

The malefey exchanged another uncertain gaze, unsure what or who The Watchers or The Waiting Ones were, but she took up her conversation with the Dark One before they could inquire further. The two Dark Ones spoke uninterrupted for several moments before she drew back. Shaking her head and snorting to clear her senses of his foul reek, she stooped to pick up a handful of snow and pressed it to her nose, inhaling the fresh, clean scent deeply before explaining that he was referring to a small band of rebel Legionnaires who lived in secrecy among the Dlalth. "The Watchers study the ancient writings, although doing so is forbidden, and search for evidence of the one who will lead them out of bondage. They wait for any sign of his existence, constantly on guard. They are an obscure faction who live in even greater fear than most Dark Ones and the risk of being discovered keeps their numbers to a minimum."

"And if they are discovered?" Bryth inquired, attempting to understand her by confirming what he already suspected.

"They would be named a traitor, which means death by inexpressibly horrific torture. None dare risk it, even if they believe the one spoken of in the ancient texts exists."

"Evidence of The One?" Reydan repeated thoughtfully and the malefey stared at each other hesitantly, unwilling to speak what they all were considering until Mardan smiled ironically.

"Evidence of the *Fierce* One, even if it was you, Bryth, who gave him that name." The Fey Guard's skepticism faded as a wry smile turned his lips, but their unpredictable tempers kept the Legionnaire watching them with the vigilance of a trapped animal. They debated the possibility that the Reviled also knew of the Prophecy of Reclamation that foretold the coming of 'The One who walked in Light and Shadow'.

"So, you now believe Gairynzvl *is* The One?" Bryth intentionally taunted, once again asking something he already knew the answer to and Mardan nodded.

"I certainly would not have followed him into the Uunglarda if I did not. The prophecy says '*Out of the Darkness, Light shall burst forth, Indomitable, Guiding the Innocent from shadow and the irresolute from placidity.*' Surely this speaks of Gairynzvl. Has he not done all these things?" His answer surprised them all.

Reydan looked at the young Legionnaire and continued thoughtfully, "and it does sound like the Reviled are awaiting the fulfillment of this prophecy upon which we acted. But why should the Dlalth, who were once Fey of the Light, not also know of it?" Reydan's proposal left them staring at each other in silence again as they contemplated something none of them had considered previously. In their hush, the young Legionnaire began to thrash violently once more and his determined chaos tipped the tenuous balance Mardan had gained over his frustration. Stalking forward to stand within inches of the flailing Dark One, he stared at him with blatant exasperation before he growled ferociously at the younger fey. Extended his wings outward in an intimidating threat as his cerulean glare blazed with animosity, his reaction to the tiring ploy of the young Legionnaire only made the others laugh. Reaching forward, Bryth clapped the bristling Celebrant-Warrior across his shoulder.

"Irascible Tryngalith." His taunt brought Mardan's glare to his own, but Bryth's smile never faltered. "Gairynzvl was right in calling you that, so now we have named you as well."

In full agreement with his jibe, Reydan and Rehstaed joined Bryth's good-natured taunting, their laughter prompting Mardan to glare at them as well, though with a less than convincing scowl than he had directed towards the Legionnaire. Despite his annoyance, he could find no grounds to protest the title given to him and he relented from his display of irritation. Joining their mirth, his laughter transformed the vexed glower of his expression into a charming smile, but as the malefey released their tension with humor, Ilys could not help staring at them with undisguised bewilderment. Their behavior was unpredictable and perplexing and her guarded cerulean gaze locked upon the sparkling blue of another.

* * *

As the noontide sun reached its apex and balanced precariously on the pinnacle of its course through the brilliant winter sky, pausing to survey its dominion before continuing onward, the Hasparii pulled cart passed through the remainder of the snow-laden forest quietly. Its fair driver was respectfully silent while Evondair sought to reconcile the revulsion he felt at taking another's life. Regardless of the reason such an action had been required of him, he could not lay aside the notion that he had intentionally disregarded the oath he had taken upon the commencement of his Dedication as a Healer to serve with humility and to revere all life.

As they passed through the vast gates of the Temple and entered its precincts, Evondair got to his feet from the place he had taken sitting beside Gairynzvl in pensive silence, and stood behind Kaylyya. Quietly he provided direction through the winding avenues and across the snow-covered grounds of the complex, guiding her to come to a stop before the broad doors of the Healing Wards where they were met by a group of Fey Guards. Instantly upon stopping, Evondair vaulted down from the cart and called in insistent Celebrae for Healers as he moved towards the bed of the beautifully constructed conveyance where he watched over his friend who had lapsed into unconsciousness once more.

Recognizing the Healer, one of the Fey Guards signaled to another keeping watch in the ramparts overheard and, at his indication, the vast bronze doors swung slowly open. Several Healers hurried outward to speak with Evondair and Kaylyya watched with curious amazement as he conversed with them, hastily describing with proficient detail the particulars of Gairynzvl's condition and injury. He also suggested the intercession of the Temple Surgeons and specifically requesting an audience with The Elders who were expecting their return.

Turning to gaze thoughtfully at Kaylyya, he asked one of the Fey Guards to help her see to the care of the great Hasparii who had transported them through the forest and, once he was properly stabled, to escort her to the Nursing Chamber where he would be tending Gairynzvl. After assuring her agreement with such a proposal, he and one of the other Healers lifted his unconscious friend from the cart and proceeded inward hurriedly. The dim, quiet environs surrounded them with a soothing calm Evondair had missed since the moment he left it and he could not hold back a deep sigh of relief.

They were joined by several other attendant Healers, one of which prepared a place for the injured Fey they carried while the other hurried away into the inner chambers to request the attention of one of the skilled surgeons. As they lay Gairynzvl onto the treatment bed and drew several lamps closer in order to inspect his injuries more thoroughly, Evondair began to carefully remove the bandages from one of his hands. The constriction of the wrappings had slowed the flow of blood, but it increased at the removal of the binding cloth and, although he remained unconscious, Gairynzvl moaned in observable pain.

"He has lost a great deal of blood." Evondair repeated what he had told them just a moment before, his anxiety conspicuous, but his fellow Healers only nodded with composed deliberation. Several of their gazes fell to inspect Evondair's gray-mud spattered clothing and the blood stains still evident on his hands and sleeves, but their raised brows and curious expressions did not prompt him to speak as he stooped to gaze at his patient's injury.

The most senior of the Healers fixed a steady gaze on him. "How did this occur?"

Evondair hesitated, unsure how to answer because they had all been asked to keep their crossing into the Uunglarda, as well as their purpose for going there, in strict confidence. After an awkward silence, he answered somewhat elusively. "Razor-edged blades. I am sorry, but I am not at liberty to explain further."

The other straightened to stare at him, perplexed by his atypical ambiguity, but the surgeon who was approaching the Healing Ward from one of the interior studies overheard their conversation and inquired further even as he crossed the floor. "Razor-edged blades? Did he inflict this injury upon himself or suffer it at the hands of another?"

Evondair stepped back from the treatment table in deference to the approaching Healer's greater knowledge and authority, as well as in response to their joint gazes of consternation at his conspicuously disheveled state. Before he could answer, however, the surgeon continued more definitively. "You have been in battle. Whom did you engage? Are you badly injured? How long as he been unconscious and when did his injury occur?"

Shifting uncomfortably, Evondair gazed round him with apparent uncertainty if should answer and his peers took note of his hesitancy with marked curiosity. "We opposed the Reviled in the early hours just this morning. This is when his injury took place and he fell unconscious shortly afterward as a result of traumatic blood loss. I then was forced to engage a Legionnaire alone, from which conflict I have sustained minor injuries...outwardly," he paused, visibly unsettled by his account and he swallowed with difficulty before continuing. The Healers glanced at each other with amazement, though the surgeon seemed to suspect as much and nodded while he listened to Evondair continue, even more guardedly. "Do please forgive me. I do not intend to be obstructive, but I cannot say more unless granted permission by The Elders."

Upon hearing his response, the others shared a speculative glance, but nodded and undertook the cleansing of their patient's wounds in preparation of closing them, but when they began to unwrap his other hand and his cries of distress became more pronounced, Evondair could not stop himself from questioning their attentiveness with disturbed mutters as he paced beside the treatment table with nervous agitation. Flexing his expansive wings repeatedly in an uncharacteristic display of irritation, he found suppressing the growl of frustration rising from deep within him nearly more challenging than his temperance could manage.

Working with as much vigilant haste as possible, the Healers did all they could for Gairynzvl, but his obvious suffering, even in his unconscious state, was more than his friend could abide. A shocking wave of ire and frustration crested within him with the sudden ferocity of a summer storm and he turned sharply on his heel, seeking to escape the situation in any manner possible. As he strode out into the corridor, his troubled, viridian gaze met Veryth's. Drawn by the sounds of distress emanating from the ward, the older Healer had come hurriedly to see if he could lend further aid, but when he saw Evondair and realized it could only be one of the Liberators whose voice was ringing through the side wards and down the otherwise quiet corridor, he stopped abruptly. Greeting his friend with his customary welcome, his tone quickly filled with concern.

"Valysscopta, Evondair." His salutation was returned with a brooding glare filled with restive emotion and exasperation, and this caused Veryth to gaze pensively at his friend. "The Darkness has exacted a costly toll."

It was not a question, but a definitive statement meant to express his understanding. While they stared mutely at each other, they listened with dismay to Gairynzvl's cries, which continued to increase to a point that made Evondair shake his head in helpless vexation and curse with unexpectedly harsh language. Moved by sympathy for both his friends, Veryth strode past him purposefully and crossed to the treatment table in order to assess the situation for himself and offer any supplementary aid his own unique gifts might provide. He quickly suggested the use of several herbal tinctures that were known to rapidly provide a sedative benefit and the Healers discussed the option briefly before concurring. Then one of the attendants hastened away to collect the appropriate distillation while Veryth stepped forward to place his hands upon Gairynzvl. Closing his emeraldine eyes, he began to speak a gentle incantation that had an instantaneous effect and through his softly spoken words of Celebrae, Gairynzvl's shouts and wails of pain diminished considerably.

From the corridor, Evondair watched in silence. He had witnessed Veryth's spell casting ability on several previous occasions with similarly distraught patients, although he had never found himself more appreciative of his skill before that moment. Shortly after Gairynzvl's cries ceased, the youthful attendant Healer returned with several small bottles and he handed them to one of the practicing Healers who combined their contents in the proper proportions to administer to their patient. When they began to cleanse his wounds once more, however, Gairynzvl's unremitting moans and gasps indicated the measure of his pain that remained unabated and it became a torment Evondair could not tolerate. Unable to quell the violent frustration intensifying within him, he turned to glare out of the closest window and clamped his hands over his highly sensitive pointed ears as the emotions within him spiraled into a maelstrom he was incapable of comprehending.

Chapter Five

Drawn by the echoing cries of distress filling the Temple Healing Wards and reaching even the seclusion of the Devotionary, the Elders came quietly along the corridor. They found Evondair standing glaring in forced silence upward at the sunlight that was shimmering in the afternoon winter sky. So lost in introspection was he that he did not take any notice of them until the youngest of the Three, Zraylaunyth, touched his shoulder lightly and drew back his hood to gaze at his friend with open concern.

Evondair recoiled from his touch instinctually, but when he turned and gazed into the youthful Elder's remarkable pale cerulean eyes dappled with gemlike cobalt and saw in his empathetic stare all the dismay, revulsion, fear and frustration he felt himself, he could no longer withhold the flood of emotion that had been threatening to overwhelm him for the better portion of the day. Covering his face with trembling hands, he moaned in misery as the turbulent battle between Healer and Warrior lashed within him. He knew he did not need to speak a word in explanation. As the Elder gazed at him, he also gazed into him, touching the essence of his being and comprehending the vicious onslaught of opposing emotion and purpose that had beset him from the moment he stepped into the Devotionary to join Gairynzvl's band of Liberators.

"The Shadows have usurped the harmonious proclivity of your nature, Evondair, but do not despair. Your Purpose is being fulfilled. Draw strength from this knowledge and from we who support you." Zray-launyth's soft voice filled him with a sense of relief and belonging and Evondair sighed heavily, but a sharp cry of pain pierced the hush that answered these reassuring words. As they turned to gaze into the Healing Ward with apprehension, Kaylyya was led from the outer vestibule to stand with them. Her snowy-jade eyes met Evondair's deep viridian and he did not reach to hide the tears still evident in the depths of his stare, but as they shared the unsettling moment with unspoken understanding blossoming between them, one of the Healers shouted in surprise.

Forced into a state of combative agitation by the pain the cleansing of his wounds caused, Gairynzvl had once again revived into semi-consciousness. Cursing in furious Dlalth blended with vehement Celebrae and incensed common tongue, he knocked aside the attendant Healer who was rinsing one of his hands in a solution of salt, curative minerals and water. The Healer tumbled backward, the basin he held clattering noisily across the floor even as Gairynzvl rolled sideways in an attempt to escape the treatment table.

"*Chrys*-galnuth raach *lyyr*-echtuk, viperous Healer! Volgralnuch *shalee!*" His insensible speech and fierce determination to be free from them betrayed the gravity of the situation and it took three Healers laying over him to begin to subdue him. Flailing his wings, arms and legs viciously, he struck the surgeon full in the face and sent him reeling before he twisted beneath the weight of the Healers piled on top of him. Biting another of them with all the ferocity of a trapped wolf, he hissed aggressively while the other Fey screamed in pain and retreated.

Together with the remaining Healers who were drawn by the noise of the startling commotion and rushed into the chamber, Evondair attempted to help restrain his friend, but, in spite of his unstable condition his strength was bolstered by survival-driven instinct and sheer panic. Cursing at the golden-haired Fey with belligerent Dlalth, Gairynzvl lurched upwards forcefully. He knocked his head against that of the nearest Healer and sent him stumbling backward in dazed confusion. Twisting, kicking and hissing malevolently at them, he struck another Healer ferociously over the head with his wing. He then grasped one of them who was sprawled across his chest and began throttling him with both hands, cursing at him with shockingly vulgar Celebrae.

In the midst of the chaos, Evondair turned and looked at Kaylyya curiously, his thoughts returning to the tranquility with which she had enchanted him, entirely soothing his distress and leaving him in a blissful reverie unlike any he had ever experienced. Capturing her astonished gaze with his, he shouted to her over the chaos filling the chamber. "Are you able to calm him?"

His question drew the attention of the Elders, who had placed themselves between the dangerous malefey and the graceful newcomer. When they turned their united stare on her, the weight of their joined gazes was nearly more profound than she could bear. She looked beyond them, however and watched the panic-stricken, wounded Fey with an expression of uncertain trepidation. For an interminable moment, she seemed only to stare at him and Evondair wondered if she had even heard his question amid the pandemonium Gairynzvl was causing, but then she closed her eyes and, very quietly, began to sing.

Initially, the delicate, ethereal sound of her voice was barely perceptible; a whisper in a crowded, noisy room. In spite of the onslaught of profanity spewing from Gairynzvl's mouth, she did not increase the volubility of her song, nor did she move closer to ensure the struggling, incoherent Fey to whom she sang would hear her. After a moment, the others turned to stare at her, transfixed by the melodious intonations softly filling the Healing Ward and, released from their restrictive efforts, Gairynzvl flailed wildly for an instant.

Gasping loudly for breath, he paused at last, turning his head as his unfocused gaze sought the source of the entrancing music filling his being with surreal calm. His lavender-ice stare met hers and his entire body visibly slumped with relaxation. The language she used was unknown to any of them; even the Elders stood motionless as the sound of her captivating song blended in their thoughts with an underlying, harmonious tone that echoed softly with the beguiling sound of distant birdsong.

Shaking his head, Evondair forced himself to look away from her, fully aware of the beautiful void into which she could lure him if he listened too intently. Jostling the Healer at his side, he gestured at their patient who was gasping from exhaustion, but had otherwise become calm and was lying on his back with his wings spread wide across the table and hanging lax over its sides while he stared blankly at Kaylyya. He was utterly transfixed by her mesmeric singing.

Refocusing their attention away from the enchantress who continued to harmonize with nature itself, he suggested they take full advantage of the spell under which their patient had fallen in order to close his wounds, but before the surgeon could take up his implements, the Elders stepped forward. "How did he come to bear these wounds?" They looked to Evondair and he no longer hesitated to answer.

"They were produced by the ironwork of the Great Gate."

Several astonished gasps answered this pronouncement and no one moved. Bending closer to See the injury to Gairynzvl's hands more clearly, Zraylaunyth closed his eyes with poignant emotion as the moments leading up to the collapse of the gate replayed in his mind. Straightening, he turned to meld telepathically with the other Elders, sharing what he had Seen so they, too, understood the significance of what had taken place.

The First spoke. "The Gate was created as an impenetrable barrier between the Darkness and the Light, without lock or key. Constructed by both sides to protect each dominion from infiltration by the other, the Ancients fashioned a spell of protection that no Reviled could contravene. Only through an act of inestimable self-sacrifice could the Gate be sundered."

He said no more, but in his silence, the Second continued. "The Reviled, as is their nature, utilized a more ruthless and unsophisticated deterrent by inlaying the ironwork of the Gate with blades that would not grow blunted by the passage of time."

Astonished beyond comprehension at what she was hearing, Kaylyya's song wavered and then stopped as she stared around her in wonder, but, in her silence, though it was mere seconds, Gairynzvl once again began to moan.

"Sing, Enchantress! We must close these wounds before he loses the use of his hands." The surgeon prompted with urgency marking every word, but before she could even draw breath to begin again, the Second Elder stepped forward and raised his hands.

"Your skills are not required, Surgeon."

A dubious expression answered this declaration, but as the other Elders also stepped forward the remaining attendants and Healers retreated with inquisitive reverence.

"*The One shall face an Insurmountable Challenge. The Capacity of his Love will be Measured by the Depth of his Wounds.*" The First spoke, repeating a prophecy from the days of the first Ancients as he raised his hands slowly.

Then, the Second continued. "*Sacrifice will Liberate when Hope falls into Shadow.*"

The Third nodded sagely and completed the ancient prophecy. "*Light shall Heal where Skill stands staring, but the Wounds will Remain, Testament to the Purpose of The One who walks in Light and Shadow.*" Raising his hands as well, their conjoined aura's melded into a shimmering, radiant glow. As if summoned by the influence of the resplendent glistening, the winter sun broke through the veil of clouds that had filled the sky throughout the afternoon and its unhindered intensity streamed into the Healing Ward through the open shutters of its many windows. Scintillating ribbons of light reached downward, kissing the crown of Gairynzvl's head and spreading outward to envelope his entire body. The dazzling glow reflected from his nebulous wings and sparkling across his mud-spattered clothes, and when the luminous glimmer reached his hands, he gasped sharply.

Arching upward from the treatment table upon which he lay, he was held suspended, cradled by the Light as it enwrapped him, circling his hands, his arms and his entire body much as it had done during the Prevailation. Those gathered round watched in awe-struck wonder as the deep lacerations crisscrossing his hands began reflecting the shimmering light as if glowing from within. Then, as the Light's incandescent glimmer seemed to amplify through the influence of the Elder's unified auras, the wounds on Gairynzvl's hands inexplicably began to close.

* * *

The winter sun broke through the veil of clouds overshadowing the forest at the base of the mountain where the Liberators stood guard. The early afternoon radiance shimmered over the now quiet clearing. Having satisfied themselves that the young Legionnaire posed no threat, Rehstaed and Mardan bound him to the trunk of a massive evergreen in the hope of removing themselves some short distance from him to escape the noise his incessant blathering. Reydan had taken up a discussion with several of the villagers regarding their plan to guard the open portal, which was still spiraling in a state of flux at the base of the mountain, until the Fey Guard arrived. Many of the villagers had retreated into their homes a short distance away beneath the hanging boughs of the forest, taking the childfey with them so they could warm them and tend to their needs. Several shefey gathered at the village center to prepare a suitable meal and provide for the little ones, as well as the fierce warriors who had risked so much to rescue them.

Bryth stood at a distance from the others, his jet-black hair and the feathers of his equally dark wings tousled by the winter wind. His bright cobalt gaze was fixed upon the base of the mountain where shouts in Dlalth echoed through the slowly turning portal. Drawn by the sound, he had crossed the clearing to stand gazing into the vortex and listened as keenly as his hearing might allow for any intimation of what was happening in the opposing realm. Regardless of his vigilance in guarding the opening, he was nonetheless astonished when several Legionnaires walked cautiously through the portal.

Their wings were tightly folded in a clear sign of deference. Their heads were bowed and they walked forward with their hands extended outward, indicating they held no weapons of any kind. As they approached, the first stopped to glance up at the warrior in golden armor who was staring at him with obvious confusion as the grime-laden Legionnaire lowered himself to kneel before him respectfully. Those behind him paused as well before, they too, although begrudgingly, took to one knee while Bryth stared down at them with a fiercely incredulous expression. Across the clearing, Rehstaed and Mardan turned to watch with startled curiosity, but it took only a moment for the former Fey Guard to draw his sword. As the Dlalth leader began speaking to the golden warrior at whose feet he knelt, Rehstaed took to wing in order to cross the distance between them in the least amount of time and he was followed closely by Mardan.

"Golden Warrior, we come unarmed, seeking neither conflict nor destruction, but only your help." Senzuur spoke with his gaze purposefully averted, attempting to display in all possible manners that, although they were Legionnaires, they posed no threat. Bryth scowled and turned his head to watch his comrades alight to a running pace as they came to stand with him against their foe.

"What aid can I possibly offer you?" he answered doubtfully, entirely perplexed by their behavior, but the antagonistic stance Rehstaed assumed beside him with his sword poised for battle instigated a more predictable response. Behind their leader, the subordinate Legionnaires shifted nervously, unable to keep their gazes turned aside from the aggressive Fey of the Light in their midst. One even reached towards his hip where his sword would have usually hung, having forgotten they had disarmed themselves before crossing over. His instinctual reaction was all the motivation Rehstaed required. Brandishing his sword, he stepped towards the kneeling Dark One menacingly, his voice an intimidating growl.

"He conceals a weapon." His accusation caused the Legionnaire to recoil in dread as the taller, more powerfully built Fey reached down to grasp him by the back of his coat as he raised his sword in a threat that could not be ignored. Bryth stepped forward as well, reaching out in an attempt to impede his comrade's zealous actions while both he and Mardan shouted his name.

"No, Rehstaed!"

"He reacts out of fear alone! I assure you, we bear no armament of any kind!" Senzuur protested sharply, vowing they were unarmed, but Rehstaed would not be persuaded.

Thrashing to escape the Fey of the Light holding him and preparing to deliver a killing blow, the subordinate cursed repeatedly in rancorous Dlalth, but he did not draw any form of weapon, nor did he unfurl his wings to utilize their formidable spines in defense. Instead, the young Legionnaire hissed belligerently and shouted at their leader. "I told you they would never trust us!"

Glaring down at him with implacable hatred, Rehstaed visibly shook with the effort of control required to force himself not to strike. "Treacherous Demon, you canno' prove t' me in any manner tha' I can trust you!" he hissed at the cowering Legionnaire, ignoring the insistent appeals of his friends to take no action as he raised his sword over his head once again.

"They are unarmed, Rehstaed!" Bryth shouted, his more commanding tone causing him to turn his head so he might argue more vehemently.

"They are Reviled, need I som' ot'er reason?" he growled, turning his head back and cursing in his native language at the struggling Legionnaire even as Ilys raced toward them. Drawn to the fray from the balm of the overhanging evergreen boughs offering the only measure of shade in the glimmering light of afternoon, she answered his profanity with equally harsh Dlalth as she alighted beside him and grasped his arm with both hands in an attempt to deflect the arc of his sword.

"He is no threat to you!" Her insistent tone only caused him to hiss viciously at her. Shoving the Dark One aside, Rehstaed turned to glare down at her furiously. His entire demeanor shifted from the even-tempered Fey who craved nothing more than the pleasure of Temple wine into a merciless warrior and he rebuked her harshly.

"All Reviled are a threat, whether or no' they be armed!"

The Legionnaires forced themselves to remain motionless and watched through furtive upward glances as Ilys returned his glare with an equally fearsome scowl, though she barely reached the height of his chest. "I am one of the Reviled. Will you kill me as well?" she goaded with venomous ire. Beyond the limits of his patience, he grasped her tightly, forcing her to release his arm by exerting an unbearable pressure upon her small wrist. When she yelped in surprise at the pain with which he threatened her and relinquished her hold upon him, he wrenched his sword free from her and raised it over her head.

"Do no' tempt me, sheDemon!"

"Peace, Rehstaed." Mardan injected in as temperate a tone as he could manage, placing his hand upon his friend's shoulder so that the scowling Fey turned his glare upon the Celebrant. Burning violet melted into crystalline cerulean and for a moment they stared at each other obstinately, but Rehstaed shoved Ilys forcefully away and lowered his sword.

"Ach, she is so irksome!" he muttered angrily, to which Mardan nodded. Turning his head to gaze upon the sheDemon standing only a few feet from them rubbing her wrist briskly to ward off the lingering pain from Rehstaed's fearsome grasp, he watched her for a moment before answering.

"Agreed." He said with greater thought, the expression in his eyes altering from the intense glare he had fixed upon his comrade into a far more penetrating stare as he looked upon her with consideration she had not seen in their depths before. Cerulean melded into cerulean as they stared at each other, but when Rehstaed muttered to himself in his own beguiling language, Mardan turned back to him once more. "You of all people understand the horrors the Reviled can unleash. Have you not considered that, perhaps, she needed to be this way in order to survive in the Uunglarda? Perhaps Legionnaires were as ruthless to her as they were to your beloved?"

Rehstaed scowled fiercely at Mardan for an intense moment before he looked past the Celebrant at the sheDemon before them. The hatred that burned in his violet glare diminished as he recalled the vile atrocities Legionnaires had inflicted upon his beloved and may have, also, forced upon her. In the silence that filled the clearing, the malefey looked at her with perception so apparent in their stares that, for the briefest moment, she could barely breathe. Even the Legionnaires still kneeling before the Fey of the Light turned to look at her with such unmistakable compassion that she could not combat the onslaught of emotion that suddenly overwhelmed her. Gasping audibly, she closed her eyes against the tears attempting to overpower her and stalked away abruptly.

Although he was stirred by an unexpectedly powerful desire to follow her and offer any means of comfort he might provide, Mardan shook his head and looked back at his companions. They said nothing, nor did the Legionnaires, as the comprehension of what she must have suffered filled their thoughts, yet after what seemed an eternity of silence, Bryth turned his piercing cobalt gaze onto Senzuur once more.

"What is it you want, Dark One?"

Shifting uneasily in his kneeling stance, the Legionnaire looked up at the warrior in golden armor, then glanced round the clearing curiously. "We want to speak with your Leader."

"Our Leader?" Mardan repeated incredulously. He and Bryth shared an uneasy glance, but it was not Senzuur who answered. Behind him, the Legionnaire who had narrowly escaped Rehstaed's wrath responded with a distinctly constrained tone.

"Aye. Where is Gairynzvl?"

Chapter Six

Senzuur twisted round to glare back at the subordinate, silencing him with a sharp hiss and staring at him so threateningly that not even Bryth interrupted his wordless form of discipline in order to inquire further. Only when he was satisfied that his lieutenant would interject nothing further did the leader of the small band of Legionnaires turn to look up at the Fey of the Light once more. "Will you allow us to speak with him?" he inquired with surprising diplomacy.

Bryth shook his head and glanced sideways at Mardan even as he answered. "You must speak with us first and answer our questions before you are given access to our Leader."

Behind him, the Dark Ones shifted and hissed impatiently, but Senzuur nodded, indicating his acceptance of the structure of their hierarchy and waited for whatever queries the Fey Guards might put to him.

"Why are you here?" Bryth queried first.

"Why have you crossed into our realm during the daytide and what have you to discuss with Gairynzvl?" Mardan added with equal authority. Closing his crimson eyes with an effort of retaining his composure, Senzuur considered briefly before responding with far greater eloquence than any of them expected.

"We are here, Golden Warriors, because we witnessed what occurred at the Great Gate; what Gairynzvl did to open the portal and the actions your group took to protect and rescue younglings. We chose to drive the Legionnaires who pursued you through the portal so you might know our purpose is true. We crossed over before nightfall to prove our intentions can be trusted and to demonstrate that our objectives are not volatile. Had we crossed under the cover of darkness, you would never have spoken a word to us and it is imperative that you do and that you permit us to speak with Gairynzvl."

Again, Bryth turned to gaze contemplatively at Mardan, whose cerulean stare never wavered from the Legionnaires before them, but Rehstaed growled. Unimpressed by the Legionnaire's display of lucidity and resolutely unconvinced, he listened with a doubtful expression even when Senzuur continued more informatively.

"Only the one spoken of in the ancient texts could have sundered the Gate and liberated so many. As Watchers, we have waited a very long time to see such evidence of the Day of Liberation."

Scoffing impatiently, Rehstaed turned aside. "Day o' Liberation. Liberation from what? Yer appallin'ly ab'orrent existence?"

Unable to constrain his vexation any longer, a subordinate at the back of the group who had up until that moment forced himself to keep silent lowered his head and muttered in a beguiling language that was distinctly not Dlalth.

Upon hearing him, Rehstaed turned sharply to look at the Legionnaire with a penetratingly Discerning glare. "Ye' ha' som'tin' t' say, treacherous demon?"

Looking up at the Fey of the Light who glowered at him with his bronze-feathered wings spread wide aggressively, the Legionnaire glanced across at Senzuur. When he received no reproof for his actions, he got up from his kneeling position and glared back at him tenaciously. "For a Fey o' the Light, yer hate speaks wi' suprisin' clarity."

Rehstaed's comrades stared at the subordinate with astonishment, recognizing the accent with which he spoke that distinguished him as being native to the northern lands of Vrynnyth Gahl, in spite of his blood hued eyes and immense dragonhide wings. Rehstaed moved closer to him with an infuriated growl and would have taken him by the throat if Bryth had not stepped between them.

"Rehstaed has justifiable cause to hate." he warned the Reviled One who stood as tall and as powerfully built as they and who did not step back from their antagonistic posturing, regardless of the fact that they both bore weapons that could easily have taken his life.

"As ha' we, Fey Guard, but we are no' the ones makin' threats."

Bryth returned the Legionnaire's crimson stare pensively, then spun about, showing only his back to the Legionnaires as he spoke in a low voice with Rehstaed. "We must discover their purpose for being here and if we can use it to our advantage. Your ferocity in the face of the enemy honors you, but can you stand down?"

Giving Bryth a sideways glare that might have sent shivers through a Reviled Centurion, Rehstaed curled his lip in a silent hiss and stepped backward. Turning towards the Legionnaire glaring at them obstinately, Bryth stepped back as well before continuing their interrogation.

* * *

Glittering winter sunlight streamed through the shutters of the Healing Ward, reaching to envelop Gairynzvl in its life-giving vitality long after the deep lacerations inflicted by the ironwork of the Great Gate had closed. As if by its own sentient decision, regardless of the advance of the afternoon and the sun's declination in the sky, the Light's tender touch swathed him in luxurious warmth that renewed and invigorated his life force while he slept, exhausted by the trauma he had endured. The Temple surgeons and Healers visited his bedside often, monitoring his steadily improving condition, stooping to examine his hands with quizzical wonder, and discussing the marvel of it in hushed whispers and speculative tones. Even Zraylaunyth returned after several hours to scrutinize the continuing influence of the Light. He nodded in silent contemplation when he discovered the fully healed, yet lingering scars upon his hands, just as the prophecy had foretold.

Evondair spent much of this time in the company of the Elders, speaking with them at length to describe how the portal of the Great Gate was opened and how that breach now threatened the adjacent woodland. He warned them about the Reviled who were marshalling for a full-scale attack, and requesting the intervention of the Fey Guard who could protect the villagers and the many childfey they had succeeded in rescuing. Not surprisingly, they agreed that deployment of the Guard was appropriate and immediately sent word to the division on duty to make preparations and to advise them to coordinate with Evondair about the particulars of when they would depart. It was only after the Elders ensured the involvement of Fey trained in fighting skills and military strategy that they could begin to assuage the hesitations of the Healer who was less than keen to return to the site of an impending battle. Reassuring him that he was fulfilling his purpose, despite their silence on the specifics of that role, the Elders soon afterward retired to the Devotionary to mediate on events further.

As the afternoon advanced, Evondair stood in the corridor outside the Healing Ward with Kaylyya beside him, both gazing outward at the sunlit winter gardens surrounding the Temple, but although she stood in wonder, taking in the finest details of the exquisitely pruned and tended gardens, his thoughts were brooding and conflicted. He knew his fellow Liberators were anticipating his return. He knew they would require a Healer when the battle commenced and he was certain his skills would be necessary to help tend the needs of the neglected and abused younglings they had rescued. He had given his word he would return, but he longed to remain in the tranquil environment of the Temple where he could find some measure of peace to combat the turmoil within him that had begun tormenting him the moment he stepped through the portal into the darkness of the Uunglarda. He also wanted to participate in his friend's full recovery, rather than leaving him behind in order to return to the portal and the mounting threat of conflict with the Reviled.

Although she was neither telepathic nor empathic, Kaylyya could easily sense his agitation and interpreted the frown that overshadowed his otherwise handsome features. Unwilling to disturb him with idle chatter about all she had seen and heard when his thoughts were so clearly troubled, she said little and waited for him to break the silence as they stood wordlessly. In the hush, the afternoon sunlight shifted behind clouds, then broke through with brilliant determination. The lustrous glimmers played across the lavender and dark jade of her wings and sparkled through her bright blond hair, drawing Evondair's attention away from his contemplations at last. Turning his head to gaze down at her for a protracted moment, he forced the melancholic gloom of his thoughts aside and drew a deep breath, though he said nothing.

"Will you be returning to the village?" she questioned softly, neither turning to face him, nor raising her gaze to his own, but focusing her attention on the light outside as it sparkled across the snow and danced amid clusters of small plants trimmed with icicles. Again, he breathed deeply, closing his eyes when he nodded subtly.

"I must. I gave my word," he answered in a perfunctory tone that brimmed with reluctance and it was this obvious hesitation that caused her to turn and look up at him.

"Returning troubles you?" Her inquiry made him sigh a third time as he struggled to suppress the frustration he felt over the prospect of having to face another battle with the Reviled, but she did not wait for him to respond before continuing in a far softer tone. "Because of the Legionnaire."

It was not a question and her perceptiveness made him grimace as a wave of revulsion and grief swelled within him. It stifled his voice and when he attempted to answer, his response was diminished to a heavy whisper burdened by poignant emotion. "I have never killed before."

She stared up at him with a pained expression, not having known him long enough to draw him into a comforting embrace, although she could think of nothing else to do.

Drawing a shuddering breath, he shook his head and opened his eyes. The brilliant viridian of his stare pierced her. "I am a Healer, not a warrior. I do not belong on a battlefield."

"Are there not many on a battlefield who might require the skills of an exceptional Healer?" The deep voice of the speaker echoed along the empty corridor, surprising them both so they looked about with bewilderment. To their even greater astonishment, they found Gairynzvl standing in the Healing Ward doorway with a wry smirk turning the corner of his mouth. He gazed back at them with a clarity of expression that belied the trauma he had suffered and Evondair could not keep from turning his head to the side to stare at him with amazement.

"Gairynzvl?"

The Healer's disbelief made his friend smile. "Were you going to leave without me?"

Evondair shook his head, his mouth agape as he stuttered to find something intelligible to say, entirely flummoxed by his unanticipated recovery. "I did not...I should not have supposed you would be in any condition to return... so soon."

Gairynzvl shook his head. "Soon? Have I not been asleep for days?"

"No, hours only." Evondair corrected him, moving closer and looking down at his hands when he held them up to examine them with a thoroughly puzzled expression.

"Hours? How can that be? I am fully healed." They gazed at his hands more closely, marveling at their condition. They were healed to such an extent that anyone would have believed he had sustained the injury months prior.

"It was the Light," Evondair explained somewhat cryptically, struggling to put into words something he did not fully comprehend, but when Gairynzvl stared at him with confusion, he tried again. "Though I was not present at your Prevailation, I understand that, during the rite, the Light surrounds and pervades in order to transform. It was much the same today."

Again, they gazed at his hands, fully healed though permanently scarred. Unable to stop himself, Evondair asked his friend to perform several functional tests, checking his dexterity and flexibility before he stepped back and shook his head with even greater amazement. "I confess, I did not expect you to ever regain the full use of your hands, but there is a magic at work here that far exceeds my understanding."

"There is a story to be told," moving to join them from further along the corridor where he had been speaking with one of the Fey Guards, Veryth interrupted their conversation with his characteristically even-tempered manner. "One you can surely share while partaking of the evening meal. I came in search of you to inform you it is being prepared early so those Guards joining your company may bolster their strength before setting off. As it may be some time before you have the benefit of a full meal again, should a battle ensue, it may be wise to join them."

Agreeing they were indeed hungry, they shared a brief moment of introduction as Evondair presented Kaylyya and explained how she had offered her kind assistance when they were in need. Greeting her amiably, they moved together towards the dining hall, but Evondair stopped abruptly. Looking down at himself with a critical gaze, he scowled and shook his head. "Forgive me, but I cannot go a moment longer without changing these blood-soaked clothes. Go without me and I shall rejoin you presently."

Laughing in good-natured jest at his friend's fastidiousness, Gairynzvl shook his head before he turned to Kaylyya to inquire about the childfey they had rescued. "Have you seen the younglings we rescued? Are they... alright?"

She answered softly, "I confess I know little about them, except that they have been taken into the homes of the villagers who were caring for them. Our immediate concern was you."

Gairynzvl smiled somewhat uncomfortably at her, but at the mention of the little ones, Veryth interjected once again, "Could the cart you used to bring Gairynzvl to the Temple be utilized to transport the younglings back to us? It could be outfitted with a covering to protect them from the cold."

Kaylyya smiled and nodded as if she had already presumed they would. "Of course."

"Could it not also be used to carry additional weaponry and supplies to the village? If a battle does break out, villagers armed with hay-forks and scythes will offer weak opposition to Legionnaires equipped with heavy swords and archers trained to strike at distance." Gairynzvl added and, when Veryth agreed, their conversation shifted to talk of armaments and provisions for extended conflict. As they walked along strategizing, they were joined by the captain of the Fey Guard, who introduced himself and, upon hearing their discussion, added a few supplementary requests of his own.

The evening meal quickly turned into a planning assembly. Hav-ing finished her small meal quietly, Kaylyya excused herself from the table of malefey whose conversation veered between battle tactics and a sport she had heard of, but never actually witnessed, known as Vladokhyssum. Having little interest in either topic she wandered the broad hall, inconspicuously moving from the long table at which the malefey sat to the window. There she gazed outward for several long moments until the winter's chill seemed to reach through the panes of glass to send a shiver over her. Moving again, she stepped quietly to the massive hearth centrally located in the hall and extended her hands towards the radiant blaze to warm them. Listening to the chatter of the malefey around her, she attempting to keep her thoughts from wondering too curiously about Evondair who had not yet returned.

She had spent her entire life within the precincts of her small village of wool-weavers, never having traveled even so far as Veryn Falls to celebrate Summerfest or the autumnal shifting of the seasons. Life un-der the eaves of the forest was quiet and uncomplicated, where each member of the community knew every other member and few secrets could be sustained. Here amid the complex structures of the Temple where Fey Guards, Healers, Artisans, Scholars and skilled attendants resided with the Great Elder's themselves, life seemed to overflow with drama and mystery. Certainly, whatever endeavor in which Evondair and Gairynzvl, as well as those others whom they had left at the vil-lage, were involved was nothing short of extraordinary and to find herself entangled in its plot, despite her lack of details concerning it, was as exhilarating as it was terrifying.

Smiling warmly when her thoughts shifted to contemplate Evondair more particularly, she could not stop herself from turning to gaze over her shoulder towards the entrance of the hall in search of him, but when she did not find him her attention was distracted by a group of Guards entering the hall by a door on the opposite side of the chamber, which led outside. Dressed in sparkling golden armor that glittered in the late afternoon sunlight, she could not contain a sigh of wonder. Shaking her head in disbelief that she should be standing in the same room with such an awe-inspiring group, she failed to notice Evondair returning from his quarters.

Locating her with little difficulty amid a room filled with malefey, he crossed the floor with a purposeful stride, but said nothing when he stood behind her. Not wishing to startle her, he watched while she gazed wonderingly at the Guards who had entered at the same time he had and were now collecting their dinner. Turning around at last, Kaylyya found him standing quietly, gazing down at her with undisguised admiration. She gasped in surprise at his unexpected proximity, but his light chuckle and the manner in which he inclined his head to her while offering a quietly sincere apology for unnerving her silenced any admonishment she might have considered and left her blinking up at him demurely.

She expected he would change his shirt, as it had, indeed, been heavily stained with the blood of the Legionnaire, but she had not anticipated he might entirely redress or that, in changing out of the muted grays and blacks he had been wearing, he might seem utterly transformed, but his alteration was nothing less than remarkable. His brown leather pants boasted interwoven lacings along each outward seam and defined the strong shape of his legs. His boots were embellished with both lacings and numerous buckles, which extended up to the knee and these accents were repeated along the sleeves of his dark brown leather coat. The form-fitting vest fashioned of rich gold and black brocade fabric he had donned, which hugged his trim, powerful physique in the most flattering manner, captivated her stare. Its stand-up collar, wide, sweeping lapels, and golden buttons descending along each side seemed incongruously elegant for the frontlines of an impending battle, but the ensemble accentuated his expansive white wings and the waves of his shoulder-length golden hair reflecting the firelight. She sighed at the sight of him, in spite of the fact that he stood gazing down at her, visibly pleased by her obvious delight.

"I confess it is rather a formal ensemble for the battlefield," he admitted in a hushed tone, looking down at himself with nearly as critical an expression as he had done when he wore clothes covered in blood. "I am usually in Healer's robes and own little social apparel, so it is," he paused to consider the appropriate word, but Kaylyya smiled approvingly and completed his sentence for him with guileless honesty.

"Stunning."

Laughing unpretentiously, he smiled and inclined his head once more in an expression of appreciation before he looked beyond her and noticed Gairynzvl who had gotten up from the table where he had been awaiting the Healer's return. Moving towards them with a smirk turning the corner of his mouth, although he was shaking his head, he glanced down at Kaylyya perceptively before speaking. "All is sufficiently prepared for our departure and, although I can plainly see it is not on your list of priorities, have you eaten?" His inquiry, brimming with mischievous insinuation, caused such a charming smile to brighten Evondair's features that the source prompting his friend's banter could not help staring up at him with genuine partiality.

"I appreciate your concern for my welfare, but be assured it is unfounded as I partook of a small meal in my quarters and find myself most satisfied," Evondair countered with exaggerated courtesy, at which both malefey laughed with an easiness of spirit neither had enjoyed since the evening after the game of Vladokhyssum in the village tavern, but the Healer's countenance shifted when their mirth subdued and he stepped round Kaylyya to speak with Gairynzvl more directly.

"Before we depart, there *is* something I must say."

Chapter Seven

"You are the one with the gift of Discernment. Are you not able to determine if they speak truth or lies?" Reydan queried in a nearly indistinguishable whisper, moving closer to Rehstaed as nonchalantly as possible while his comrades continued to interrogate the Legionnaires, but Rehstaed shook his head. Gazing at them for a protracted moment in silent consideration, he shook his head once more, confessing just as quietly that his own roiling emotions were impeding his sensitivity. They listened as Senzuur provided details about the numbers of Dark Ones mustering for battle, as well as the places the battalions of Legionnaires might cross, hoping to win the Fey Guard's trust.

Mardan scoffed at the mention of such statistics and turned aside. "All this could be deliberate deception. We have no reason to believe them."

Hissing impatiently at his accusation, Senzuur turned to face the fair Fey and, although he had been attempting to maintain a purposefully tactful tone, it then shifted to a far more customary pitch of impudence as he stepped closer to Mardan with a menacing glare. "Had you any reason to believe Gairynzvl when you decided to follow him?"

Mardan's cerulean gaze sharpened with animosity and he glared back at the Dark One wordlessly, daring him to more violent action through the hostility of his defiant stare alone, but the Legionnaire constrained his anger and spoke through bared teeth, though he shook with restraint. "Why will you not permit us to speak with him? He could, at the very least, corroborate the fact that The Watchers exist and we speak the truth."

"B'cause ye' are contemptible, deceitful, worthless Reviled!" Rehstaed spat in anger, stalking forward to glare balefully at Senzuur.

His retaliatory actions spurred the subordinate at Senzuur's side to stare fiercely back at him with an equal measure of hostility and he spat back his own slanderous reply. "An' ye' are no' but a blood-thirsty, vengeful monster, consumed by yer' own pain, an' eager t' be killin' yer' own brot'ers b'fore 'earin' a word o' their own!"

Hissing viperously at the Dark One who stood mere inches from him and returned his scowl of detestation, Rehstaed reached forward suddenly to grasp him by the throat, but, rather than seeking to escape, the subordinate leaned closer and hissed further accusations through clenched teeth. "Ye' think ye' are t'only one t' ha' suffered? Can ye' e'en imagine the brutality we ha' endured since our younglin' years? Starved for food, for water, for the touch o' a mot'er's lovin' 'and. Raped an' ravaged, an' forced to do the same t' other's or face far worse. Beaten an' bludgeoned an' tortured, 'til e'en our scars bear scars!" Looking down at himself, the subordinate wrenched open his shirt, sending its few remaining buttons scattering in order to reveal the intertwined scars that covered nearly every inch of his chest, his stomach and wrapped round his sides to suggest they extended across his back as well. They told a horrific story of repeated abuse and, as the Fey of the Light stared at him with visible dismay, he stretched out his wings to display the latticework of scars they bore as well.

"By the Ancients!" Bryth breathed in shocked amazement.

The subordinate continued undaunted. "If ye' be wishin' to prove me right, then throttle me an' be done wi' it; for ye' shall be doin' me a kindness!"

Rehstaed's deep violet gaze pierced the blood red of the subordinate's and narrowed as he struggled to put aside his hatred. With his hand still encircling the Legionnaire's throat, he looked into his eyes, then past them as he delved to read the essence of his being and, although he had not asked permission, the subordinate did not resist him. Opening his thoughts to the other's Discernment, he allowed him to seek, and the two Fey stared at each other intensely while those around them waited.

His gift of Discernment allowed him to keenly understand the subordinate, to judge the level of his honesty and know the truth of the other's nature with as much certainty as he understood himself, but Rehstaed had not considered the Dark One's own gift of telepathy. In connecting mentally with the Legionnaire, he became aware of disjointed memories that were not his own. His thoughts filled with screams of pain and the distinctive sound of a lash as echoing cries for mercy melded with cruel, sadistic laughter. The flood of painful memories closed in on him, surrounding and filling his thoughts until he could barely distinguish them from reality.

Gasping loudly, Rehstaed squeezed his eyes tightly closed even as the subordinate's filled with tears and ran over to streak the grime covering his pallid cheeks. His hand relaxed and Rehstaed drew back, shaking his head as the truth of the other's existence pierced into him like a blade. The pain he had endured when he had been forced to watch Legionnaires rape and murder his beloved and his only son was a single day; one solitary event. It had stolen the joy of life and the reason for breath from his spirit, but the subordinate had suffered similarly devastating torments and brutality since he had been abducted as a childfey and the memories of his Integration, which had transferred to Rehstaed, were more appalling than the former Fey Guard could bear. He stared at the Legionnaire horrified by the truth he had discovered and mortified by his own prejudiced hatred.

Withdrawing his hand from the other's throat, he placed it, instead, upon the Dark One's broad shoulder and inclined his head, folding his wings in an indication of deference as he spoke with a tone of esteem none of them had ever heard him use. "Countryman."

The subordinate raised his head to look back at him with a vivid mixture of confusion and surprise. Blood-red and dark violet locked as Rehstaed drew an unsteady breath. "Friend."

Turning his head slightly to one side, the Legionnaire shook his head once, attempting to understand the Fey Guard's unanticipated actions, but the emotion conveyed in his voice eliminated the Dark One's skepticism. When he had spoken, Rehstaed stepped forward and embraced him, removing any doubts he may yet have had while utterly astonishing the Fey of the Light who stood watching in dumbstruck silence.

"Brother."

* * *

Gairynzvl focused his awareness, though he refrained from extending his still heightened senses to read the Healer's thoughts when the sudden gravity of Evondair's tone betrayed the turbulent emotion with which he struggled.

"I shall return with you to the village. I will tend any who may become injured in the impending conflict and I shall, of course, participate in relocating the childfey to the Temple if my skills should be needed, but I will not," The Healer paused, closing his eyes to briefly combat the rising tide threatening to undo him. Shaking his head, he fixed his penetrating gaze upon Gairynzvl once more and continued in a far more poignant tone. "I cannot fight."

Gairynzvl turned his head slightly to one side, regarding the Healer more contemplatively. "The blood that covered your clothes was not my own," he returned decisively, receiving only a shake of the head in answer so that he delved a bit deeper. "Was it the Legionnaire's?"

Evondair stared at him, surprised he might remember events that had occurred while he had been insensible, but before he could respond Gairynzvl added more musingly, "I thought I was dreaming it, a delirium brought on by my injury." His tone was halting as he sought the illusive memory slithering through his thoughts like a shadow slipping between the forest trees.

"No, it was far too real." The burden of emotion evident in the Healer's tone shook Gairynzvl from his musings and he looked back at him, comprehending perfectly what Evondair was trying not to say. The malefey considered each other silently while Kaylyya looked up at them, but the former Dark One answered him with certainty.

"He would have killed you, perhaps all of us, if you had not acted."

Sighing prodigiously, Evondair turned aside, as if weary of the argument, despite the fact that the only one with whom he had debated the point had been himself. "I am not convinced of that," he breathed heavily. He walked around Kaylyya to face his friend and the intense lavender-ice of Gairynzvl's gaze locked with the Healer's brilliant viridian in a piercing stare.

"Why do you not believe it?" Gairynzvl's tone was not incredulous, but curious and Evondair drew a deep breath, reconsidering the judiciousness of sharing his reasoning because he was certain his compassionate perspective would only bring him under scrutiny, but the words forced their way past his lips as if with a will of their own.

"If I had given him *any* assurance that I would not harm him, perhaps he would not have acted as he did." Unable to keep silent any longer, the diminutive shefey standing with them spoke out at last, defending Evondair's actions in spite of his own condemnation.

"He tried to remove your head, Evondair! He certainly would have crushed Gairynzvl's hands under his boots if you had not stopped him, and the Ancients only know what he might have done with me." Both malefey looked down at her, considering her assertions, but when Gairynzvl's icy gaze melted into hers she could not keep from shuddering under its intensity and silenced any further protests.

Evondair shook his head another time. "Perhaps he anticipated I would attack him and so, to protect himself, he attacked us first."

Gairynzvl turned his stare upon the Healer once again, regarding him with an unreadable expression and pondering the insight with which he spoke as his visibly distraught friend continued.

"I do not know," the Healer sighed sharply and shook his head another time, continuing even more uncertainly. "Perhaps I am doing what I, as a Healer, do best; I am over-thinking the matter." His exasperation was as plain to hear as it was to see, but he had gained his friend's full attention and the former Reviled Fey did not interrupt when Evondair continued with a halting, more repulsed tone. "The only thing I know with certainty is this: when I held that Legionnaire by the throat and his blood poured over my hands- hands that I have taken an oath would *never* do harm to another- he looked at me with tears in his eyes."

"Tears?" Kaylyya repeated with evident confusion.

"Tears. Not hatred, not anger, but tears." His voice quavered as the gruesome moment replayed in his thoughts and Gairynzvl watched him as intently as he listened. The Healer plunged on, the words spilling from him like a long-guarded confession. "He may have been one of the Reviled, but as he died his body responded to the trauma that *I* inflicted just as yours or mine would have done and my training made me keenly aware of it. I should have thought he would have resisted in some manner; that he would have fought against me to prevent his death, but he did not." Again, he paused and the deep viridian of his gaze locked with the liquescent lavender of his friends'. When he continued, his voice shook with tremulous emotion. "As the life force left his body, the only thing he did was look into my eyes...and smile!"

The utter disconcertion of his tone betrayed the reasons for his turmoil. Shaking his head repeatedly, the Healer covered his face with trembling hands to hide the bitter regret swelling within him, but his actions could not be ignored and it was not only his companions who watched him with astonishment. Raising his gaze from his platter, the Fey Guard Captain still seated at the table with Veryth regarded him with incredulity and then nudged the Guard beside him who looked up from his rapidly disappearing meal to stare at him as well. They could not entirely overhear the conversation, but the unanticipated, emotional display from a Healer who was well-known and respected for his calm serenity and level-headed demeanor was cause enough for them to strain to hear what was being said.

"There is only one reason I can think of why he should smile." Evondair continued through the splayed fingers of his hands.

"What reason is that?" Gairynzvl asked purposely, his qustion causing Evondair to uncover his face and stare at the former Legionnaire as if he ought to already know the reason.

"You of all Fey should know. Because death was preferable to his life, and if his life was so intolerable that he should look upon death as some form of release, then perhaps," his voice trailed off when he was unable to complete his thought because he did not truly understand what such a death might signify, but Gairynzvl nodded.

"You are, indeed, perceptive, Evondair. Having lived the intolerable life of a Legionnaire, I can tell you that death is very much preferable." Gairynzvl's confirmation brought a pained expression to the Healer's face and those who sat around them listening unreservedly to their conversation could not help looking at each other with marked uncertainty. Such a notion had never been a consideration. It was merely taken as fact that Legionnaires were ruthless monsters whose only desire was to inflict harm upon another.

When she heard Evondair indicate that his friend had once been a Legionnaire, Kaylyya stared up at the white-haired, nebulous-winged malefey before her with an expression of such foreboding that both he and Evondair looked down at her with surprise. Unable to contain her natural inclination to step back from him, her ingenuous reaction made both malefey smile. Gairynzvl inclined his head and lowered his wings in a non-threatening gesture while Evondair reached out for her.

"Forgive us, Kaylyya. There is much to explain to you when time better permits, though for now you must trust me when I say that Gairynzvl would never seek to harm you." He spoke reassuringly and smiled with warm affection when she nodded hesitantly, but before either could say anything further, Veryth got up from the table where he had been sitting and moved to face Gairynzvl.

"Please forgive my intrusion into your conversation, but I must speak with you."

Gairynzvl looked at the well-respected Healer whom he felt humbled to be able to call his friend and turned his head slightly to one side with obvious curiosity.

Veryth spoke with a tone of determination, "If battle is inevitable you will undoubtedly require the skills of more than one Healer, and even if the only way in which I might serve is to watch over the little ones you have rescued, or to return them here for care and nurturing, then I should like to volunteer to join you."

The eager reception that greeted his offer made the Healer smile more easily, at which time he gave assurances that he would meet them at the stables in little more than a candle mark so he might change from his Healer's robes and make some few preparations. Delighted to wait upon him, the malefey returned Kaylyya to her Hasparii so she might ready him for their departure and, within the hour, the entire ensemble was underway. Fey Guards winged overhead and the malefey accompanied Kaylyya in the cart, now laden with armaments, blankets, supplies of food, and provisions for use by the Healers.

Hoping to set any trepidations she might have to rest, Gairynzvl undertook the explanation of his history, much as he had done in the garden room of the Temple with those he now called friends, and the young shefey listened with earnest fascination to the tale. Evondair listened with similar interest, having pieced together most of what he knew about the former Dark One from various conversations with Veryth, Bryth and Zraylaunyth. Through hearing his story, the young Healer understood more fully not only what he had Discerned about the Fierce One during their earliest interactions, but the irresistible compulsion he had felt to join his endeavor.

As they listened to his tale and while the malefey related to Kaylyya the events leading up to the sundering of the Great Gate, which had opened the portal beneath the mountain, the miles between the Temple complex and the small village of Lyyshara disappeared beneath the runners of the Hasparii drawn cart. Having acquired the name of the village before setting off, and familiar with the community of wool-weavers, the Fey Guard had wasted little time traversing the distance to its borders, but those with the cart did not arrive until after darkness had fallen. As they approached the barns, calls echoed through the indigo dimness from villagers carrying torches and lanterns rushing from the many cottages nestled in the nearby forest.

Jumping to the ground before the cart had even come to a full stop beside the stables where the wool-weaver's livestock were housed, Gairynzvl called to one of the malefey hurrying by them. "What is happening?" He feared he already knew the answer, that the Reviled were surging forth from the portal, but to his surprise the villager hurriedly replied.

"The Fey of the Light have built a great fire and we are going to join them with provisions for a meal and to see the Legionnaires who are with them." Turning to gaze at each other with confusion, they could not help standing in dumbstruck silence as the villagers passed them, heading in the direction of an enormous blaze radiating its ruddy warmth into the frosty winter evening.

Chapter Eight

Blaylscith scattered in all directions through puddles of murky, gray water as a battalion of mud-spattered Legionnaires tramped into the bustling encampment. Straggling behind the main group and panting with over-exertion, a second unit followed closely, but unlike the former who marched in unison and carried their weapons with strength and purpose, those who followed were ragged and in visible disarray. Many of these bore scars that stood out in vivid contrast against their pallid complexions and others nursed fresh wounds. They were a testament to their harrowing existence, which was exemplified when the unit came to a halt and many stragglers stumbled or nearly collapsed out of fatigue.

When the battalion of Demonfey ahead of them stopped, they stamped the ends of their spears into the ground or clapped their swords against their shields as they voiced a growling, unified exclamation that echoed along the mu-smeared road and sent shivers of fear through any who heard them. "Raah!"

These were the Legionnaires of the Realm. They were fiercely loyal to their Centurion and vicious of nature, not only in battle, but with any who crossed them. Their uniforms were spattered by the mud of the road, but they were in good repair, made of finely worked leather treated with oil to repel water. Their weapons were fashioned of exceptionally-wrought steel by skilled Dlalth hands in the forges of Vrasduuhl, the centermost and chief city of the Uunglarda.

In contrast to this disciplined, brutally efficient regiment, those who followed behind were under-nourished, poorly equipped with second-hand, over-utilized weapons, and wore clothing that had been repeatedly patched, were soaked through from the pouring rain and distinctly unclean. These were also Legionnaires, but they had been forced to undertake their oaths of service after years of harsh punishments and deprivation. They were the insignificant and the irrelevant; the expendable vanguard who would suffer the greatest number of injuries and fatalities before the highly-trained, ferocious Demonfey ever stepped onto the field of battle.

As icy rain leeched down in heavy torrents, the battalion of Demonfey were rapidly processed and sent off toward the tent where hearty provisions awaited them. The remaining Legionnaires were left standing in the downpour with little thought to their comfort or the fact that several had fallen out of utter exhaustion. Lying in the pooling rain, their needs were ignored by those standing round them. They were all fully cognizant of the fact that any display of compassion for their comrades would only result in further torment or punishment. Although they were weary beyond measure and, in spite of the fact that some had not eaten for days, they stood in the downpour with grim, mute endurance and waited.

Long after the Legionnaires of the Realm had enjoyed a satisfying meal, one of the captains returned to those still waiting in the rain. They were now shivering violently from weariness and exposure to the elements. Compelling them to undergo an inspection, the captain first released only those who were still able to follow his instructions while he callously ignored those who had fallen or who could no longer force themselves to obey. Sending the first group off to the provisions tent to scavenge whatever food and drink might remain, the captain then summoned one of his lieutenants who carried a barbed lash. Mercilessly, he stalked through those few who remained hunched against the deluge, handing them the lash and forcing them to beat those who had fallen until they scrabbled, wailing, to their feet. Only when all the remaining nonessential Legionnaires were once again standing did the captain give consent for them to join the others in search of any provisions that might yet remain.

* * *

The sweet scent of fresh snow mingled with bright, crisp evergreen as the evening breeze whispered through the clearing and surrounded the Fey who had gathered around an enormous bonfire. The villagers had returned to the clearing from their homes carrying with them large earthenware crocks filled with hearty grains and winter vegetables, freshly baked breads, deep jugs of mead, and great joints of meat for roasting over the fire. Although most Fey of the Light rarely, if ever, consumed the flesh of an animal those gathered were not opposed to the villager's surprising generosity, particularly when the scent of roasting venison began to fill the air.

In spite of the fact that they had crossed to Lyyshara without weapons, the villagers were reluctant to trust those Legionnaires who were now in their midst and remained as far from them as possible, but the Liberators had come to an understanding with them and stood around the blaze they had constructed together without further hostility, warming their hands and wings and sharing tentative converse. When the Fey Guards of the Temple arrived, they were greeted by Bryth and Mardan who shared what had occurred during the course of the day. They described in detail not only the repeated Dlalth horns they had heard echoing through the portal, but also the information the Watcher Legionnaires had given them about the Reviled's plans. Although sentries had been posted to guard the portal, the Watchers insisted that the Reviled were still mustering their forces and would not cross that night to engage them in battle.

Far from willing to trust any Legionnaire, however, the Captain of the Fey Guard spoke with Senzuur at some length, attempting to satisfy his own misgivings about relying on information from a Dark One. In spite of the leader of the Legionnaire's readiness to answer his questions and his knowledge about the stratagems of the mustering Reviled, the Captain of the Guard remained unconvinced. He had spent too many years learning to distrust Dark Fey to suddenly have confidence in the dubious enticements of a handful of disheveled Legionnaires.

Those Guards who were not immediately stationed at the base of the mountain to stand watch over the open portal were released to join the growing group converging round the fire; yet, like their Captain, most could not set aside everything they had been taught as childfey or through their training with the Guard and, as a result, they did not mix with the Legionnaires lingering hesitantly near the intoxicating warmth of the fire. Eager to enjoy the company of their fellow Guards and listen to the Liberators recount their tale of daring, they were, nevertheless, unwilling to trust the determination of their comrades that these particular Legionnaires posed no immediate threat. They shared the simple feast provided by the villagers, but they did so begrudgingly.

As the crocks of nourishing grains and vegetables were passed round and jugs of mead circled in the opposite direction, the Liberators went so far as to give extra portions to the visibly ravenous Dark Ones and they brought a young Legionnaire, who babbled incessantly and could not be quieted, from a nearby tree where he had been bound during the daylight hours. Encouraging him to eat, they left him in the company of the Watchers where he finally managed to silence himself so he might eat what he was offered. The Legionnaires shared with him from their own portions, as it was very apparent he had not seen food in many days, and this unanticipated act of generosity between Reviled Fey garnered many stares from the Guards who watched with disbelief. In spite of their growing curiosity, however, they did not speak with the Dark Ones.

Returning from the village with those who were eager to gather about the fire and share the small feast with the Liberators of childfey, Ayla and Ilys strolled with several other shefey who were not presently tending the younglings rescued from the Uunglarda. Talking quietly, they walked past the barns and stable yards without as much as a second glance. As they moved toward the roaring fire and bantering malefey, Ayla stopped abruptly, her mind filling with a soft, drawn-out whisper she recognized only too well.

"*Ayla.*"

Gasping in dismay, she covered her face with her hands as her heart lurched with dread. Fearing the worst, that Gairynzvl had succumbed to his injuries and was reaching out to her one final time, she could not contain the sudden rush of tearful emotion that assailed her. Turning to gaze back at her with annoyed confusion, Ilys scowled fiercely and inquired with a distinctly impatient tone just what was the matter, but before Ayla could gather enough composure to answer, Gairynzvl stepped from the dimly lit entrance of the closest barn, flexing his wings unhurriedly as he moved closer to the shefey.

Catching sight of him, Ilys smiled in surprise with an expression of greater relief than she might have typically chosen to show. To disguise her uncustomary display of emotion, however, she turned abruptly and continued toward the fire with the other shefey.

"Do not cry, Ayla. I am here," he spoke to her softly, the sound of his deep voice causing her to jerk her head up in surprise as she looked round in all directions. When she located him, the tide of emotion that had sought to overwhelm her shifted, but did not dissipate and she turned to face him even as her tears doubled. Fully anticipating such a welcome from her, he laughed quietly in amused forbearance with her sentimentality and embraced her. Bending to encircle her with his strong arms as well as his expansive wings, he drew her close to muffle the sound of her crying against his chest as he hushed her with quiet words meant only for her.

After several moments, he drew back and looked down at her in the flickering light of the nearby radiating fire, ignoring the tumbling questions that poured from her thoughts and capturing her perplexed, amber gaze with an intense stare. Slowly raising one hand to her chin, he held her gently as his own thoughts spun in a feverish whirlwind that sent both their senses reeling.

"You are here?" she whispered breathlessly, bewildered by his unforeseen return, but he did not answer. Moving barely an inch at a time, he drew closer, then closer still; his breath coming deeper, his heart pounding faster and his desire focused on the rosy blush of her lips.

"I am here," he whispered back to her. Another fraction of an inch closer, he paused to stare ardently at her mouth as hammering passion spread through his body and he did not restrict the sensation from transferring to her. In response to the blaze of his desire, her eyes closed and her head tilted back as she offered herself for his kiss. He could not contain the deep moan that escaped him before pressing his mouth to hers so tantalizingly lightly that she sighed sharply and fluttered her wings in blissful abandon. Moving closer, he pulled her against the warmth of his body, his hands cradling her as his soft kisses lingered longer, then longer, until the passion that swirled around them in a dizzying maelstrom prompted her to sigh even more profoundly. Moaning another time with intense pleasure, his thoughts filled with the notion of lifting her into his arms and carrying her into the closest barn to make better use of the darkness and shadows, but even as his desire intensified into a rampant haze, he pulled away. Looking over her into the distance, he posed an unanticipated query. "Why are there Legionnaires here?"

Gasping breathlessly, she shook her head while attempting to refocus the clarity of her thoughts. He had straightened and was looking beyond her at the group encircling the fire, turning his head slightly to one side when he saw the band of Legionnaires standing near his friends, eating voraciously and warming themselves a safe distance from the fire.

"I cannot tell you. I have been in the village with the childfey much of the day," she answered in an unsteady tone that refocused his attention onto her. The icy-lavender of his fervent stare pierced into her with such yearning that she shivered and closed her eyes as he drew closer to kiss her lingeringly another time. The intensity of his yearning could not be denied, yet, he stepped back and sighed with undisguised resignation.

"There is nothing I desire more, my sweet Ayla, then to fill the nighttide with my passion for you, but I know," he breathed deeply, fire glimmering in the icy sheen of his stare, "it is not the right time or place, is it?" His question was little more than a whisper, but he did not require an answer. He already knew it was not. Gazing up at him with longing she could scarcely manage to conceal, she shook her head slowly, reluctantly agreeing with him even as his gaze shifted once again to seek the faces of the Legionnaires.

"Much has happened since we left this morning." Evondair's voice came from the darkness behind them and Gairynzvl twisted round as the Healers and Kaylyya stepped out of the barn where they had unharnessed and stabled the great Hasparii.

"I must speak with these Legionnaires. I may know who they are."

"It appears you will have that opportunity," Evondair returned with a grin, looking beyond his friend at several Dark Fey who had stepped away from the fire and were speaking amongst themselves while gazing and pointing in the direction of the barns. Their vision was far better suited to seeing into the darkness than the Fey of the Light who had not yet noticed the return of their fellow Liberators. Gairynzvl closed his eyes, stretching out his thoughts to read those of the Legionnaires and instantly smiling when he recognized the inner voice of the one he sought who answered his questing with a familiar and abrasive retort for delving without permission.

"Impatient hravclanoch!"

Fixing his gaze on this Dark One who was walking toward them hastily, Gairynzvl turned briefly to place Ayla behind him before he strode forward with a grin. The Healers stepped around the shefey to stand between them and the potential threat the Legionnaires posed, but watched with curiosity as Gairynzvl and the unknown Legionnaires greeted each other.

"I should not be surprised to see you, but what, by the Ancients, are you doing here, Senzuur?" Gairynzvl's tone was openly disbelieving and Senzuur smiled crookedly, his expression brightening his otherwise sallow features. They met each other as friends who had spent much time apart and it did not take long for the remaining Watchers to approach as well, the Dark Ones staring with amazed conjecture at their nearly unrecognizable friend.

"Is it really you, Gairynzvl?" They drew closer, reaching out to touch his nebulous wings tentatively.

"It is; I assure you."

"By Hvyyrbachvra's demons, I'd ne'er ha' reco'nized you!"

Gairynzvl laughed openly, though his gaze fell to skeptically take in the subordinate Legionnaire's torn clothing. "Nor I you, Dravahl. Why are you half naked?"

It did not take long for Rehstaed's countryman to explain why he had torn his already poorly mended clothes or to remark on the efficiency of the Liberators who had kept Gairynzvl so well guarded during the course of the entire afternoon. This prompted the former Legionnaire to some measure of explanation and he assured them that they had been prevented from seeing him because he had not been there.

"I have just returned from the Temple where the injuries to my hands were tended."

Having witnessed the sundering of the Great Gate and the injuries it had inflicted upon him, they stared at him with even greater astonishment, but any further questions were cut short when a shout pierced the darkness that compelled all of them to reach for weapons, even in spite of the fact that the Watchers did not carry any.

Rehstaed's distinctive inflection rang through the darkness. "By th' Ancient's, Fierce One, I ne'er expected t' be seein' you back 'ere this eventide!"

Gairynzvl turned to watch as the remaining Liberators hastened into the dimness beyond the light of the fire to welcome him. Their evident delight at his return astonished him beyond measure, but although they were curious to hear about his unfathomable recovery, they urged them all to return to the warmth of the fire so the Fey Guard might also hear. Thus, as the evening progressed, the Healers recounted those events that Gairynzvl could not while he, in turn, queried about the arrival of the Watchers, and the jugs of honeyed-ale went round and round.

* * *

Icy rain fell upon the inhospitable encampment of Legionnaires until the deepest hours, mid of night. When it subsided, it was replaced by seeking, numbing cold that permeated to the bone. Those among the ranks of the Demonfey received ample protection from the biting chill in tents that were sufficiently weatherproofed and they were supplied with warm woolen blankets to fend off the cold while those recently mustered, who were deemed expendable, were left to huddle together with a meager, sulfurous fire their only source of warmth.

In order to gain any measure of comfort and to avert the worst of the fire's fumes, most of the new recruits covered their faces with bands of cloth torn from their already shoddy uniforms, but others were unable to tolerate the malodorous reek of the insignificant fire. These frequently retreated into the darkness where the air was less foul, but being any distance from the conflagration meant they were forced to endure the permeating cold unprotected, which lead them to wrap their wings round themselves in a vain attempt to keep warm until the queasy sensation produced by the sulfur fumes abated and they could return to the ineffectual warmth of the fire. Restively passing the long hours of the night in this exhausting manner, these ill-fated Fey greeted the gray-green light of new day with weary gazes and limbs numbed by the frosty conditions as they awaited their fate with the grim resolve of the hopeless.

Morning in the barren 'scape of the Uunglarda was bleak, heralded not by melodious birdsong and the suspirations of trees tossing their emeraldine heads in the crisp fresh breeze, but by discordant calls of Dlalth horns recalling from whatever fleeting measure of comfort they may have found during the night those held captive under the strict domination of the Centurion of their ranks. He was not, however, a preeminent dictator, but was required to swear allegiance to the district Overmaster who governed the entire province in which the Legionnaires were encamped. This territory, which was dark and foreboding on the best of days, also housed those Reviled who bore more servile positions in Dlalth society; those who were forced to undertake the preservation of weaponry and repairs to uniforms for the Demonfey, as well as the preparation of meals and any cleaning that might be deemed necessary. If there existed a menial duty, these servile Dlalth were the ones to perform it. They had no rights, no liberties, and very few basic necessities. They were the lowest in the social structure. They were the forlorn and dejected, and they were, invariably, the ones who bore the brutal sport of the Demonfey when they were in camp.

There was one, however, who ruled over the Demonfey, the Centurions and the Overmasters. One who was both venerated and feared because he was without mercy of any kind. His domination was inescapable; his words were immediately decreed as law; his demands required urgent obedience and his every thought was of manipulation and exploitation. He was the embodiment of sadistic cruelty and unswerving hatred. His essence was said to be rooted in absolute darkness. There was no hint of the Light left within him and none, regardless of rank or station, ever dared challenge him.

The fortress from which he ruled was known to all Dlalth as Hvyyrbachvra, which meant in the common tongue Abyss of the Lost. It sat at the centermost point of Vrasduuhl, constructed upon a mammoth, artificial outcropping. The walls of the fortification were twenty feet high, but they were built upon the sheer drop of the outcropping, which plunged nearly one hundred feet to ground level. There at the vast citadel's base, the city of Vrasduuhl sprawled outward proliferating commotion and unrest on all sides, consuming every resource it could acquire while wheezing out putrid fumes and excreting tainted water like a grotesque living monster whose only purpose was to serve the Imperial Praetor. Those who resided within the precincts of the cramped, overcrowded city lived in the foulest of conditions, suffered hunger and thirst on a daily basis. They were oppressed by masters who sought only to satisfy their own needs or who were themselves under the dominion of those select few who were appointed to personally serve the Praetor.

Only this small handful of Reviled were granted access to the citadel. They were the most powerful, most ruthless and brutal of all Demonfey. They were among the very few to ever survive contact with the Praetor and, although few ever dared look upon him, rumors of his mesmerizing beauty, which was impossible to oppose, filtered down through these select servants to the ranks of Legionnaires and every member of Dlalth society. Appalling tales of unfortunate Reviled, who were either seduced by his beauty or were sacrificed to him as some form of tribute only to find themselves victims of his unimaginable sadism, were as common as the recurring accounts of the delight he took in torturing with horrifyingly methodical cruelty any who denied him.

The Legionnaires who had passed the cold night beneath the gray, starless sky, knew these accounts well. They were reminded of them every day when one among their ranks was unwilling or unable to obey the commands of the Lieutenants and the remaining Legionnaires were then forced to carry out some unthinkable act of violence against the one who refused. It was a daily occurrence designed not only to ensure strict obedience, but to harden them against any thought of mercy or compassion and to subjugate any glimmer of Light surviving within them. It was meant to shatter hope. It was a nightmare of pain and anguish from which each Legionnaire sought respite by any means necessary and from which none could ever truly find escape.

Chapter Nine

Several days unraveled in preparations for the inevitable as the Fey of the Light bolstered the ranks of the Fey Guard with able-bodied malefey willing to undertake the risks of battle. The Healers, Kaylyya and Ayla, as well as a number of shefey from the village, spent a day transporting the childfey who had been rescued to the Temple where they could be more properly cared for and would be safe from the impending battle. During that time the Captains of The Guard met on more than one occasion with The Watchers and the Liberators who had forged the alliance with the atypical Legionnaires and many hours were consumed in debate over the information they provided.

The statistics and combat stratagems of the mustering Reviled were contemplated and weighed against the ranks of The Guard. The most advantageous crossing points the Reviled might utilize in order to infiltrate the realm of their enemy in the most oppressive manner were suggested and, summarily, the swiftest emissaries were sent upon the wing with messages to those local Fey Guard battalions to fortify against attack. The numbers of Demonfey presently known to the Watchers were reported along with accurate depictions of their horrifying brutality and how they differed from common Legionnaires. Even after the many hours they spent in these discussions there were those within The Guard who could not lay aside their suspicions over the Watcher's true purpose. The doubts that remained invariably spawned tension among the malefey that could not easily be ignored.

"It is not that I wish to question your judgment, my friend; rather, I seek to provide proof for those Guards under my command who are unwilling to trust the Legionnaires as you do." The Captain of the Fey Guard spoke with Bryth surreptitiously and at some distance from the others, who were themselves quarrelling about the distances between crossing points over an extensive map of Jyndari.

Bryth shook his head. "If I were in your position, Varka, I would feel much the same way, certainly. How do you suggest we test them?"

The two captains stood silently considering, their gazes falling on Gairynzvl who cursed unexpectedly in exasperated Dlalth and stalked from the map table where the others continued to disagree. Flexing his wings with furious agitation, he moved away from them, muttering under his breath even as he approached the silent captains who watched him. Looking up at last, Gairynzvl noticed their joint stare and glared back at them with a mute challenge, his instinctive inclination to meet the unknown with audacity sparking the fire behind his icy gaze into a blaze, but Bryth smiled charismatically and raised his hand, palm upward, to gesture at the bristling malefey.

"Our dithering frustrates you, Fierce One?" he asked in a tone that clearly indicated he was already aware of the answer, but Gairynzvl cursed in abrasive Dlalth another time just to confirm their suspicions.

"Vrach saulagcth myrgowthran hyyrloth!"

Laughing heartily at his unmistakable aggravation, the dark-haired Fey Guard clapped his arm round the former Legionnaire's shoulder and shook him in a consolatory manner. "I understand completely. Ilys called us a pack of squabbling ravens and, although our friend the Healer took offense at such a comparison, I think she was not far from the truth. Nevertheless, Varka and I were just discussing something that may interest you far more than the location and distances of portals."

Varka's eyes narrowed with uncertainty and he listened to Bryth explain their conundrum to the former Legionnaire.

"Many of the Guard are hesitant to trust Fey they have been taught all their lives are untrustworthy. We are attempting to determine how best to substantiate the veracity of the Watchers." While he spoke, Gairynzvl's gaze darkened with further irritation. Hissing at Bryth with vexation, he threw off his embrace of camaraderie and stepped back with a another curse of anger.

"Gurkaulraech! Do you doubt my word that they are trustworthy?"

The Fey Guard returned his hostility with even greater charisma and charm, shaking his head and raising his hands in a negating gesture. "Never, Fierce One, never. I assure you, we would not be here if we doubted you, but there are those among The Guard who do not know you as we do and who are justifiably hesitant to trust Legionnaires. Certainly, you cannot blame them?"

The former Legionnaire glared at his friend, but Bryth stepped forward and continued in a conversational tone as if nothing at all might be wrong. "I have heard you say you wish to return again into the Uunglarda to find and rescue additional younglings. Is this so?" His change of direction was no less confusing than his tone was suddenly dismayed. In truth, he was not the least bit surprised by such a fact. He had come to understand that his friend was a compassionate as he was fierce. Nodding sagely when Gairynzvl agreed with him, Bryth once again wrapping his arm about the former Dark Fey's shoulder and drew him closer, as well as nearer to Varka, so that all three might devise a plan together.

"Then let us set a plan into action before the cursed Childwraiths have a single moment longer to work their horrid schemes and, in so doing, utilize the Watchers in some manner that might put to rest any lingering reservations about them."

* * *

Ayla, Ilys and Kaylyya stood among a group of shefey who were gathered round an immense cauldron, the contents set to boiling over a ruddy fire. Situated centrally amid the thatched houses of the village, the communal cooking pot was used each day by a different group of shefey who prepared the meals for the village as a whole on that day.

By sharing the responsibility, as well as their collective resources, the community existed together in a balance of harmony that provided for all.

Watching the chattering shefey from a distance, Gairynzvl leaned with his wings spread wide behind him against the mottled trunk of an elder evergreen, his arms crossed over his broad chest and his gaze fixed upon Ayla. He could not help noticing the subtle motion of her hair as it blew with the breeze and the delicate sway of her hips as she helped to bring the gathered ingredients from a nearby basket and give them to the shefey putting them into the kettle. His lavender-ice stare strayed repeatedly to the bodice of her woolen coat, cinched round her small waist with a braided belt of flaxen and deep emeraldine leather. The blush of her cheek and inviting rose hue of her lips tantalized and tempted him until he could no longer refuse the urging of his body.

"*Ayla.*" Without moving from the tree upon which he reclined, he sent his thoughts to her in his familiar draw-out whisper. She paused and looked up from the cauldron, scanning the cluster of houses for him and the wide avenue that stretched out between them, but could not find him. He smiled wryly when he saw her shake her head dismissively, attempting to return to her work before the sound of his voice filled her mind another time.

"*Sweet Ayla.*"

She smiled this time and closed her eyes, returning a sigh of such distinct pleasure to him that he immediately pushed himself up from leaning upon the tree and took several steps away, heading towards the barns situated around the perimeter of the village. "*Come with me, Ayla.*" The longing in his thoughts could not be denied. Locating him at last, she excused herself from the shefey and moved quietly away from them, following the soft enticement of his whispers and the less perceivable vision of him as he moved silently through the trees ahead of her.

Query?

Certainty.

Desire!

Sigh!

* * *

The Liberators, Fey Guards and villagers were gathered around another large bonfire, such as they had built each night since the Liberators had opened the portal and stepped out of the Uunglarda. They stood basking in the warmth of its radiating glow as the pale glimmer of a full winter moon slipped between the fringes of the forest. Weapons were at hand and the Fey were prepared to undertake combat with the Reviled should they choose to cross from their dark realm that night, but those gathered had been assured by the Watchers, who sat with them enjoying the radiant warmth of the blaze, that such an event was unlikely to occur for at least several nights. Senzuur had made it clear to them that the Reviled were still mustering and it would take time for the fullness of their forces to be gathered and then dispatched. In spite of the questionable reassurance such information provided, the Fey were vigilant and stood watch over the portal beneath the mountain.

The evening meal had been heartily enjoyed by all, as was the steaming mulled wine passed round and round after being prepared by the Healers and fortified with bolstering Quiroth to see them through the unusually cold night. Friends gazed contentedly into the blazing conflagration and conversations drifted from trivial to poignant, but the quiet night smiled down on the gathering as a gentle winter zephyr caressed blushing cheeks and tousled hair. Amid those gathered, Ayla and Gairynzvl stood together, he at her back with his arms and warming wings wrapped round her to protect her from the chill. Although they did not speak outwardly and it appeared they were listening to the chatter around them with quiet amusement, their thoughts and emotions mingled intimately. The light-hearted conversation the Fey were sharing diminished unexpectedly, however, and was replaced by an intense hush as those who had not yet retired to the comfort of their homes or tents listened to an intensifying argument between the Liberators and the Fey Guards.

"It is perhaps difficult to contemplate and most certainly dangerous to consider any measure of compassion when speaking about Legionnaires, but I believe we must." Evondair's resolute tone was unwavering as he proposed what many considered to be absurd. Recounting the attack by the Legionnaire he had killed, the Healer opened a conversation he knew would have serious repercussions and could easily divide loyalties, but he could not in good conscience ignore the insistent voice within him to share his perspective on slaying Dark Ones indiscriminately.

"You are fortunate he did not kill you and treat Kaylyya with unthinkable cruelty." Mardan's tone was as resolute as his friend's, but the Legionnaire from Vrynnyth Ghal, Rehstaed's countryman and more recently his friend, shook his head in disagreement.

"I agree wit' th' 'ealer. The Legionnaire may 'ave broken off if 'e 'ad known 'e was safe." Dravahl spoke with certainty and the remaining Watchers nodded in agreement, but a Fey Guard sitting near them got to his feet and assumed a confrontational posture as he rebuked their claim with his broad wings arched assertively.

"I have never known one of the Reviled to break off an attack simply because he was given quarter."

Dravahl's rebuke was instantaneous," 'ave you e'er gi'en quarter t' one?"

"If Evondair had not acted to protect himself and the shefey, they would both certainly be dead." The Guard maintained defensively and those seated close to him nodded and agreed heatedly. The division between the group widened, but Evondair raised his hands to quiet the intensifying argument and persisted with his original assertion.

"Whether he would have killed me or harmed Kaylyya is not my point." He spoke with the measured calm of a seasoned Healer and the listening Fey gazed at him more curiously, unsure of his meaning. "I only wished to share what I observed. As a Healer, I am keen in observation. I have been trained to notice what many others might overlook or ignore. Even as his life force was extinguished, I could not blind myself to what I saw and it was not a vile monster or demon intent upon harming me." He paused, waiting for one or more of those listening to disagree with him, but only their uncertainty spoke in the hush.

Finally, one of the villagers broke the silence. "What did you see, Healer?"

"What I saw was a Fey, bleeding and in pain, His eyes, blood-red as they might have been, were not filled with hatred or malevolence, but with tears."

The Fey Guard who still stood in opposition scoffed at his poignant description and several of his comrades looked at him disapprovingly, but he could not silence his refusal to accept what the Healer was trying to tell them. "Are you saying you felt sorry for him, Healer?" The disparagement evident in his tone garnered even greater censure from those seated around him. The Healer who spoke to them was highly regarded in spite of his young age, but it was clear that the Guard voiced a commonly accepted sentiment. "I have never known a Legionnaire to feel sorry for anyone. Why then should we feel anything for them?" The outspoken Guard made Evondair's point for him and he turned to stare at the visibly agitated Guard, his viridian glare piercing the other like a blade.

"Because if we who are Fey of the Light do not live by the code of moral conscience we profess, how are we different from those we condemn? That Legionnaire acted out of hostility because he assumed *I* would act out of hostility. Where shall it end? Do we not profess to live harmoniously and peacefully? How else might we achieve peace if we do not become peace?" The Fey round him grew so quiet that only the rustling crackle of the blaze issuing pillars of sparks into the cold night sky filled the leaden hush. Evondair continued passionately, "one thing further shall I say. When I grasped that Legionnaire to take his life from him, he neither fought against me nor spewed vulgarities with his dying breaths. He did not scratch or claw at me with his talons or the spines of his wings. He knelt in the growing pool of his own blood, gazed up into my eyes with tears filling his own, and smiled."

Silence fell upon the gathering so heavily that no one dared move, yet after a protracted moment Rehstaed's new friend who was both a Watcher and a Legionnaire stood and broke the intense hush with a provocative question. "'ave you any notion why 'e should 'ave smiled at you, 'ealer? Wha' would 'e 'ave t' be pleased about?"

Nods of like-minded curiosity went around the ring of those gathered, but Evondair did not falter. "I believe, Dravahl, as I am sure you are already very well aware, that he was thankful."

An outburst of disbelief swept round the circle as forceful as a rushing flood and Fey Guards as well as villagers jumped to their feet to cry out against his suggestion.

"Thankful you killed him?"

"What, by the Ancients, would he be thankful for?"

"Your sentimental perspective clearly shows you know very little about the Reviled."

"He was crying *and* thankful? I dare say, Healer, you were entirely taken in by him. It is lucky you had your blade in his throat or he would certainly have had his in yours."

Beyond the point of vexation with their refusal to hear what his friend was trying to tell them and unable to keep silent a moment longer, Gairynzvl broke from the embrace he shared with Ayla and flexed his expansive wings wrathfully. Hissing loudly at the lot of them, he leaned towards the blazing inferno and the sound resonated off the flames of the fire mutating into so fierce a noise that they silenced their protests and stared at him in astonishment. "He smiled because he could no longer bear the thought of living! Because his life was utterly intolerable."

The same Guard who had interrupted Evondair turned to challenge Gairynzvl. "Intolerable? How then do you explain the sadistic pleasure a Legion takes in plundering innocence, torturing and killing?" Although he spoke with enmity, he voiced what many of them might also have asked and none attempted to quiet him, but looked back to the former Legionnaire and waited on his answer with equal measures of curiosity and skepticism. He gazed about the gathering, the lavender-ice of his eyes reflecting the flames of the fire and glittering intensely.

"You all seem to think when a Fey of the Light is taken by the Reviled they somehow instantly change and desire only violence and cruelty. Have you forgotten so quickly what you have seen firsthand: the effect the Integration has upon childfey?" No one answered his painful question. "From the moment you are abducted, you are mistreated and I can tell you how cruelly the common Legionnaire is made to suffer, so why should you doubt that life becomes utterly intolerable?" Drawing an unsteady breath, he shared one of his own experiences, his description holding them captive from his first words and not a single Fey, not even the argumentative Guard, sought to silence him.

* * *

Three years after his abduction, when he had turned ten years of age, he was released from the Integration and fledged into the life of a Legionnaire. The night was bitterly cold and a sleeting, freezing rain was falling. Several other halflings, as they were called when they were neither childfey nor proper Legionnaires, had been released with him and the small group was forced to march to their new encampment that was a full ten miles from The Braying Caverns. The rain leeched down on them, freezing in their uncovered hair and forming icicles on their half-transformed wings that were no longer feathered, but did not yet bear spines. When they were thirsty, they were forced to drink whatever water pooled at their feet and when they were hungry, they were ignored.

Several hours passed and the youngest of them, a boyfey barely eight years of age, fell to the ground out of exhaustion. Not permitted to help him, the rest were forced to continue marching. He was left behind, but when he realized he would be utterly abandoned if he did not force himself up, he struggled to his feet and clambered after them, wailing. Being the oldest and, by far, the strongest among them, Gairynzvl stopped and pleaded with their commander. He was a Lieutenant DemonFey twice his age and he stood impassively when he asked permission to run back for the boyfey.

"I can carry him. We will not lose any time and I will not ask for extra rations." It was all he could think of to say, but his request was deemed insubordination. Without even bothering to consider his offer, the DemonFey stalked closer and handed his barbed lash to the boyfey standing beside him.

"Beat his disobedient hide until I tell you to stop." His growl caused the boyfey to cringe in terror and in his fear, he was unable to take the lash from the DemonFey's outstretched hand. Hissing at him viperously, the Lieutenant turned balefully to Gairynzvl and thrust the lash out to him. "Since he refuses, you will beat him instead." The terrified boyfey crumpled to the ground in horror, crying out so noisily that the DemonFey hissed at him again and kicked his little body hard enough to lift him from the ground. "Beat him!"

Horrified and unable to think how to respond, Gairynzvl took hold of the lash and reluctantly carried out the unthinkable order, his eyes filling with tears each time the lash struck. He was not told to stop until the small boyfey's clothing had been shredded from his body and he lay unmoving in the crimson-stained slush. Snatching the lash from his shaking hand, the DemonFey snarled viciously into his face, "now you can carry something." Without looking back to see if he obeyed or not, he ordered the group onward.

Struggling to raise the body of the childling to his shoulder without causing him additional pain, Gairynzvl followed as quickly as he could, but the DemonFey increased the speed at which the remainder of the group marched until they were nearly running and within a mile he was also left behind. Determination and fury spurred him forward, in spite of the tears blurring his vision and the blood running down his arms and chest from the boyfey who lay unconscious over his shoulder. In his mind he spat all manner of vicious curses, but he never spoke a word. Each breath was too valuable to waste on speaking when no one was close enough to hear. Each step he took became a torment as the freezing rain transformed into stinging sleet that pelted down on them mercilessly.

Behind him, he could hear the one they had left behind squalling loudly and he stopped to wait for him, but he knew better than to call out. If he was heard calling after the abandoned, his punishment could be even more severe than it already was. Though he waited as long as he dared, the little one never caught up and the sound of his cries eventually faded into the intensifying storm. He was lost, utterly and completely, and he knew he would not be mourned by anyone. Anyone other than him. Tears fell, but he forced his footsteps forward, following the smeared trail through the deepening slush towards the encampment.

He could see the light of fires in the distance and knew he was not far, so he pushed himself to his limit, and then beyond. By the time he reached the camp, his breathing was so labored it rasped in his chest. His body shook from over-exertion and his empty stomach was a tight knot of sickness. The rest of the group stood around a small Sulphur fire, warming themselves despite the horrid stench emanating from the ruddy glow. He staggered forward with his burden and pushed closer to the blaze, but as soon as he reached the front of the ragged circle, a belligerent shout from behind them made them all turn in dread.

"You stubborn blaylscith! What makes you think you deserve warmth?" Stalking towards the cringing group of halflings, the DemonFey Lieutenant glared at Gairynzvl mercilessly. Though he was shivering violently and his hair and wings were coated by a layer of ice, Gairynzvl turned to face the taller Legionnaire and made the mistake of returning his malicious glare. "You'll learn." Wrenching the halfling he carried from his grasp and hurling him to the ground, the DemonFey called for one of his comrades who stood nearby beneath a tarp that protected him and several others who watched from the freezing downpour.

The older Legionnaire obeyed his commanding officer and came out into the deluge to glare at Gairynzvl furiously. He had been warm and dry, but no longer and his resentment was unmistakable. The Lieutenant grasped Gairynzvl by the shoulders and presented him to the older Legionnaire. "He wants to be warm," he explained as if such a thought was unbelievable and the Legionnaire smiled sadistically.

"Does he?" His glare became a heated stare that dropped to take in Gairynzvl's body as a lecherous smile curved his lips, "I can make sure he's warm." Gairynzvl's insides twisted violently at the thought.

His threat made plain, the DemonFey forced him towards the small boyfey who lay crying in the slush a few feet away. Pointing at him, he posed an unthinkable, ruthless ultimatum. "You can get warm one of two ways, dravlug. Take him or be taken."

Gairynzvl shook his head in revulsion. "I cannot. Please," but his petition was ignored. Shoving him towards the Legionnaire who stood watching with an increasingly lecherous stare, he was not given a chance to reconsider. "Fine. Enjoy yourself Mrinvallin. Just have him back here by roll call." Thrashing violently to escape the Legionnaire who took hold of him with an inescapable clasp, Gairynzvl resisted being led away into the Legionnaire's tent, but the older and stronger Dark One could not be opposed.

* * *

Silence met his shocking account, although the Legionnaires beside him nodded mutely as if, they too, had suffered similar atrocities. Those listening grimaced in dismay to hear such horrifying details and glanced at each other with mortified expressions or close their eyes or look away, but Gairynzvl continued.

"Each time the choices are harder, more shocking, and far more terrifying. The misery of your life becomes a nightmare from which you seek to escape through any means possible, but there is no bottle large enough, no drug potent enough to detach you from yourself, at least, not for long enough. If you show your weakness through depression, which is inevitable, or despair, which is unavoidable, you are punished." The Liberators, who knew him better than the villagers and

Fey Guards, looked at each other with pained expressions, hating every word they were hearing because they knew without any shred of doubt that he had borne each nightmarish detail he was describing. As they forced themselves to continue listening, Gairynzvl's voice began to shake with honest emotion; his depiction inescapable.

"Punishment is often far more brutal than any act of savagery they might contrive and your life becomes a pit of vipers biting you from every direction. When the time comes for you to choose again - because it always comes back round to you - you do not even think. Whatever it is, you do it. You force yourself not to feel, and, yes, some laugh because it is the only way they can convince themselves they do not care. But unless you are a Demonfey who is twisted into a monster by years of repeated abuse you cannot stop yourself from caring. That is when your nature as a Fey of the Light begins to tear at your sanity because you have no choices. You simply do whatever they demand, no matter how appalling. You know iit will be appalling because that is their intention; to either shatter whatever is left of your spirit or to drag you further down into the pit of desolation into which you are falling."

Unable to bear the thought of such complete misery, Kaylyya sobbed audibly and covered her face with her hands. Beside her, Ayla wept as well, having felt his pain the first night he revealed himself to her, but he had never described it so explicitly. The Guards sitting around the shefey closed their eyes as if the sounds of their distress verbalized their own dismay, but Gairynzvl continued; the depth of his emotion compelling him like a tide that builds momentum under its own influence.

"Some simply cannot bear it. Some slip beyond the reach of the Light when something inside them snaps and they twist into monsters, into Demonfey. Others lose their wits entirely," he paused, looking at the young Legionnaire they had captured who was, even then, muttering unintelligibly to himself. "These become sport and prey for any seeking to unleash their anger or despair and they suffer callous mistreatments and neglect. Life in the Uunglarda is an abyss from which there is no escape. There is nothing you can do for yourself and you are helpless to help anyone else because such aid would only lead to further punishment. So, you wait and you pray you are fortunate enough to encounter a Fey of the Light because when you do, you will do everything, *absolutely everything* in your power to ensure they kill you."

Chapter Ten

Darkness settled deeply over Lyyshara, the sky heavy with a new winter storm's burgeoning clouds crowding together above the quiet village and blotting out the light of the moon. Most of the wool-weavers who resided in the small community had returned to their homes in silence with thoughts of bitter neglect and harrowing violence filling their minds. Many of the Guards who had come to the small hamlet to keep watch over the portal and await the unavoidable incursion of the Reviled had also retired to their tents. The Watchers, as well as the Liberators, remained gathered around the fire, neither able to sleep nor interested in trying to after hearing so vivid an account of their friend's former life. Brooding over their own miseries, the Watchers sat as close to the blaze as possible, attempting to lose themselves in the bliss of its radiant warmth. They were far more accustomed to waiting out the biting chill of the nighttime hours without protection of any kind and the fire was as intoxicating as it was warm. Near them, Gairynzvl and Ayla, as well as Evondair and Kaylyya, huddled close together, speaking softly with each other and sharing the deepening nighttide.

Looking round him with sudden curiosity, Mardan searched the flickering firelight for Ilys, whom he had only seen briefly during the past several days, but he could not find her. Moving closer to Bryth who stood with his eyes closed, facing the fire in a standing doze, he inquired softly if he had seen her, but in answer the dark-haired

Fey Guard merely shrugged and shook his head. Glancing across at Gairynzvl, Mardan considered inquiring of his friend, but chose not to disturb him after seeing the close embrace he shared with Ayla, the sight of which caused him to hiss under his breath and turn away.

Only a few yards from the fire, the darkness of the forest village was thick and all but impenetrable. His fair cerulean eyes were not well suited to seeing in such blackness and, for a moment, he considered abandoning his search and retiring to the warmth of his tent, but her absence among them troubled him, even if he could not justify the reason why. Uncertain if he doubted her loyalty or if his concern lay more in the realm of her unexpected display of emotion that had unintentionally revealed the truth of her past to them all, he continued trudging through the snow and strain his eyes against the darkness in search of her distinctive form. Aware that her gift of light bending meant she could easily hide herself from him if she wished, he decided to explore the borders of the forest and the nearest complex of barns, making a large circular sweep of the area that would, ultimately, return him to the place where the tents had been set up. If he did not find her in that time, he would not deny himself sleep by seeking any further. To his dissatisfaction, the margin of the dark and silent forest stood empty and the first cluster of stables housed only sheep and goats.

A chill wind nipped across his face, stinging his cheeks and tousling the platinum-blond curls of his hair as the storm congesting in the sky above began to kindle its impending fury. Arching his wings against the bluster, he muttered to himself with exasperation and shook his head. 'Predictable of her to go missing', he mused tetchily as he passed the next set of barns housing sheep and their herding companions. Called Maaygras, they were large, domesticated felines nearly equal in size to the sheep they guarded. They were often grey and white in color with spotted coats and long flowing fur in the winter months. Gazing through the doorway into the darkened interior for only a moment, Mardan hissed under his breath a second time and turned aside, but a glitter of light deep in the shadows of the barn's hayloft caused him to stop and gaze inward once again. The shadows would not typically have reflected light of any kind and the corner of his mouth curved upwards in a knowing smirk.

Listening keenly for a sound other than the snoring of sheep and the occasional purr of Maaygras while he stared inwards, he tried not to stare at the loft in the hope that she would move and give herself away. As the light of the bonfire streamed into the barn through the hayloft window, it was inadvertently refracted by the veil she was able to draw round herself; it's sparkling giving her away even in complete darkness. Stepping inside the warm barn, Mardan shook the chill from his wings and rubbed his hands together briskly, lowering his intense stare as if he had not taken notice of her and for several moments he stood quietly, gazing nonchalantly at the animals before returning to the doorway to peer out at the hushed encampment.

Then, without preamble, he spoke. "Sheep are certainly safer than nearly one hundred malefey." Silence answered his words, but he expected nothing else. After a prolonged moment, he spoke to her again. "I know you are there, Ilys. I saw you up in the hayloft." Pausing to allow her a moment to consider her options, he smiled dimly at her stubborn silence. "Even you cannot hide the reflection of light from your bending of it. Come down and speak with me." His invitation was ignored, although one of the Maaygras got up from its place in a nearby corner, glared at him through half-closed eyes, and slunk off into a quieter part of the barn. Its sullen attitude made him grin and he turned to look up into the hayloft once more, seeking the glimmer of light he had seen previously, but she had hidden herself better. Her diligence, however, did not deter him. "I can be equally stubborn, you know. There is only one way in or out of this barn and I am standing in front of it." His tone took on a more impudent edge and to his amazement, she answered him, though she did not divest herself of the shadows that disguised her.

"What do you want from me?" Her voice was a low growl issued through clenched teeth and, if he had not witnessed her softer, more vulnerable side for himself, he might have been daunted by her show of aggression.

Slightly. Instead, he shook his head. "I do not want anything from you. Are you not tired of lingering in the darkness, cold and alone?" His unintentional expression of sympathy brought a derisive hiss from the dimness beside him.

"What do you expect me to do, dissolve into a puddle of tears like my predecessor simply because you say you care?" Her acerbic response sparked anger within him, but he scoffed at her hostility rather than acknowledging it further.

"You may choose not to believe me, but Ayla's emotional-instability irritates me as much as it does you. Unlike you, however; she cannot help it."

"And that makes it alright?"

He shrugged, realizing just how skilled she was at turning the focus of any conversation away from herself. Smirking at the discovery, he shifted their discussion back onto her. "It makes it understandable, but I did not come in search of you to discuss Ayla."

A protracted pause met his words and when she answered him, the sound of her voice was farther off. She had backed away from him. "Why did you come searching for me? What do you want?"

He sighed. "Just to talk with you. Will you not come out of the shadows?"

"Why?" she hissed more assertively, "you have no love for the Reviled. Why then are you so concerned about me?"

Unsure how to answer her because he could not fully comprehend the reasons why he had undertaken the search for her in the first place, he turned to gaze out of the open door. A bluster of wind caressed his cheek and ran its hand through his hair. The feathers of his magnificent wings rustled in the rush of cold air and the unfastened coat he wore blew open and billowed behind him for a moment, pressing his shirt against his broad chest to define his powerful physique. The silhouette of light streaming in through the doorway displayed his attributes to her and she could not force herself to be blind.

After a protracted silence, he offered honestly, "I am not sure, but I did not come here to hurt you, Ilys. We of the Light are not like that."

Her laughter echoed in his perfectly pointed ears as she rushed towards him from the back of the barn, a brilliant ripple of light blazing behind her like a streaming star as she unveiled herself and alighted directly behind him.

"All malefey are like that," she hissed resentfully. The closeness of her caustic response startled him, but he constrained the more instinctive reaction of flinching that rushed over him and, instead, turned to look down at her with a purposefully unhurried motion. His fair gaze was darkened by the shadows of the barn and, in spite of her brazen display, she could not stop herself from taking a single step away from him as the weight of his stare pierced into her. They looked at each other for a brooding moment, cerulean locked with cerulean, before he shook his head subtly.

"No, Ilys, they are not." Inclining his head to her in a gesture of consideration, he turned with an equally deliberate action and strode quietly from the barn without looking back. As he walked into the dark night, she stood in the doorway gazing after him.

* * *

Three Demonfey stood outside the massive iron doors of Hvyyr-bachvra, gazing up at its mammoth walls with unspoken dread. Even they, the most callous of all Reviled Fey, could not completely disguise their fear of so dreadful a place or the one who resided within its walls: the Imperial Praetor, Uxvagchtr. More beautiful in appearance than any other Dark Fey, his magnificence to the eye was as false and treacherous as his essence that held no measure of compassion, no inclination for mercy, and a violent animosity that threatened any who drew near him.

"The Braying Caverns are empty. He must be informed about the robbery of the childfey," one of the Demonfey ground out in guttural Dlalth. His crimson gaze shifted from one of his companions to the other, clearly indicating his unwillingness to undertake so dangerous a task. They looked at each other as well, undecided and palpably hesitant.

"Who wants to lose their life today?" One of the remaining two asked, revealing a truth they all anticipated. Bringing bad news of any sort to the Praetor was a certain death sentence that kept them loitering at the entrance of the fortress, arguing amongst themselves rather than entering inward.

"We're not to blame for the Lighter's audacity. Why then should we be punished for it?" The third hissed under his breath, cautious to raise his voice even outside the massive walls of the Praetors lair. He knew the scope of dark gifts their master possessed; knife-like telepathy and inescapable discernment, as well as spell-casting magic and dream-stalking. He did not need to speak at all for the Praetor to hear him, even from so great a distance. He knew he could not employ enough caution and filled his mind with hatred and loathing in an attempt to block any obtrusive telepathy.

"Because someone must be punished and we'll be present," the first snarled resentfully, continuing before either of his companions could argue further. "I'll go in with you, but I'm not risking my life by saying a word."

The others glared at him, despising his cowardice while at the same time thoroughly comprehending it. Staring at each other for an intense moment, no one moved until the third shook his head and cursed. Spitting upon the mud-smeared stones at the foot of the gate, he steadied his resolve by bolstering his hatred with new abhorrence for his spineless comrades, set his broad pinions with determination, and reached for the latch of the gate. "Cowering blaylscith! You're an insult to the uniform you wear. I'll tell him."

"Nunvaret, you'll be skinned alive or worse!" they shouted after him, but he glared back at them contemptuously.

"I exist to serve the Praetor and he must be advised of this outrage." Yanking upon the heavy ironwork of the gate vehemently, he shot them a sideward scowl before he strode into the darkness of the fortress. Traipsing after him unhelpfully, the others followed at some distance as he trod tenaciously along the dim corridor that was lighted only by torches spaced at intervals too great for their light to make a significant impact against the darkness. Providing just enough illumination for navigation through the labyrinth of tunnels that led to the great hall, the torches sputtered sulfurous blue light and putrid fumes that filled the entire complex with a stomach-turning reek.

Coming into the great hall, the triplet of Demonfey were met by twelve guards who were clothed in black leather that bulged and rippled in a formidable display of their musculature. The result of extensive, grueling physical regiments that built strength and endurance far beyond the limits of average Fey, they stood round the perimeter of the chamber in mute guardianship none would dare oppose. They bore weapons unique to the Praetor's ranks: long spears with curved, serrated blades on one side and heavily barbed bludgeons on the other.

"Halt!" they growled together as one unit in a commanding tone impossible to disobey and the Demonfey stopped instantly. "State your purpose." The guards spoke in unified antagonism.

Shifting uncomfortably behind their comrade, the two stragglers failed to say anything, but Nunvaret arched his wings aggressively and replied, "I bring vital intelligence from the borderlands for the Praetor."

Closing their eyes in a coalesced action, the guards communicated this information through a telepathic connection with their master, then reaffixed their blood-red stares upon the three. Speaking nothing further to them, they waited in menacing silence for an interminable length of time before a black shadow undulated through the darkness that filled the main portion of the hall. At its arrival, terror leeched into Nunvaret's being like icy water pouring over his head and he could hear his companions shuffle behind him as they suffered a similarly chilling experience.

It was Uxvagchtr.

Chapter Eleven

Closing his crimson eyes briefly, Nunvaret focused his hatred into an even more intense sensation. As he did the shadow rippled sinuously towards them, reflecting sparks of indigo torchlight and wavering smoky dimness as the Praetor released the darkness surrounding him. It fell to his feet like a discarded robe, pooling around him upon the floor where it continued to waver like heavy smoke stirred by hot air instead of dissipating entirely. The moment he extricated himself from the cowl of blackness, every guard standing in the dim hall closed their eyes and lowered their heads, neither able to look upon him nor willing to risk doing so under any circumstance, but the triplet of Demonfey stood in abject horror and astonishment; struck into silence by the sight of him.

Uxvagchtr was every bit as stunning as the rumors had led them to believe and was equally as terrifying. Standing fully six and a half feet tall, his physique boasted of perfectly defined and proportioned musculature that was brazenly displayed by the fact that he wore little more than exquisitely soft, brown leather pants that were cinched low across his hips by a crisscrossing belt of braided silver. The paleness of his complexion was accentuated by bold, black tattoos that formed dramatic designs across his cheeks, along his neck and outward across his entire body. His fearsome dragonhide wings spanned twenty-five feet from tip to tip, their imposing spines adding another two feet to each. They were studded with metal barbs and pierced with rings and jagged spines in decorative patterns, but his most arresting feature of all were his immense, double set of horns. Situated at the crown of his head, one pair twisted upwards into broad spirals of black while the others, arching outward from above his temples like those of a tryngalith, stretched nearly three feet from tip to tip and glistened with a silvery sheen.

He stood facing them and, in spite of the fact that he wore an elaborate headdress fashioned from intricately worked silver that covered the crown of his head and completely obscured his eyes, all three Demonfey could feel the weight of his intense stare. He reached up slowly and took hold of the thick, single braid of his waist-length white hair that fell over one shoulder and stood holding onto it absently while he considered them.

"Nunvaret, Captain of the Bathracht Demonfey, what news do you bring?" he asked in a tone barely louder than a whisper. To their surprise, his voice was neither grating nor harsh. Rather, his rich tenor was inescapably alluring, yet the fact that the Praetor knew his name, rank and station, although he had not given it, sent a shiver down the Demonfey's spine. He knew he dared not hesitate to answer and forced himself to speak, despite the fear threatening to strangle him.

"I'm certain, Excellency, you're already aware of the news I bring so late; that the cursed Fey of the Light have crossed into our realm and emptied the Braying Caverns." As he suspected, this shocking news had no outward effect upon the Praetor at all and his lack of any response forced Nunvaret to haltingly continue. "In order to escape us, they sundered the Great Gate and crossed back through a portal that now stands open. In anticipation of your wishes, we've begun the muster and we three have come to receive your orders." Falling silent, the Demonfey waited as Uxvagchtr stood staring at him, unseeing, yet seeming to see everything about him. Turning his head slightly, he appeared to be considering the Demonfey Captain's unusual uniform of dark crimson leather, rather than the black that was far more customary. He smiled a terrifying approval of the brazenness of his garb before he seemed to gaze right through him at the others who loitered many paces behind him.

"Why do your comrades not stand beside you?" Outwardly unconcerned about the loss of childfey, the sundering of the Gate, or the muster, the Praetor turned his head slightly, as if to gaze around Nunvaret in order to see his companions more clearly. At this slight movement, the two behind him scuffled backward even further. Unable to concoct an answer quickly enough and unwilling to offer excuses for them, Nunvaret made no response and his silence brought Uxvagchtr's piercing stare back upon him. "The Gate, sundered? The way open, you say?"

Nunvaret briskly inclined his head once in answer, but dared not engage him in conversation. His succinct reply seemed to frustrate their Dark Master, however, and he stretched out his wings to flex them violently in a terrifying display of displeasure. Nunvaret grit his teeth in order to force himself not to react with any sign of fear. Pouring hatred upon the flame of his already raging mind, he blocked any telepathy directed at him with intense emotion while the two behind him scrabbled backward even further, then thought better of their retreat and falteringly returned. The viperous hiss that met these actions reverberated around the hall in a crescendo of dizzying sound that not only disorientated, but filled them all with absolute dread.

"Your fear sickens me! How did you rise to the rank of Demonfey through such cowardice?" Stalking forward, Uxvagchtr directed his remarks past Nunvaret, who braced himself with every measure of wrath he could manage, and hissed like an enraged and snarling beast at the two cowering in the darkness behind him. Before either could formulate an answer, he turned to his guard and, although he did not speak, two leapt from their stations to detain the pair before they could turn-tail and run. Smiling with satisfaction at their panic-stricken expressions, the Praetor then turned to look down at Nunvaret, watching him with inexorable attentiveness for any sign of fear or compassion for his fellow Legionnaires, but the Demonfey captain's expression did not waver.

Mounting hatred and abhorrence high upon the raging conflagration of his emotions, Nunvaret gave no outward indication of his dismay, though he hardly found the Praetor's actions surprising in the face of such weakness. He was unprepared, however, when Uxvagchtr reached out to place his hand upon his shoulder and it took all of his composure not to crumble in terror. Baring his teeth against the touch of the Dark Master's hand, Nunvaret goaded himself into turning his head to glare at him. He was certain such an impudent act would earn him some appalling form of abuse, but to his astonishment the Praetor only smiled. Lowering his unseeing gaze, he took in the young Demonfey's appearance in an unhurried inspection that set Nunvaret's skin crawling, though he dared not allow his revulsion to show through the anger with which he sought to defend himself. Unable to look at the Praetor while he openly drank in every aspect of the youthful malefey, Nunvaret fixed his gaze upon the obsidian throne inset with silver that stood upon a raised dais at the front of the chamber. Uxvagchtr licked his lips with lascivious pleasure, then turned away. He stepped back to the place where the darkness he had discarded earlier still rippled and swirled upon the floor, awaiting his command as surely as the rest of them.

"I have no use for those who fear," he said offhandedly, gesturing at one of his guards who responded to his nonverbal cue and jumped from his place to hand Nunvaret his spear. Turning back to watch, then, Uxvagchtr issued a command that was as gruesomely chilling as it was calmly spoken and it took every ounce of control Nunvaret could wield to keep from displaying the slightest indication of his horror.

"Open them so I may watch them bleed."

* * *

When he finally decided to retire for the night, Evondair lay down beneath the woolen blanket given to him by Kaylyya, which he had spread over one of the treatment tables in the Healer's tent. Attempting to fend off the penetrating chill of the winter night, he pulled the blanket over his head, tucked the edges of it beneath him, and wrapped his wings around himself to keep his body warmth close, but to no avail. During the long hours of darkness, the gathering storm in the dark spangle above the quiet village continued to congest, gaining potency like a flood constrained behind some unseen barrier and the numbing cold it bore upon its shoulders was inescapable. Curled up against the sinking, frosty atmosphere he sought some few hours of sleep, but he could find no comfort either in body or in mind as his thoughts replayed over and again all Gairynzvl had told them, forming images far too distressing to be conducive to sleep. Though he persisted in his attempt for what felt like days, it was not until the first hints of lavender-gray light tinted the sky with hues of morning that he could subdue his restless contemplations and then, just as he managed to capture the elusive phantasm of sleep, Gairynzvl stole quietly into the tent.

"Evondair." His deep voice was barely a whisper so as not to disturb Veryth who lay curled upon the other treatment table beneath his own woolen blanket. Neither Healer stirred. Shaking his head, Gairynzvl drew closer and laid his hand upon what he presumed to be his friend's shoulder. "Evondair, wake up."

A petulant hiss answered his entreaty, which caused him to grin impishly and try again, shaking the Healer vigorously as he bent close and spoke in a more urgent tone. "We need you, Healer; wake up."

Accepting the fact that he would enjoy no measure of sleep that night, Evondair sighed profoundly, but drew the cover back to glare up at Gairynzvl wearily without bothering to lift his head. "Who requires my aid?" his conscientious inquiry, in spite of his evident fatigue, caused his friend to step backward and fold his wings culpably.

"No one, not exactly, but we need you."

Puzzled viridian locked with lavender-ice and Evondair did not need to question further to make his confused frustration evident.

"The storm is growing in intensity and may soon be upon us with even greater force than the one that preceded it."

"So?" The Healer's lack of concern was stinging.

"The Reviled can cross into a storm during the day as well as the night."

"I know that."

"So, we must act quickly if we are to rescue any additional younglings."

Raising his head from his crossed arms at last, which had formed his only pillow, Evondair frowned with even greater bewilderment. "Rescue more? What are you talking about?"

Unable to evade the issue any further, Gairynzvl straightened and raised his wings more assertively, speaking in a far more persuasive tone. "There are other places the Dlalth confine childlings, places into which I can open a portal. Bryth, Rehstaed, Mardan, Ilys and several of The Watchers are returning with me to find them and bring them out."

Pushing himself up from his comfortless bed, Evondair sat looking at the Fierce One before him with a confounding mixture of respect and trepidation swirling within him as he struggled to decide just how he felt about such a proposition, but he said nothing and his silent stare prompted a more compelling argument.

"I know how you feel about conflict. The others shall undertake any fighting that may be required, but if one of us is injured or, when we find the childfey, if any of them require help, none of us are adept with healing arts. We need *you.*" Gairynzvl's tone was insistent.

Closing his eyes, Evondair could not conceal the pained expression that crossed his handsome features when he realized he would not only gain no measure of rest, but found himself facing the prospect of returning into the gloom of the Uunglarda; a place he had hoped never to revisit. Drawing a deep breath, he threw back the comfort of the woolen blanket and got to his feet; certain he would miss such a simple luxury in the seeking cold of the dark place into which they would be crossing.

Nodding at his waiting friend with observable resignation, he looked round at the supplies with which that filled the tent and took several moments to gather an appropriate portion of them into a pack. As he did this, Veryth awoke and, after being told what was about to take place, he inquired how he might aid their endeavor. As Evondair continued to diligently assemble the implements he would need, Gairynzvl and Veryth planned for their return from the dark realm and the likelihood that a hasty withdrawal to the Temple would be required with any childlings they succeeded in rescuing. Veryth then took up these preparations while Evondair raised one of several bottles of Quiroth from the shelf upon which they had been stored and showed it to Gairynzvl with a sly grin. The Fierce One grimaced prodigiously and shook his head.

"Is that really necessary?"

Evondair smiled deviously at his obvious revulsion. "Oh, I assure you it is and I shall take great pleasure in administering it."

Chapter Twelve

By the time the Liberators and Watchers had gathered before the small frozen pond chosen for the crossing, snowflakes had begun fluttering through the boughs of the evergreen canopy sparkling in the crisp morning air. A portion of the snow that blanketed the shadow-covered pond had been brushed away to reveal the dark ice beneath and Gairynzvl stood looking down into its frozen depths with intense concentration. Beside him, his fellow Liberators gazed downward with far greater apprehension, uncertain to their very cores about stepping into a portal made of frozen winter water, which might just as easily close around them and prevent their return to the surface than transport them to some secluded corner of the dark realm.

Several paces behind them, the Watchers stood in grim silence. They were as noticeably displeased about having to return into the darkness of the Uunglarda as the Healer who stood with them, but, although they exchanged telling glances with the Healer, none gave voice to their qualms. They were far to accustomed to keeping any complaints they might have to themselves than sharing their feelings. The only sounds that filled the winter morning were that of sheep and Maaygras greeting the morning. Turning after many long moments to face the group, Gairynzvl took a brief moment to remind his friends of the safest way to cross through the portal, as well as how not to become enmeshed in its swirling void.

"Be certain to keep moving, even if you cannot tell whether you are. Three steps should be sufficient to transport you to the other side."

"Are you certain the ice will not close and leave us trapped in the darkness, or worse, in the water?" Mardan could not contain his skepticism any more than Ilys, who stood beside Gairynzvl, could stop herself from rolling her eyes and shaking her head. Her reaction was not missed by any of them.

"Once I open the portal, there shall be no ice or water." Gairynzvl's explanation did little to appease him, but Mardan made no reply, his stare fixed upon the sheDemon so intensely that she was forced to turn aside to escape his glare. Stalking past the Legionnaires, she was unprepared when Evondair stepped forward to impede her retreat. Recalling their previous encounter and anticipating some further verbal abuse from him, she glared up at him with a baleful expression and hissed under her breath. For a brief moment, they stared at each other wordlessly, icy cerulean locked with unfathomable viridian and the silence of the shadowy grove became as loud as thunder. Behind them, Mardan turned to witness their interaction with a bearing of protectiveness he could neither deny nor fully justify, particularly since the flames of his irritation with her were still dissipating. As he turned, so too did his companions and their merged stares left her so observably unnerved that she backed away from them warily, but Evondair pursued her.

"What do you want from me, Healer?" she rebuked his actions maliciously, yet, despite her insolence he closed his eyes and inclined his head to her, lowering his wings in an unmistakable sign of regret.

"I wish to apologize to you, Ilys," he explained, his tone clear enough for all to hear and they stood in mute surprise as they listened.

She shook her head, her gaze narrowing suspiciously. "Why?"

"I was unprepared for the darkness of the Uunglarda. It overwhelmed me."

"It does that," she scoffed callously, but he inclined his head once more and continued.

"So I have come to understand. It overpowered me in ways I did not anticipate."

"Perhaps Ayla can cry for you so you'll feel better." Her caustic retort caused him to stop, an expression of annoyance darkening his otherwise handsome features. Locking his jaw to prevent himself from rebuking her just as callously, he glared back at her while attempting to refocus his thoughts.

"I...I simply wished to apologize," he offered a third time through gritted teeth, but, having never received an apology from anyone, she little knew how to acknowledge it.

"I don't care." Her quarrelsome attitude entirely confounded him so that his mouth fell agape while a fierce scowl shifted his expression into brooding contempt. Looking at his companions, he closed his mouth, then opened it again in favor of reproaching her, but he could find no words to adequately express himself. Leaning closer to the Healer from the place where he stood behind him, Rehstaed inclined his head as if to speak confidentially, but used a tone loud enough so all might readily hear him.

"I believe th' word ye' are seekin', 'ealer, is irksome."

Smirking wryly at the Fey Guard, Evondair willingly agreed, but Mardan scowled at their callousness.

"Ilys is one of us now and Fey of the Light are supposed to abide harmoniously," his chide was met with raised brows and surprise, but in spite of his defense she glowered at him as well and shook her head as if what he said made no sense to her.

Evondair disagreed with conspicuous sarcasm. "She does not seem to care about abiding harmoniously, does she?"

"You know very well she cares, Discerner, in spite of what she says," Mardan rebuked him further and to his surprise Evondair agreed.

"Why do you think I apologized? If we are going to be successful in our endeavor, we must be able to trust each other, but she *cannot* trust and I cannot convince myself that we can trust *her*."

The malefey stared at each other in silent scrutiny, but before either could expand on their thoughts, Gairynzvl redirecting their attention back to the task at hand. "We are relying upon you, Ilys. You understand what we are asking of you?"

Cursing, she brushed past them and replied through a mumble of garish Dlalth, bringing smiles of comprehension from the Legionnaires who watched the quick-tempered interactions of the Fey of the Light with astonished intrigue.

"They're more like us than they like to think." Senzuur spoke through his thoughts to his companions and they nodded in wordless reply, but did not interrupt the conversation otherwise. Casting a glare at Ilys that might have made even the most hardened Demonfey hesitate, Gairynzvl said nothing about her hostility, but turned to face the pond and began the incantation to open the portal.

"Hchrynoch drall enpach thrynnovich." The words sent shivers through the listening Liberators, regardless of the fact that they had heard the Dlalth spell once before. The pond silently resisted. Staring at it with puzzlement, he extending his hands towards it to direct as much energy as he could at its frozen surface. He repeated the phrase more emphatically before he continued the incantation to magnify its potency without pausing as he normally might have done. "Hchrynoch drynnovl enpackich thrynnul."

The visible ripple of magic directed at the pond through his hands seemed to bend and shift as a result of his scars, mutating into a powerful force that caused the ice to resound loudly as if a vast leviathan had pummeled it from below the surface. Those behind him drew closer to watch with mounting curiosity as the entire surface began to vibrate forcefully.

"Hchrynoch thalinan drynnovl chi ennovat!" Gairynzvl's deep voice sent reverberations through the heavy ice, but it was the energy propelled through his hands in an unanticipated blaze of intensity that shook the pond with tremendous influence and caused the Liberators to gaze at him in wonder. Even as the ice groaned against the powerful incantation, it turned over in the water, then turned again. Shifting and twisting with ever increasing turbulence into a warping vortex, it spiraled suddenly downward into nothingness with a resoundingly hollow sound that caused them all to step back cautiously, including Gairynzvl who looked into the void with a blazing stare.

* * *

Nunvaret obeyed the commands of his Praetor, regardless of the horror he felt in eviscerating his companions. As a captain of the Demonfey, it was expected that he should have no sympathy for another and carrying out such an act of brutality would have no effect on his state of being. Thus, when the order was given, he stifled his instinctive reaction to cringe an grimace in disgust and obeyed. Filling his mind with prevailing hatred and anger, which came easily as a result of being forced to perform such a sadistic act, he did what was required and did not balk when Uxvagchtr complained that he cut the first of his companions open too quickly and demanded he take more time with the second. It was far more difficult, however, to stand beside them afterward and listen to their suffering while the Dark Master's pleasure was satisfied by their screams and whimpering. It took far too long for the Praetor to remember the real purpose for the Demonfey's visit, which was to carry his orders regarding the incursion of the Fey of the Light into their dark realm to those overseeing the muster.

Never more thankful for anything than when he was granted permission to return to the squalor of the Bathracht encampment located outside the city walls, Nunvaret took every measure of haste in retreating, including flight, in spite of having no Tox-Guard to protect him. Every weatherworn tent and each straggling battalion was a relief to see. Even the meager rations and stale water he knew were stored in the mess tent were preferable to drinking the Praetor's wine while being forced to witness the unspeakable acts he committed upon his dying subjects. Nunvaret returned from Hvyyrbachvra in grim silence, bearing a scroll that was to be read in the presence of those in command, but instead of reporting immediately to the Centurion's pavilion, he went to his own tent. Closing the flaps and tying them securely from the inside to ensure he would not be discovered, he flung the scroll down upon a small desk occupying one corner of the dismally cramped tent.

Standing motionless in the shadowy interior, he allowed the wrath surging tempestuously within him to subside as he closed his eyes and covered his face with his hands that were still stained with the blood of his former comrades. His broad dragonhide wings, fiercely adorned along each of their immense, protruding spines with metal studs, pitched downward to lie upon the ground as irrepressibly violent shaking overtook his entire being. Gritting his teeth against the overwhelming desire to wail like a youngling, he held his silence as a deluge of tears fought their way past his defenses. In forced muteness, he listened to a unit of newly arriving Legionnaires tramped past his tent while his entire body was wracked by unbearable emotion he had no strength to constrain...

...and dared not show.

* * *

The slurking emptiness of the portal spiraled in confounding directions, blackness folding upon darkness, disorientating and robbing him of every sense. Silence filled his hearing; emptiness touched his hands and piercing blackness robbed his sight as he forced himself to step through the numbing cold nothingness. Three steps, Gairynzvl had told him. Three steps and he would be through the portal, but in the darkness where he lost all perception, including that of his own body, he could not be sure how many steps he had taken and the slowly turning abyss offered no perspective. Wholly uncertain, Evondair took another step.

The scrunch of gravel beneath his boots reoriented his senses as he took a final step and found himself standing on a dusty, barren track of grayish gravel surrounded by jagged outcroppings of bare rock. A fetid stench hung upon the thin air and, leaching downward from a colorless sky, sooty rain in the form of a heavy mist shrouded everything. As the other Liberators gathered to discuss their tactics for when they would penetrate the dark cavern just beyond the margins of the road-way, Evondair moved away from the portal and gazed around him. Even as he sought to re-familiarize himself with the empty wasteland stretching away before him in both directions and ignore the malodor-ous stench that made him snort in disgust more than once, he reached out through his exceptional gift of Discernment.

The action was instinctual; a means of understanding his surround-ings and those within it, but opening his mind to the darkness of the Uunglarda was not only an ill-conceived idea, it was a thoroughly dan-gerous endeavor and he instantly regretted doing it. With the force of a rushing tide, desperate loneliness and unremitting anguish poured into his being, overwhelming him so completely that he raised his hands to cover his face and doubled over with physical pain. Memories that were not his, but were as scathing as a lashing torment serrated through his thoughts. Recollections of sadistic brutality and remorse-less cruelty that drew a profound groan from behind his clenched teeth filled his being with the irrepressible sorrow of more souls than he could number. The desperate emotion pressed into him like a thou-sand blades.

He did not say a word. In truth, he could not, but as the waves of despair and suffering sought to drag him into the colorless shadows and ensnare him, he fought to withdraw his discernment from the darkness even as it grasped and clawed at his mind like a ravaging monster. He could have screamed. He could have cried bitter tears. He could have cursed repeatedly in fluent Dlalth as the comprehen-sion of the dark language of the Reviled filled his mind as intelligibly as his own, but he did none of these things. As the deluge of misery wrenched at his essence and the dejectedness of the lost Fey of the Light tore at his sanity, he centered his thoughts on the only thing he knew was capable of defeating the darkness. Filling his mind's eye with an image of bright, clear, sparkling Light, he focused his attention on the wails and screams shattering his thoughts and answered their cries for mercy with the strongest weapon at his disposal.

Unspoken, yet heard as clearly as thunder rolling across the languid heavens, the compassionate love that filled his entire spirit reached outward benevolently, seeking those whose minds he touched through his discernment, silencing the calamitous uproar seeking to usurp his harmonious nature and with that single action, a breathless pause stretched across the gloom.

Silence.

"Drachalych!" A Dlalth curse assaulted them as three Legionnaires lunged at the Watchers from the shadows they had drawn around themselves to disguise their presence. Senzuur and his subordinates responded ferociously, drawing the bright weapons given to them by the Fey Guard in order to provide protection for the Liberators and prove their reliability. Behind them, Mardan and Bryth stood ready to engage any who slipped past the first line of their defense, while Rehstaed and Dravahl took up positions to guard Gairynzvl and Evondair, who stood watching the confrontation with a pained expression. As clear steel rang against grime-encrusted Dlalth blades, the Healer turned to gaze at his friend, unable to hide the dismay that betrayed his intense loathing of violence, but the former Legionnaire was staring beyond the skirmish into the shadows of the cave entrance situated against a towering outcropping of gray stone.

Gairynzvl could already sense the younglings detained within that dark prison. Their desperation and loneliness penetrated the cold, bleak environment as surely as a bright ray of light on a cloudy day. Twisting to gaze at the Healer beside him, he reached out and placed his hand upon his shoulder with the hope of sharing the heartbreaking impression he sensed and as his piercing lavender-ice gaze locked with intense viridian, Evondair gasped repeatedly. The weight of the imposing emotion transferred to him was nearly too painful to bear. Even without Ayla to provide a conduit, the two exceptionally gifted male-fey were now familiar enough with each other to establish their own connection and they stared at each other in horror as the crescendo of small voices crying from the darkness pierced into them.

"They are here." Gairynzvl said with heavy emotion, his stare shifting to Ilys who had stepped off the track and was looking into the distance. "You bear the message, Ilys. We all rely upon you."

The sheDemon turned to look back at him with a scowl, but nodded curtly; then raised her hand over head and, drawing an invisible circle in the air above her, winked out of sight in a ripple of beguiling light. Her disappearance caused Evondair to recapture his friend's stare and he did not need to speak for the Fierce One to hear his undeniable misgivings, but neither said a word about the perilous situation.

Waiting just long enough for the Watchers to render the Legionnaires standing guard at the entrance of the cave unconscious, Gairynzvl moved purposefully towards the opening. His gaze sought evidence of the childfey he knew were only yards away, but the aperture that yawned before them was shielded by a spell of diffusion his vision could not pierce. Comprehending the inherent danger in plunging into such dark magic, where what lay beyond was entirely concealed, he called to Senzuur.

"We cannot risk it. The way is obscured by a spell of diffusion. You must enter first." Moving to stand beside his friend, the Watcher growled under his breath at the jeopardy they faced, but those under his command gathered behind him. Preparing to infiltrate the darkness and face certain disaster, they joined his fortifying growl, but before they could move forward into the murk of the spell and face certain peril, Mardan rushed forward.

"Wait! I know how to counter that spell." Widening his stance as he handed his sword to Senzuur, who looked at him with as much amazement as increasing respect, the Celebrant-turned-Fey Guard confirmed to all of them what many suspected. Though he never spoke of it and seldom utilized it, he had an undeniable gift of magic as a spell-caster. While his friends watched with guarded glances at each other, he raised both hands towards the dark entrance. His intense cerulean gaze narrowed with concentration and he began an incantation. "Vas hevauthycaera shavaul invaalnyyth."

Hear my voice impenetrable shadows.

"Pyyrvat sha-lindauwyn eprauvanyyl guildynn!"
Shimmering light pierce and open the way!

At the utterance of these words, the opening of the cave shimmered with resplendent light, piercing the obscuring shadows to allow them all to see what lay beyond and revealing what they had assumed. Guarding the cavern that held their future, a full legion of Reviled waited within the dimness, armored and already growling menacingly. The spell sparkled only long enough for the Fey of the Light to peer within; then faded, but they had gained the intelligence they required and Mardan did not re-employ the incantation. Instead, he turned to gaze at his comrades with a brazen expression.

"A handy gift to have, fair warrior," Senzuur quipped in a light-hearted expression of appreciation as he handed Mardan's sword back to him and the spell caster grinned deviously in response. Then the Watcher turned to his own and nodded."Trach klynnoch vla sladdin!" he shouted in fluent Dlalth.

To the courage of fools!

Chapter Thirteen

The dimness of the obscured cave entrance swallowed the Watchers like thick fog as they plunged into the interior. Dlalth curses and the ring of metal proclaimed the fact that they met the inhospitable welcome they had anticipated and, as the moments dragged by, Bryth became more and more uneasy. Turning to scowl first at Rehstaed and then at Mardan with an unspoken aversion to the situation, he shook his head and flexed his powerful, black wings agitatedly. "I understand the test we have put them to, but have we not waited long enough?" His desire to join in the fray and aid the Watchers in subduing the Reviled was shared by his warrior-spirited companions who turned as one to glare at Gairynzvl.

"Surely they have proven themselves reliable," Bryth continued, clearly unsettled by the inequitable assessment they had devised for the Legionnaires, but Gairynzvl rebuked him angrily.

"I said they were trust-worthy from the start. It was you and Captain Varka who had reservations."

"My reservations have been satisfied," the dark-haired Fey Guard looked at his companions who willingly agreed that they, too, had no further qualms about trusting the Watchers. Gairynzvl gestured invitingly at the cave, encouraging them to proceed and without any supplementary discussion they drew their weapons and stepped through the diffusion of shadows.

Unlike the Braying Caverns that had stood in darkness, damp and inhospitable, this cave was well lighted by torches mounted into the rock walls. Glowing tunnels led away in several directions and the atmosphere was dry instead of heavy with moisture. Bryth looked round him hurriedly, evaluating the situation as his thoughts filled with the tactics of combat, but an unexpected sight met his cobalt gaze. Four of the Watchers were engaged with six Legionnaires, the ringing of their swords and curses echoing from the vaulted ceiling, but Senzuur and Dravahl were not among them.

Running in opposite directions around the skirmish and holding a length of heavy rope by each end, they encircled the group, passed each other at the far end of the cave, and rounded back again; effectively containing the entire contingent, including their comrades, as they tugged the rope taut and circled once more. Realizing the trap into which they had fallen, one of the Legionnaires swung unexpectedly outward with his sword and the dark, blood-encrusted blade sliced a gaping wound in Senzuur's arm as he passed the hissing Dark One. Although he screamed as the blade found its mark, Senzuur did not drop the rope he held tightly in his hands, nor did he stop running as he and Dravahl passed one another yet again.

Comprehending their simple, yet effective tactic, Bryth sheathed his weapon and hastened to the starting point where the two Watchers returned. Taking the end of the rope from Senzuur's hands even as he stumbled away from the ensnared group, the tall Fey Guard glared provokingly at the trapped Legionnaires. Rehstaed and Mardan sheathed their weapons as well, then took up positions with their companions in order to grasp the rope and help haul the length inward to compress the struggling Legionnaires together while the remaining Watchers, threatening the Dark Ones with blades poised at throats, took the last possible opportunity to duck under the rope and escape its constriction before it cinched tightly about its quarry.

Captured, the Dark Fey cursed incessantly, flinging their weapons at the Fey of the Light in a final attempt to cause harm before the rope tightened to the point that movement, let alone breathing, was nearly impossible. Tying the rope in several places to ensure it could not be evaded, the Watchers then took up positions around the ring of hissing Legionnaires with their bright Fey of the Light weapons brandished to discourage any foolhardy endeavors.

Senzuur moved away from the group in a directionless reel, gazing down at his arm in distress even as he grit his teeth against screaming again. The Dark One's blade had cut through his leather uniform so deeply that bone was visible in the depths of the gaping wound. As he staggered towards the entrance of the cave, grasping his arm tightly in an effort to reduce the prolific blood loss, Mardan pursued him while calling urgently for their Healer.

"Evondair, come quickly; you are needed. Evondair!"

In response to his imperative shouts, the two remaining Liberators who waited outside the cave stepped through the shadow-cast entrance together. The Healer sought the one who required his skills while the former Legionnaire stopped to watch Dravahl and Rehstaed. They were retracing their steps to the entrance and indicated hurriedly as they passed him that they would collect the Dark Ones who had been left unconscious outside the cave and return with them. Then, the native Vrynnyth Ghaler's conversation shifted into their own beguiling language as they slipped through the swirling shadows and Gairynzvl stopped to look about him with a satisfied grin.

The Watchers had done precisely what they had asked of them. They had cleared the way to rescue the younglings and provided valuable protection without killing or even harming any of the Legionnaires.

* * *

The bright morning sparkled with gentle snowfall fluttering downward through embracing evergreen boughs that sighed and creaked in the brisk morning chill. The small village of Lyyshara had, in but a few days' time, transformed from a rural farming community into an encampment of Fey Guards, Healers and attendants; tents, supply wagons and massive horses with thick, shaggy winter coats and lengthy manes to protect them from the cold. As was typical for the quiet community, the early morning hours saw villagers going about the business of tending to their livestock, though they were mirrored in their ministrations by several Fey Guards who undertook the care of their own. Others prepared breakfast for the hungry ranks while the remaining contingent of guards greeted the day with customs of exercise and training. Amid the flurry of activity, Veryth stood beside one of the supply wagons with Ayla and Nayina, who had arrived in the camp just that morning with one of the supply wagons bearing provisions of food for the guards. Quietly discussing the return of the Liberators and the needs of the childfey they would, with the blessings of the Ancients, bring with them, Veryth prepared them for what to expect. "We have learned from working with the first group the Liberators rescued that patience and caution are the key to interacting with these traumatized childlings. Although they will initially rush towards any Fey of the Light, desperate for reassurance and tenderness, their ability to trust, as one might expect, is extremely limited and they must be handled with delicacy. In fact, as we transported them to the Temple through the unfamiliar environs of the forest, many became overwrought and terrified; some even attempted to flee the safety of the wagon and had to be restrained."

The shefey listened with pained expressions, eager to be of assistance in the rescue of the childfey, while at the same time finding it challenging to keep a steadying hand on their compassionate emotion. Veryth understood their difficulty all too well. "You may not be aware of this, as I tell very few, but I lost my beloved and our young daughter in a raid by the Reviled. Though I fought to protect them, I could not combat a legion of Dark Ones and they were both taken from me. It is because of this that I comprehend fully how hard it is to see what happens to these unfortunate ones and yet, try to remain detached."

Ayla muffled a whimper, then tried to swallow her emotion with an audible gulp. The Healer, who was not quite twice her age, but experienced enough to recognize the weakness in her empathic tendencies, reminded her to stay guarded. "Caution is vital, Ayla. Your gift is useful, but it puts you at risk. The emotional volatility of the younglings can and will overwhelm you, making you a potential hindrance rather than a benefit."

She gazed up into his deep green eyes and nodded, fully aware of his ability to quiet her emotion by using his own gift of empathic transference, through which he could utilize his own emotion to affect another. He could easily transfer his wealth of serenity to calm her, but he did not employ his gift unless desperation required such measures. He merely gazed at her with a subtle smile of confidence in her own ability and nodded before turning to Nayina, asking her to help Ayla collect as many blankets from the tents of the Fey Guards as they could find.

Quietly standing at the far end of the wagon, Kaylyya awaited an opportune moment to offer her assistance, but when Ayla and Nayina hurried off in the opposite direction without taking notice of her, she approached the Healer instead and smiled pleasantly. "How may I help, Veryth?"

He shook his head and returned her genial smile. "You already know the answer to that question, Kaylyya Synnowyn. The childfey will need as much soothing as your magical song may lend; you only need remain close until the Liberators return." She smiling agreed; then gazed up at him with greater considering.

"I am sorry, Veryth. Your loss must have been very difficult to bear."

He said nothing as his thoughts turned inward and he closed his eyes, inclining his head to her without offering anything additionally and she understood his unspoken request to not speak on the matter further. The Reviled had already caused so much sorrow in the lives of so many; so much grief and pain; had inflicted so much harm, there was no need to verbalize what they both already knew painfully well. Though she never spoke of her own losses, Veryth understood the connection she formed with him without speaking about it. The loss she had suffered of her own loved ones; of mother, father, and the unshakeable terror of far too real nightmares that had sent her psyche into another place where solitude had become a reality through the only source of pleasure that remained to her. Music.

* * *

Turning the shadowy corner, Ilys thought to press on, in spite of the many Legionnaires filling the encampment that stretched out before her. Crowding round its many sulfur braziers with faces half-covered to protect themselves from the malodorous fumes, they sought to extract some meager warmth from the ineffectual fires while awaiting the whims of their commanders. She remembered such a life far too clearly; remembered the endless days of harassment and the exhausting hours of training that had taught her the most valuable lessons she could ever have learned from the Reviled: how to be a danger to them.

They had thought to train her to be a killer; a mercenary by stealth through the exploitation of her extraordinary gift as a Light Bender, but they had not anticipated that by training her how to kill they would be putting themselves at risk. It was only after years of brutal enslavement that she had become strong enough, physically as well as mentally, to lay aside the harmonious inclination of her Fey of the Light nature and draw blood by her own decision; yet it was through that violent act that she had liberated herself from their ruthless control. Slaughtering the Centurion who had held her as his own personal captive, she had slipped through their grasp and had remained hidden beneath the sheath of light she wore as close as her own garments every day since.

Disguised beneath the veil of bent light she cast about herself in order to traverse the dangerous avenues of the Uunglarda unseen, Ilys stepped onward lightly, neither creating any sound nor offering any indication of her presence. Yet as she came to the end of the street where a black tent marked the Centurion's quarters and a smaller tent beside it indicated the accommodations of one of the Demonfey, she stopped short. Standing silently, she reconsidered if she truly wished to confront a Demonfey Captain with the message she bore, in spite of the Watcher's assurances that he was one of them and could be trusted. While she contemplated such a foolhardy endeavor, a Legionnaire in crimson leather strode purposefully into the middle of the street, stopped directly in her path, and glared at her.

Catching her breath, she refused to breathe so not to give herself away as her mind spun, seeking some means of escape. She remained invisible behind the ripple of light she had bent round herself, but his crimson stare pierced into her from beneath a broad, brown leather bandana that kept his long, jet black hair from falling into his eyes. In the mustiness and reek of the Bathracht encampment, he had turned the collar of his coat up and had cinched it tightly to avert some measure of the noxious fumes poisoning the air. He stood unmoving with his arms crossed assertively over his broad chest while, in an incongruously non-threatening gesture, held his wings tightly folded behind him.

Staring at her long enough to make it clear that he was aware of her, regardless of her invisible guisel, his crimson gaze sent a shiver through her. Memory served her well, but in a realm where nearly all the inhabitants had blood-hued eyes he was indistinguishable. His only other distinguishing feature, his wings, he held closed behind him and she could not differentiate him from the many other Legionnaires that had, at one time or another since her Integration, used her for sport or had been forced to do so. Fear blended with anger, then mixed with hatred within her that boiled into a rage that was nearly uncontrollable. It took every measure of restraint she could muster not to reach for the dagger sheathed along her thigh and provoke him into action. If he had not seen her he would be easily dispatched, but it was evident that, somehow, he could penetrate the cowl of bent light she wore and she was not foolish enough to think she would be capable of injuring a Legionnaire who towered nearly twelve inches over her, whose physique boasted of strength and whose stare held no light of compassion.

"Yes, I can see you." His voice was little more than a hoarse whisper, but it sent a shudder through her that made her teeth chatter. "Do not unveil yourself, but come with me and don't even think about trying to escape or I shall announce your presence and free the entire encampment to deal with you."

Chapter Fourteen

Gairynzvl stood in the center of the cave, his liquescent eyes closed as he reached outward with his senses, seeking the younglings secreted in the recesses, dark corridors and dimly illuminated chambers that stood off the main hall of the cave. The Legionnaires stood in mute curiosity, watching his actions and whispering to each other in Dlalth undertones the Fey of the Light could not comprehend.

He could hear the childfey's small voices; muffled cries of fear and loneliness that wafted through the stale atmosphere of the cave like an icy breeze. He focused on them, listening intently to gauge the direction from where it came; then whispering to them in return through the touch of quiet thought.

We shall not hurt you. Tell me where you are so we can bring you home to the Light.

A discordant horn call pealed in the distance, warning the Liberators that time was not on their side. A change of guard would soon take place and when it did, they would be discovered. Urgency prompted Gairynzvl to step closer to one of the glowing corridors. His eyes remaining closed as he sought an answer to his appeal. As he stood, silently contemplating, the Watchers glanced uncertainly at each other with very real fear. If they were discovered amidst a band of intruding Lighters, let alone found to be rendering them aid by impeding the Legionnaires tasked with guarding the childfey against rescue, they would suffer unthinkable torture as traitors to the Realm.

Scrutinizing Gairynzvl's actions with deliberate speculation, the Legionnaires spoke more urgently amongst themselves and the Watchers, comprehending their conversation, could not keep from gazing first at each other; then at the Liberators. Having bound Senzuur's wound as securely as he presently could, Evondair turned to watch the interactions of the Dark Ones, his curiosity piqued. He had touched the subconscious essence of the Dlalth long enough to remember their language, but only on the most rudimentary level. Still, he recognized several of the words the Legionnaires whispered.

Liberator. Childlings. Hope.

Crossing the dusty floor of the cave to stand before the detained group, he fixed his piercing viridian gaze upon them before turning his interrogating stare to Dravahl. "What do they say?"

The Watcher scowled at him hesitantly, setting the Healer's patience on edge. "I am on your side, Dravahl. What are they saying?" His insistence could not be avoided.

"They question if 'e is Th' One." Crimson locked with viridian even as Gairynzvl turned to gaze down one of the winding corridors, his seeking thoughts echoing into the silence as another volley of Dlalth horns penetrated the shadows swirling at the cave entrance.

"The One?" Evondair repeated and Dravahl nodded, but said nothing further, watching the Healer as he considered the information carefully. "They know the Ancient Writings?"

Dravahl growled with frustration. "Are they no' Fey o' th' Light, 'ealer? Simply because they be 'eld captive in this 'arrowin' place an' are forced t' survive any way they can; they still know ev'ryt'ing you an' I know abou' th' Ancients."

Twisting round to gaze behind him at Bryth and then at Mardan, Evondair's thoughts whirled, but before he could say anything further one of the Legionnaires leaned over the length of rope constricted tightly around them and stared at the golden-haired malefey fixedly. "Chrysvagcht byyrvanna kihlar?"

The rasping Dlalth words confounded him and Evondair turned to Dravahl for interpretation once more, yet before the Watcher could translate the dark words, the telepathic Legionnaire penetrated Evondair's mind, forcing his way past the barrier all Fey were trained to utilize to keep their thoughts their own. Repeating the phrase through inward thought as sharp as a dagger, he forced the discerning Healer to accept his knowledge of Dlalth so they could communicate. At the forceful intrusion, Evondair arched backward abruptly and squeezed his eyes closed with a growl of discomfort, but in spite of the prohibited manner in which the Legionnaire's thoughts entered his mind, he suddenly and undeniably understood him.

"Why don't you kill us?"

Staring at the Dark Fey with a conspicuous fusion of anger at being forced to accept such a violation and sympathetic horror at comprehending the Legionnaire's appeal, Evondair swallowed hard against the turbulent emotion conveyed through the Dark One's thoughts and answered in the Common Tongue. "We are here to rescue younglings, not slaughter Legionnaires."

Upon hearing this, the Reviled gazed at each other with unspoken urgency, then the Dark One spoke through his thoughts once again; his incursion less volatile, though still every bit as unrelenting as before. *"Do you think the Praetor wouldn't take measures to prevent such an act?"*

Listening to the conversation through his own telepathic gift, Dravahl interrupted aloud. "What do you mean? How are the childlings protected?" His question caused Gairynzvl to pause and twist to gaze at them intensely, his unspoken questions filling the Watcher's mind.

How are the childlings protected? Where are they? How can we release them?

Hissing impatiently, the Vrynnyth Ghaler stalked forward to glare at the Legionnaire. "Where are they?"

"It doesn't matter where they are. Even if you find them before the guard change arrives, you won't be able to free them."

Pushed to the limit of his patience, Mardan shoved the Healer aside, who stood listening to the telepathic argument pensively, and reached for the Legionnaire. Grasping him by the throat, he repeated the question with an imperative hiss. "Where are they!"

Having touched the Healer's thoughts long enough to share his dark language as well as to remember the Common Tongue, the Legionnaire responded out loud with blatant frustration. "They are in five separate locations through the caverns, locked into cages that all require different keys. You don't have time to rescue them."

Startled by the unanticipated development, the Liberators looked at each other with the grim realization that their efforts may very well be in vain. Cursing repeatedly in fluent Dlalth, Gairynzvl crossed the floor, hissing wrathfully with each step until he stood before the one held by Mardan's clenching grasp. "Do you hold the keys?"

Unable to answer verbally as a result of Mardan's tightening grip round his throat, the Legionnaire nodded mutely; then spluttered for air when he was released and pushed back violently.

"Give them to me." The Fierce One held out his hand, unintentionally exposing his scars to the captive Reviled who stared at them and then at him with amazement.

"He bears the scars."

"He is the One who sundered The Gate."

"He is the Liberator foretold by the Ancients."

"You don't have time," the one Mardan had released shouted to be heard, but before any of them could rebuke him, the Dark One did something none of them expected. Grasping the ring of keys hanging from his belt, he glanced back at his subordinates who nodded at his unspoken question and then yanked them free. "The guard change will be here in less than thirty minutes. You have no choice. The only way you can rescue all of the childlings is if each one of you accompanies one of us. Only we can guide you directly to each of the seculsionaries and unlock them. If you try to find them on your own, we are all dead Fey."

* * *

Ilys glared hatefully at the crimson clad Legionnaire staring back at her without blinking and without any outward indication of clemency. Neither of them moved initially; they merely stood locked in the intensity of each other's eyes, but he stepped backward at last, watching her suspiciously to ensure she followed him to the small tent beside the Centurion's. When she did, he glanced down at the dagger she wore sheathed along the outside of her thigh, paused, then held out his hand. "Give that to me."

"I only unsheathe it if I intend to use it. You may end up bleeding," she threatened as brazenly as she could manage to sound, but he scoffed at her display of audacity.

"If I end up bleeding, you will end up at the mercy of every Demonfey in camp."

"Mercy!?" she retorted in disbelief, but he inclined his head with a wicked smile and gestured wordlessly for the dagger with his hand still outstretched. Reluctantly, she withdrew it and turned it over to him.

"Thank you," he offered quietly; then he utilized the blade to pull back the flap of the tent and gestured for her to enter. "Inside now."

His unanticipated civility sent a shiver down her spin as the realization that she would not be leaving his tent unharmed pressed into her thoughts. At that moment, however, there was nothing else she could do. Stepping within the dim interior, she scanned the small area rapidly, seeking anything she might use as a weapon to defend herself.

A tight cord was suspended along one side of the tent, upon which were hung an assortment of swords, daggers, bucklers, and other smaller weapons. Upon closer investigation, she could see they were all securely fastened to the rope through intricate knot work, which would make snatching one hastily to use against him very unlikely. Along the same side of the tent hung a separate taut cord, utilized for organizing his uniforms and outwear; all exceptionally clean and in good repair. Turning back to gaze at him more closely, she could see he was not gaunt with malnourishment, nor was he covered in filth from over-extended periods of time exposed to the harsh environment. His gaze was clear; his hair and hands clean; even his boots were polished. With the dawning realization that he was, in fact, no common Legionnaire, but one of the Demonfey of the Realm, she watched him more cautiously. He, in turn, scrutinized her with the same constant stare he had locked upon her in the street; yet, to her amazement, he made no move against her.

"You may as well unveil yourself, Ilys. We both know I can see you." Her startled reaction at his use of her name made him chuckle hoarsely. "Yes, I know exactly who you are. Not many Light Benders to be found in the Uunglarda." His nonchalance was wearing thin, but he was right; there was no reason to waste energy concealing herself and with a rapid wave of her hand over her head the ripple of light she had drawn round herself blazed for an instant, then vanished.

"What do you want with me?"

He ignored her question. Turning his back to her, he placed her dagger upon a small desk shoved into the corner of the tent and unfastened the top portion of his jacket as he turned slowly back to face her. Observing her as she scanned the sleeping area of his tent, in which was suspended an oversized hammock with ample blankets to ward away the numbing cold, he saw her expression shift from blatant hatred to an unreadable haze. Casually, he posed a question of his own as he leaned back upon the desk and folded his arms across his chest, staring at her with all the leisure of a confident captor. "Why are you here?"

"Can't a sheDemon enjoy a stroll if she wants to?" Her acerbic reply came out not quite as biting as she had hoped and he smirked at her attempt to appear unaffected before shaking his head.

"Not through the center of the Bathracht encampment; not if she knows what's good for her."

"Most Legionnaires cannot see me, so what's good for me is to remain concealed."

He inclined his head. "I am not *most* Legionnaires." He certainly was not. His unhurried interrogation was truly beginning to terrify her, but in spite of the threats he used to intimidate, he only stared at her.

"What do you want with me!"

"I want you to tell me why you are here, Ilys, and, I assure you, I have the patience and liberty to wait upon your answer as long as I choose."

Shuddering at his relaxed demeanor, she could not help stepping back from him; then cursed inwardly at her unintentional display of fear. She had been away from the Uunglarda too long. "There is nothing to tell; I was taking a walk."

Her insistence made him sigh profoundly and he closed his eyes, shaking his head subtly before fixing a glare of even greater intensity on her. "You weren't taking a walk, Ilys. You've been missing for weeks and its common knowledge that you aided the Lighters when they encroached upon our realm to rescue childlings. I need you to tell me why you are here." The calm manner in which he clarified himself was chilling, but confusion, not trepidation, whispered across her features as she considered his words. He had not said 'to steal childlings', but 'to rescue childlings'. The distinction was glaring.

"Who are you?" The impudent question slipped from her lips before she could contain it and his reaction was terrifying. Moving in a blur of speed, he was one moment reclining against his desk and the next grasping her around her throat with one wing spine poised over her heart, ready to plunge inward. His crimson stare penetrated the cerulean of her startled gaze and he hissed at her viperously before rebuking her insolence with a low growl.

"You will answer my question, Ilys, or I shall bind you and summon every Demonfey within twenty miles to take sport with you. They have gone a long time without recreation and I can promise it would be particularly unpleasant. Is that what you want?"

It was no idle threat and she knew it. Shaking her head emphatically before she took time to consider any alternative, she cursed inwardly once more for betraying her fear another time, but his response to her unspoken answer was not at all what she expected. He did not hurl her to the ground to enjoy her fear himself. He did not strike her or injure her through the strength of his hands or wings, although he certainly could have, and he did not shout at her to impose his will in a threatening display that would have invited any Legionnaire passing the tent to join in. Instead, he relaxed his vice-like grip around her throat and moved his hand to caress her cheek instead.

"Good." Though his tone was softer, it sent a tremor through her just as surely as his threat had done. Smiling, he withdrew the spine of his wing and closed them once again behind him in an unthreatening gesture as he stepped back from her to watch her attentively. "Now tell me, Ilys, why have you returned to the Uunglarda and what brings you into the encampment of the leadership of the Dlalth?"

She stared at him, altogether indecisive. Without knowing positively who he was, she could not risk relaying the message she bore; although it seemed apparent he was one of the Demonfey. Still, there was no evidence anywhere in his quarters that might proclaim his identity as the Captain she sought and without knowing this crucial fact she had no choice but to continue to evade his questions, even if it meant provoking his anger another time. "You have comfortable accommodations." She stated flatteringly, turning to gaze round her as innocuously as she might appear and her unexpected change of tactic amused him. Laughing unguardedly at her stubbornness, his smile transformed from hostile to handsome and she could not help glancing sidelong at him more than a few times in astonishment at the abrupt alteration.

"Yes, I have, but its comfort is deceiving. It may hold clean clothes and warm blankets, but it also contains chains used to detain captives and a lash that would tear that pretty outfit of yours to shreds, so I suggest you answer me before I decide to put them to use." With each word his smile faded and she knew she stood upon dangerously thin ice. Her mind spun, seeking some means of tricking him into disclosing his identity, but he was losing his patience toying with her and it was obvious he was just as skilled as she was in the art of evasion.

"I...I was looking for...seeking the..." she stammered demurely, but his stare did not falter.

"The Centurion?" he offered obligingly. "We all know how much you enjoy slaughtering them."

She regarded him through a flutter of eyelashes. "Actually, I was looking for the Captain of the Demonfey."

His stare widened for a brief instant, then narrowed suspiciously. "A new target for the light bending, traitorous mercenary? How intriguing." His response did not betray him; not enough to be certain.

"I'm not a traitor," she purred in an exhibition of hurt feelings as she stepped closer to him, then round him while reaching to place her hand lightly upon his shoulder. "I'm an infiltrator, sent into the enemy camp to learn their weaknesses."

He smiled wryly. "Sent by whom, Ilys? And which enemy are you referring to; the Lighters or the Reviled? We can play this game as long as you like, but one way or another you're going to answer my questions." Turning to face her, he ran his fingers along the fastenings of her corset as the hostility of his gaze melded with unmistakable fire and her blush of confidence paled.

Chapter Fifteen

The Legionnaires stood at the opening of three of more than half a dozen tunnels leading into the darkness of the system of caves. Beside each Legionnaire stood one of the Liberators and, because there were not enough Liberators, Dravahl accompanied one as well. Each Liberator held a key to unlock the seclusionaries that secured the childfey they sought to rescue. The remaining Watchers had taken up positions just within the swirling shadows obscuring the entrance to the main cavern; awaiting the arrival of the guard change. As the Liberators set off down the network of tunnels, Dlalth horns serrated through the thin atmosphere. They were much closer than they had been just moments before and the Watchers glared at each other with unspoken trepidation.

Time was running out.

The corridors were narrow and twisting, much as the ones they had followed within the Braying Caverns, yet they were illuminated by torches mounted at equidistant positions along their lengths and, as a result, felt less cramped and disorienting. The groups hurried at a half running pace without speaking. The uneven terrain undulated treacherously, threatening to tumble the unwary passerby and throwing intermittent blockades of large boulders in their path, which they had to clamber over or squeeze around. Several moments after they set off, two of the Legionnaires stopped and gestured at separate tunnels that snaked away in opposing directions and the Liberator paired with them followed in determined silence.

Stretching out his senses, Gairynzvl sought to touch the younglings and reassure them of their safety. Arriving in the company of Dark Ones would do nothing to allay their fears and justifiably might lead some of them to seek escape once the bars of their prison were opened, but there were no alternatives. Just as they had to trust the Legionnaires to do what they said they would, so too did the little ones; although even as this thought filled his mind and then reached outward into the emptiness of the caverns, Gairynzvl could not contain a scoff at such a ridiculous notion. He remembered only too well the terror Legionnaires instilled in childfey.

"Here." The Dark One leading him stopped abruptly and pointed at what appeared to be a blank wall. His guttural Dlalth broke into Gairynzvl's thoughts and scattered the coalescing whispers he had encountered as they came upon the spell-enshrouded seclusionary. He gazed at the wall curiously, his senses assuring him the childfey stood within arm's reach, although he could neither see, nor hear them. Looking at the Legionnaire, he extended the key toward him wordlessly as the piercing ice of his stare demanded action without the need for him to speak.

"You should; they will be afraid of me." When the Legionnaire spoke, a rustling echo filled the corridor. The pattering of many small feet hastened away from the sound of his voice, then the Dark One raised his hand and hurriedly spoke the incantation to expose what stood obscured. "Hchrynoch ennovat, vraylscalth guldrar." At his words, the illusion of blank wall wavered like candlelight just before it is extinguished, then vanished to reveal a small, cramped grotto into which no light from the torches several yards away could reach. Across its entrance, a heavy iron gate barred the way and an immense lock hung from its latch. Gairynzvl stared at it angrily, hating all it represented, but then he peered into the dimness and spoke quietly to the younglings.

"We are here to help you; you must not be afraid." Stepping closer, he raised the key, placed it into the lock and turned it sturdily. The sound of the latch unbolting was satisfying, but before he swung the door wide, he looked deeper into the shadows. "This Legionnaire will not hurt you. He has guided me to you and I shall not allow him to harm you. Will you come with us so we may return you to the Light?" His reassurance drew one small boyfey towards the front of the fissure. The small childling looked up at the tall malefey before him with monumental trepidation shaking his uniquely bronze-hued wings, although hope sparkled in his brilliant, violet eyes.

"He gave us extra bread," the little boyfey whispered, looking past Gairynzvl at the Legionnaire who had stepped further away from the iron bars of the prison in an obvious attempt to set their fears to rest. Staring at him curiously, Gairynzvl nodded and pulled the gate opened slowly, then waited as a dozen or so younglings scrabbled out of the darkness to gaze up at him expectantly.

The other Liberators had similar interactions with their little ones; each malefey setting aside the ferocity of his nature in order to deal gently with the frightened childfey and reassure them of their safety. Dravahl, however, could not convince his group of younglings that neither he nor the Legionnaire at his side would harm them. Even after swinging the door to their prison wide and stepping backward several paces, the terrified childlings refused to come out of the shadows, but pressed against the inner wall of their prison and wailed in distress. The sound echoed through the tunnels in all directions, alerting the others that not all was well. As the Liberators hastened back towards the main cavern with their groups of childlings, Evondair paused at the tunnel into which Dravahl and his guide had diverted. Llistening intently before bending to one knee in order to collect one of the childfey of his group into his arms, he spoke quietly in a soothing tone that reassured and calmed him.

"I must help those who are crying. Will you follow this Legionnaire out into the main cavern where other Fey of the Light will meet you? I promise; he will not harm you. Can you trust him?" The little childling gazed at the golden-haired malefey with evident fear before he looked up at the fierce Legionnaire standing at his side. Trembling with uncertainty, the boyfey shook his head.

"Do you hear the others crying?" Evondair asked patiently and the boyfey nodded. "Should I not go to help them? Do you want us to leave them alone in the darkness?" The Healers steady tone and unhurried manner eased the boyfey's fear enough for him to shake his head, at which indication, Evondair turned to look up at the Dark One standing over them. "Walk in front of them at some distance," he suggested and the Legionnaire nodded silently to agree, moving past the Healer and the boyfey to wait several paces further along the corridor while Evondair looked once again at the little one he held. "You can follow him at a distance so he cannot harm you. He *will* lead you to safety." He waited as the youngling considered and those who had congested round them whispered fearfully, yet when they agreed he smiled encouragingly, leaned closer, and kissed the little one's dirt-smeared forehead tenderly. Standing then, he turned to gaze down the tunnel from which emanated increasingly distressed shrieks of fear and, without glancing back, he ran in the direction of their cries.

Dravahl and his guide stood glaring at each other helplessly, fully comprehending the childlings fears while, at the same time, entirely frustrated by them. Regardless of his reassurances, Dravahl could not convince the younglings of their safety and he stood in the opening of the seclusionary considering the rash, yet seemingly unavoidable alternative of dragging the squalling childfey out of the darkness and forcing them to obey.

"That's not a good idea," the Legionnaire warned, attempting to dissuade him after reading his un-verbalized musings. He received a harsh glare and a berating of viperous Dlalth in admonishment for his uninvited delving, but before he could return the Watcher's anger, Evondair came from the dimness of the distance, slowing to a walk even as he spoke above the childling's wailings.

"You could hear those little ones in Lundoon."

* * *

Staring into her cerulean eyes, the Demonfey smiled deviously as he unfastened the topmost binding of her corset, watching for the slightest indication of fear to betray her, but he was unprepared for the rage that stabbed back at him through her glare. His crimson gaze narrowed as he reconsidered his course, but shouting coming from outside his tent distracted his attention. For the briefest moment, he looked past her and it was the only opportunity Ilys needed.

Raising her knee violently, she found her mark and his shocked gasp of pain betrayed the force behind her attack as he doubled over to protect himself. Exploiting this motion, she brought her hands together over her head; then swept them downward against the back of his neck, brutally driving him into her knee as she brought it up again, this time into his face. She had not thought, however, about how accustomed to pain he had grown throughout his years as a Legionnaire. Hissing at her like an enraged demon, he twisted unexpectedly and reached for her waist, wrapping his arms securely around her as he lunged forward towards the center post of the tent. This action sent her backward into it so forcefully that her breath was expelled from her lungs and her head slammed backward against the heavy wooden beam as her senses went reeling, but she was not left defenseless.

As he struggled to ignore the pain her knee had bestowed and attempted to straighten, she brought one wing around her, slashing at him with its barb and catching him full across the chest. Ripping open his already half unfastened coat, her wing barb tore through the shirt he wore to leave a bleeding gash in his pale skin. Looking down in unwary surprise, he left himself unprotected yet again and she impelled herself forward in a headfirst charge, utilizing her horns to pummel into him viciously and send him tumbling backward.

Cursing furiously at her skill in the Common Tongue, then Dlalth and then incensed Celebrae, the Demonfey shook his head to reorient himself and she would have hurled herself into him again to press her advantage, but his use of Celebrae made her pause. No common

Legionnaire or Demonfey knew the high language of the Ancients. As he struggled to focus his glare on her, she stared back and reached out with her hands in a gesture indicative of stopping.

"Who are you?" She posed the brazen question another time, prepared for the anger of his response, but, although he looked up at her and bared his teeth ferociously, he did not answer. Outside, a scuffling of boots upon gravel approached his tent and his immediate concern became gathering his senses and composure before they entered. Fumbling to close his coat in spite of the rending it had received and cover his bleeding wound, he stepped toward the entrance even as those outside stopped and addressed him urgently.

"Captain Nunvaret. The Lighters have stolen the childlings from the Goralnicht Seclusionaries."

Stiffening in his tracks, he turned to glare at Ilys with clearer comprehension, but did not say a word to her. Instead, he addressed the subordinate outside awaiting his instructions. "Advise the Centurion. I'll join you directly." Turning to his captive, he moved closer as his glare shifted from threatening to astonishingly indulgent. "You should have told me, Ilys."

She stared back at him, realizing at last that he was, in fact, the Captain of the Demonfey she sought.

"Now, however, you need to veil yourself and get out of here."

"But I need to tell you," she attempted, but he ignored her as he moved to collect weapons from the opposite side of the tent.

"You had your chance. The Centurion will demand retaliation and it will come swiftly. Return and warn your companions to flee while they can."

Staring at him in disbelief, she shook her head. "But I have a message."

Again, he disregarded her. "There is no time. Wait until I've joined the others in the Centurion's Pavilion; then go." Turning his back on her, he moved towards the opening of the tent and left her behind without another glance.

Growling under her breath at his indifference, she stood in silence for only a moment before enshrouding herself in bent light once more. Then, she gazed thoughtfully at his desk. She could write the message she had been sent to deliver and leave it for him or she could wait until he returned to share the vital communique entrusted to her. Looking at the tent opening, she hissed under her breath instead. "Disregard me all you like."

She would not wait for him to return just to deliver a message he did not deserve in the first place. Cursing under her breath at the uselessness of the entire endeavor, she retrieved her dagger from his desk and slipped out of the tent, heading back in the direction from which she had come.

* * *

The Liberators gathered in the main cavern, obscured from view by the swirling shadows still cast across the cave's entrance, but the sounds of an approaching unit of Legionnaires drew ever closer, heralded by disharmonious Dlalth horns and the unmistakable sound of unified marching upon parched ground. Hastily, the malefey prepared their strategy. They would herd the childfey against the far wall where they could be protected behind the expansive wings of the Healer who had come out of the last tunnel bearing several of the squalling younglings and ushering half a dozen others before him. Dravahl and his guide followed behind them, scowling fiercely to dissuade any of the childlings from hurtling past them back down the corridor.

Unable to join in the resistance as a result of his injury, Senzuur took up his sword and moved to stand with Evondair in order to guard the little ones, but his approach caused them to wail in shrill distress. Turning to look down at them with a measure of placidity only a true Healer could wield in so stressful a situation, Evondair crouched down to speak to the crying younglings. His tone was both soothing and mild despite the fact that, around them, the remaining Liberators and Watchers were shouting battle tactics and organizing their defensive posture. Reaching for one of the closest wee fey, Evondair drew her close and spoke with gentle purpose to the frightened group in a tender and unhurried manner while he turned to look up at Senzuur.

"I know he is fearsome, but do you see his bandages?" The little ones gazed up at the Legionnaire towering over them and considered him as Evondair continued, "he was injured while protecting *you*. *He made* it possible for we of the Light to find and rescue you. He will stand with me before you, guarding you with his wings and his sword, even as I shall. There is no reason to fear him."

Comprehending his intention, Senzuur lowered his head in a non-threatening gesture and slowly spread his massive, dragonhide wings, revealing their many scars, as well as their ornamentation of metal studwork. The sight was predictably terrifying. Several of the childfey backed up abruptly, pressing themselves into the cold stone of the cave wall while a few on the periphery of the group made motions to flee, but their fear of the Legionnaire was nothing compared to the horror they experienced when, from beyond the shifting, spell-cast entrance, a brazen exclamation of joined voices broke the dismal, Uunglardan murk.

"Raah!"

Dravahl and the other Dark Ones glared at each other with honest apprehension. These were no common Legionnaires coming to change guard. Only the Demonfey of the Realm marched in such precise unification and announced themselves with so characteristic a call. Orders in Dlalth echoed through the swirling obscurity of the entranceway even as the Liberators formed a second line of defense behind the Watchers.

"We will join you, Liberator!" One of the Legionnaire guides hastened to Gairynzvl's side, raising his weapon to his chest while grasping it with a clenched fist. "We can help you defend the younglings so they can return home. All we ask is to be granted permission to return as well, should any of us survive."

At this request, the Liberators glanced at each other in surprise while the scrunch of boots upon rough gravel approached the mouth of the cave. Looking past the Legionnaire addressing him, Gairynzvl's icy gaze sought Evondair's, Mardan's, Bryth's, and then Rehstaed's; questioning in rapid succession without words either spoken or conveyed through thought.

"If we remain, we will not be killed. You know what sort of torture awaits traitors. Are you not the Liberator? Will you abandon us simply because we are not younglings? Will you not allow us to help you; to help them?" The Legionnaire pointed his weapon at the childlings huddled behind the splayed wings of both Healer and Dark Fey. Gairynzvl's icy lavender pierced viridian, blazing cerulean, intense cobalt and flaming violet; seeking; asking; unwilling to make an independent decision that would affect all of them, but he met no resistance. Turning to face the Legionnaire once more, he nodded.

"Stand before the Watchers. You must form our front line, but know this; through such a willing sacrifice you will prove yourselves and gain our trust. When we cross back to the Light, if you have not fallen in honor, you shall cross with us." They glanced hesitantly at each other; then each one of the Dark Fey thumped their weapons across their chests in a sign of loyalty and moved to stand directly in front of the cave entrance where certain death waited.

Chapter Sixteen

"Hchrynoch ennovat drylvaunacht khrilnaarr" The guttural Dlalth invocation to withdraw the obscuring shadows from the cave entrance leached through the main chamber and each malefey standing, waiting, braced himself against the inevitable clash to follow. The smoky mantle of darkness dissipated and the Demonfey waiting outside came into view; not a straggling handful; not a single unit, but an entire legion numbering twenty or more sent to ensure the continued captivity of the Fey of the Light younglings. Yet even they, as dispassionate Demonfey of the Realm, could not conceal their surprise upon discovering three lines of opposition with weapons raised to greet them.

Just as the swirling murk vanished into the heavier ether of icy mist and soot descending from the leaden sky, two of the Legionnaires who had taken up positions at either end of the front line, turned slightly inward, their crossbows raised, and began firing arrows into the unsuspecting Demonfey who cursed violently, drew their weapons and rushed inward against the assault. Hastening to meet them, the remaining four Legionnaires engaged the heartless Reviled with every measure of retaliatory wrath they could muster; freed at long last to take vengeance for the countless cruelties, mistreatments and ravagings they had suffered at the hands of remorseless Demonfey. Their fury was unparalleled and the unsuspecting Demonspawn fell before them, yet even as the initial lines collided and metal skirled against metal, a second line of Demonfey surged past them towards the Watchers.

Screaming in panic-stricken dread, the childfey protected behind the broad white wings of the Healer and the expansive dragonhide pinions of the Dark One jostled against each other seeking to escape, but the two guardian malefey pressed close to them, keeping the barrier they had set in place even as little ones attempted to flee in all directions. Behind the battling Dark Ones, the Liberators prepared to join the fray, pushing forward and hissing belligerently in an undaunted display of bravado; forcing the entire writhing mass backwards towards the entrance of the cave through the sheer intensity of their onslaught. Another line of Demonfey swept inward, seeking to gain the advantage by going around the raucous conflict and straight towards those guarding the childlings.

Readying himself, Evondair raised his sword, but Senzuur stepped forward, creating a supplementary barrier with his own body in front of the Healer who stood his ground to protect the younglings. Seeing the wounded Legionnaire, two Demonfey howled with glee at his audacity and hurtled directly for him, yet even as they ran Senzuur raised his injured arm, ignoring the jagged pain such action caused, and extending his hand towards them as he spoke in an arcane language. The moment the words left his mouth, a turbulently compacted ball of blazing energy shot from the palm of his hand into the attacking Demonfey; spreading across their bodies like a swarm of enraged bees. Instantaneously, they screamed and lurched backwards in agony, the tumultuous plasmatic force enveloping them from head to toe to wingtip and increasing in intensity as long as Senzuur continued to speak the incantation of the spell. Those Demonfey intent upon bursting into the barrier of feathers and dragonhide protecting childfey paused and stepped back with unconcealed hesitancy as the unanticipated magic wrought havoc over their comrades.

Pressing the converging skirmish further out of the cave through the vehemence of their attack, the Liberators then turned to deal with the Demonfey who stood unhelpfully watching their comrades suffer.

Rehstaed's sword swung in a precise arc, the rage that still lingered within him over what Legionnaires had done to his beloved and only child taking hold with a force neither he, nor the Dark Ones he engaged, could resist. As his blade severed the wing and then the throat of the first Demonfey he saw, Bryth's weapon swung in the opposing direction, leaving a bright gash across the chest of the other; yet his reach was not sufficient to take the Dark One's life. Growling in fury, the Demonfey lunged forward rather than staggering backward, impelling the blade he wielded deeply into the Fey Guard's shoulder. Bryth's curse of pain melded with the Child Wraith's sadistic laughter and echoed through the cavern, but the Dark One had not seen Mardan.

Coming up behind Bryth, the Celebrant-Warrior raised his blade high; then brought the hilt of it down with crushing force across the crown of the Demonfey's head, the impact causing his eyes to roll upward as he crumbled to his knees. Reaching to grasp him by the lengths of his dusky brown hair, Mardan encircled it round his clenched fist and stepped closer, yanking the Dark One's blade from his hand even as he moved to within inches of his face and growled menacingly at him. Not intimidated, the Demonspawn hissed in return and snatched a dagger from a sheath laced against his thigh, sinking its ten-inch blade into his opponent's leg and laughing derisively when Mardan threw his head back and screamed. "Vile demon! Cruciavaeryn!"

Curling inward to grasp at his body in desperate pain, the Demonfey released his hold upon the dagger and cried in distress as the Spell of Inflicted Pain filled his mind and body with wave upon wave of unrelenting agony. Behind them, childfey screeched in terror and Mardan opened his eyes to see the remaining two Demonfey rushing towards Evondair with blades raised high. Senzuur turned to follow their course, but as his focus shifted, the magic he utilized to subdue the first pair of Demonfey began to weaken. Speaking the incantation a second time, another furious bolt of energy blazed from his hand even as his sword tumbled through the air, turning end over end before it sank into the back of the closest Child Wraith. His magic, however, missed its intended mark and that Demonfey collided forcefully with Evondair.

Crossing his arms before him with fists extended, the Healer lunged forward into his attacker as the impetus of their combined momentum doubled the driving power of both his fists into the Demonfey's throat, knocking him backward as he choked and wheezed for air. Unwilling to lower the defense of his wings, Evondair straightened abruptly, raised the blade still held in his hands over his head, then swept it around and down, driving the handle into the temple of his adversary and rendering him, instantly, unconscious. In the midst of the calamity, however, childfey fled in multiple directions.

Successfully driving the remaining Demonfey out of the cave, the Legionnaires who had joined them and the Watchers who fought to defend The One were quickly surrounded. Dlalth curses and screams of rage and pain shook the Uunglardan gloom. Several had fallen and one of the Legionnaire's crossbows was confiscated. Sneering viciously, the Demonfey Lieutenant who absconded with it rushed back into the cave, swerved to escape the defensive line the Liberators had reformed, and began targeting those childfey who had bolted from behind the protection of the Healer's wings.

The unspeakably horrifying cries of the little ones who could not escape the Demonfey's cruel intent were more than Gairynzvl could bear. Cursing in rancorous Celebrae, he grabbed Bryth's blade from his hand and shouted to his companions even as he charged headlong at the Demonfey slowly turning and loosing arrows at the scattering younglings.

"Drive them out of the cave. Drive them out now!"

Hearing his voice, the Lieutenant turned to focus his aim on his assailant, but Gairynzvl's speed was greater than he had anticipated and the last thing he saw was The One, twin blades pointing forward as he charged into him with such intensity of momentum that both swords buried themselves to the hilt in his chest. Not bothering to wait for his reaction or watch as the Demonfey froze in an arch of traumatic pain, Gairynzvl tugged the blades out again, turned on his heel, and delivered a sideward kick directly into the fatal wound he had just bestowed that sent the Dark One sprawling. Rushing toward the mouth of the cave, he shouted to his companions once again, repeating his directive as he spread his wings and impelled himself upward, away from the conflict, into the leeching, toxic sky.

Heedless to their injuries, the Liberators moved as one unit, forcing any remaining Demonfey out of the cave into a chaotic disarray of feathers and wing spines twisting on itself in a slowly turning circle. Standing his ground, Evondair watched as Senzuur pursued the few childfey not mortally wounded by the unthinkable cruelty of the Child Wraith, attempting to return them to the safety behind the resolute Healer's wings. Furious battle and wrathful growls and hissing rent the murk as the Demonfey fought remorselessly. Two, then three of the Watchers fell before their brutal proficiency, as did another of the Goralnicht Legionnaires. Unable to use his sword arm, Bryth stood as a guard at the cave entrance to prevent re-entry. In addition to the knife-wound to his thigh, Mardan had taken an arrow through his forearm when he leapt in front of a childfey marked by the now dead Demonfey Lieutenant. He leaned against the caves mouth, gasping for breath and watching helplessly as Rehstaed and Dravahl stood back to back, defending each other from four Demonspawn.

Several hundred feet above them, Gairynzvl choked for breath in the filth-poisoned Uunglardan sky. Turning dexterously, he folded his wings and plummeted back towards the battle in an energy-building stoop that shook him mercilessly, demanding every ounce of strength and control he could achieve. Screaming in fury, his speed increasing exponentially, he focused on the center of the conflict. The speed with which he descended created visible swirling trails in the heavy ether behind him that spread outward into the gray sky. Looking up, Mardan watched the bizarre phenomena with undisguised amazement, but only for a second before he comprehended their source. Shouting to his comrades, his warning allowed the Legionnaires and Watchers to drop to the gravel beneath them as winged fury fell from the sky.

Fifty feet from the ground, Gairynzvl spread his arms wide, grasping the twin blades he held with a vice-like grip. In the last possible moment, he opened his wings and, with a powerful, direction-correcting wing beat, swept into and through the writhing mass of rage and hatred. The swords he carried rent dragonhide, severed limbs, and scathed across throats as his trajectory sent him through the Demonfey with inescapably destructive force. Dropping the swords that had done their work, he struggled to break his fall with vigorous, reverse wing beats even as he careened through the mouth of the cave and crashed to the compacted, dusty earth, somersaulted repeatedly in a chaos of wings and limbs, and landed face down at the Healer's feet.

Those Demonspawn his valiant assault did not dispatch were rapidly dealt with by viciously hissing Vrynnyth Ghalers. As the dust settled and the surviving Liberators, Watchers and Legionnaires regrouped, Evondair closed his wings carefully and gazed down at his unmoving friend with undisguised concern. Crouching down to lay his hand on his friend's shoulder, he spoke his name worriedly. "Gairynzvl."

The Fierce One did not move.

"Gairynzvl."

Drawing round them, the others watched with similar anxiety as the Healer attempted to rouse their leader, though for many long moments he lay insensible. Several younglings sidled closer to the group, looking first at the formidable warriors with clear trepidation and then gazing with genuine curiosity at the one who had acted so courageously to protect them and now lay in the dust, unmoving.

"Will he be all right?" One little boyfey inquired furtively, tugging on Rehstaed's coat in a timorous action that caused the formidable Fey Guard to look down at him through a haze of still calming, violet fury.

"I don'nay," he began, but never finished as his uniquely hued gaze met similarly blazing violet. He stared at the boyfey, transfixed. His bronze wings, reddish hair and dimpled cheeks produced a deep furrow in the warrior's brow as his mouth fell agape. Stooping to gaze at the little one more closely, Rehstaed dropped his sword into the dust with a clatter and raised a trembling hand to touch the childfey upon his cheek, turning his head gently to inspect a lightly-shaded, sable birthmark near his temple. The shape and size were irrefutably distinctive, like a bird in flight, and his breath caught in his throat.

The distinguishing mark was just as his beloved's had been.

"Lorszan?" He spoke the name through a torrent of emotion that crested over him with the force of a spring flood, but the childling only gazed openly at him, blinking without understanding. Rehstaed shook his head. Of course, he would not understand. His son had been lost to him as an infant. The youngling would not know the name he and his beloved had given him. Even as tears welled in his eyes and he stared at the boyfey, unable to speak, his comrades watched in breathless silence.

"Wha' be yer name, lit'l one?" Rehstaed forced the question from behind clenched teeth; both yearning for and fearing his answer, but the childling shook his head.

"I don't have one." His unthinkable answer was all the Liberator needed to hear. Wrapping his arms round the wee boyfey in a sudden embrace that buried him in the depths of the warrior's strong arms, he left the tot gasping in surprise and weeping, though he scarce comprehended why.

"Ye' 'ave a name, dear one," Rehstaed assured him with a tone so brimming with elation and poignant emotion and so unlike himself that those standing watching could not keep from gazing at each other with heart-warmed smiles and glistening expressions. Looking down once again into the boyfey's violet gaze, he spoke the words he never dreamed he might ever have the opportunity to speak.

" 'Tis Lorszan. An' I am yer' lovin' father, long parted from'ee." Confounded, the childling stared at the Rehstaed hesitantly; yet he had never seen another Fey with violet eyes like his own, nor like his bronze-toned wings or copper-hued hair. The childfey stared at him for many long moments, perplexed by such a declaration. Then he squealed in astonishment and glee, the echo dancing through the cave more sweetly than any music any of them could remember hearing as he threw his small arms round his father's neck and embraced him for the first time in their lives.

Smiling with harmonious emotion, Evondair got up and crossed the cavern floor purposefully, found the medical pack he had set aside after treating Senzuur, and stooped to rummage through it quietly. Retrieving what he sought, he returned to his friend and knelt down on one knee as he requested the aid of his companions to help him turn their unconscious friend onto his back. When they had succeeded, he drew closer, propping Gairynzvl's head on his bent knee as he withdrew the cork from the bottle of Quiroth he held. Then, with a wry grin, he administered as much of the invigorating amber liquid as he could before Gairynzvl shook his head and raised his hands to fend him off.

"Viperous Healer!" he cursed wrathfully, twisting to spit out whatever of the foul-tasting medicinal tonic he had not already unconsciously swallowed while those standing around him laughed with amused relief. Evondair responded with all the calm detachment typical of a Healer, though his smile conveyed an unmistakably devious delight.

"You are welcome, Fierce One."

Chapter Seventeen

A bracing wind mingled with the dance of snow flurries throughout the endless morning hours as those who anticipated the return of the Liberators and Watchers finished their preparations; then had little to do except wait. The pale winter sun climbed slowly to his zenith, paused to survey his kingdom, then began his descent toward the horizon as his radiant gleam sought to penetrate the barrier of congesting storm clouds in the leaden winter sky. Largely unsuccessful, however, the colorless sky merely shifted in brightness as his daily sojourn proceeded and it was not until late in the day when the glimmering disc of light balanced over the lip of the horizon that sounds of activity close to the portal heralded the return of the Liberators.

Ayla and Nayina had taken up sentry at the unattended crossing early in the afternoon, speaking quietly amidst the gracefully descending snowfall, sharing much with each other after many long days apart. They spoke of the impending battle and the fears they both shared at such a prospect, but invariably, their discussion turned to less portentous matters. They spoke of malefey; they spoke of love; they spoke of Gairynzvl and how he had irrevocably altered Ayla's life. Everything she had been, she now was not; yet all she was remained. He had taught her the meaning of courage, the true purpose of hope, and had shared his strength with her in ways she could not begin to explain. Her emotional turbulence did not irritate him or annoy, as it did so many others; as it had Mardan though he never spoke of it. In fact, through the soft whispers of Gairynzvl's thoughts, he encouraged her to be all that made her unique and to find strength through her weakness.

In the later hours of the afternoon they were joined by Kaylyya. She kept to herself and paced the length of the small pond again and again eager to see Evondair again and anxious that she could possibly not building within her. After the hour of tea, they were also joined by Veryth who spoke with the shefey companionably; his conspicuously soothing nature quieting their apprehension, although they all gazed at the waiting portal more than a few times with impatience for the return of their friends.

Unexpectedly, the ice groaned prodigiously and shuddered. A deep distortion in the portal bulged outward, as if a vast force were pushing against the unseen plane of crossing from the other side; then a torrent of younglings burst from the writhing emptiness. Squeals of glee and shrieks of joyful abandon pealed through the clearing as the childfey scampered and tumbled in the clean, soft snow. They played with delighted ecstasy while the shefey and Veryth stood watching them with radiant smiles, offering welcoming hugs to many who instinctively approached the adult Fey who vigilantly guarding the borders of the forest to keep the little ones from becoming lost in the darkening and unfamiliar woodland.

The Watchers stepped through the billowing vortex next, hastening to clear the way for the three Legionnaires who had survived the skirmish and could cross with them back into the Light before the Liberators stepped from the Uunglardan darkness into the twilit clearing. Last to return was Gairynzvl, who immediately turned to gaze back at the portal, speaking into the void urgently as if she could somehow hear him. "Hurry Ilys, we must close the portal. Make haste!"

Beside him, Evondair stood shaking his head, but said nothing. Icylavender locked with piercing viridian and no words were required; they both feared she would not return, although neither voiced their reservations. Behind them, however, Rehstaed did not hesitate to say what they were both thinking. "Tha' sheDemon'll no' be comin' back,

I'll warrant. How long d' we leave the entire village a' risk waitin'?" Silence answered his words when they turned to gaze at him with obvious uncertainty.

"Does not Ilys have the ability to open portals on her own? Is it not best to close this one rather than risk the safety of Lyyshara?" Bryth asked from beside his companion, his first priority as a Fey Guard Captain to protect those under his authority. Gairynzvl nodded reluctantly, but turned back to gaze into the warping face of the portal once again, focusing his thoughts into a dagger that he directed into the darkness.

"*HURRY!*"

Turning from watching the frolicking younglings, Kaylyya caught sight of Evondair standing with his fellow Liberators at the portal entrance and could not contain the rush of delight that swept over her, prompting her to take wing with a glowing smile as she hurried to greet him. At her approach, Bryth turned to impede her progress; then, noticing her focused gaze upon the Healer, smiled perceptively instead and bowed gallantly to her as she passed by him with a determined pace.

"We must gather the childfey so they can be transported to the safety of the Temple before retribution falls on our heads." Evondair advised diligently even as Gairynzvl's gaze shifted to look behind him. Before the Healer had time to realize she was there, Kaylyya alighted beside him, reached for the one for whom she had been waiting all the day long and turned him by the shoulder with audacious urgency.

The warmth of her embrace scattered any thoughts of tending younglings he might have had and, regardless of the fact that every one of his closest friends stood watching, Evondair could not deny the pleasure of pulling her close to him any more than he could prevent her from tilting her head up to him invitingly. Smiling at her with honest affection, he wrapped his strong arms around her small waist and willingly obeyed her unabashed incitement. Leaning closer, then closer still, their warmth tantalizingly mingled as he brushed her lips with his own. Smiling at her with a soft moan of pleasure, he drew her against him, closed his eyes, and allowed his kiss to deepen; expressing his intensifying bond with her in a manner that required no words and left no hint of ambiguity.

Cheers and exclamations of encouragement rang around them, but neither noticed as the soft music of her aura began to sing a transcendent, wordless song that made his head spin. Extending his wings about her to shield them from view, he hugged her closely and whispered in a barely audible tone to her. "You honor me, sweet Kaylyya. I was not sure you shared the connection I have felt growing between us."

She sighed and smiled brightly, able only to nod wordlessly before he turned his head to kiss her once again, yet she opened herself to him willingly and through his gift of Discernment he became aware of the full measure of her affection for him.

Clapping him on his shoulder approvingly, Gairynzvl stepped away from his pleasantly diverted friend; his lavender gaze searching the clearing for the most beautiful amber he had ever seen and when he found it locked upon him with expectation, he smiled broadly.

"*Jshynjshar ovaerydd.*" The hushed whisper of his thoughts crossed to her in a blissful caress that made her sigh and close her eyes as he hastened to her side. He did not slow when he reached her; did not pause to constrain the earnest emotion pounding through him. He did not restrict himself from sweeping her up into his embrace as he pressed his mouth fervently to hers.

"*Sweet beloved one.*" He whispered again in the Common Tongue, the potent touch of his impassioned thoughts spinning her senses in myriad directions as his yearning united to dance with her own.

"I was so afraid you might not return," Ayla whispered beside his perfectly pointed ear, the tremor of her voice betraying the trepidation that had spun her thoughts during the course of the day.

"Hush. Never worry. I will always return to you," he responded gently as he molded her to himself, completing his thought non-verbally as his mouth found far more pleasing occupation. "*I have no intention of becoming a victim of the Dlalth again.*"

She clung onto him tightly, her thoughts tumbling as the memories he had shared with her of his time among the Reviled serrated through her thoughts. At their touch, predictable tears sprung anew in her, but he wrapped his wings round her and redirected her anxiety with the fervency of his passion.

The ice of the frozen portal shuddered convulsively as the undulating crossing billowed outward briefly in a vibrant flash of light, then contracted just as unexpectedly with ripples splaying across its surface. Mardan smiled wryly and watched the snow at the edge of the pond for telling signs of footsteps that would betray with certainty Ilys' return and he was not disappointed. Small indentations formed in the snow as it seemed she paused to take in the scene; then came directly towards him. Not bothering to unveil herself, she circled him unhurriedly, allowing her hand to trace the contours of his broad chest and shoulders, run down the length of his arm and linger mischievously upon his hip, but feeling the caress of an unseen hand was not what surprised him the most. He knew she was there, hiding beneath the light she bent around herself. What astonished him more than anything was the teasingly light kiss he felt brush his lips and the tender touch he felt upon his cheek before she vanished into the chilling twilight.

* * *

"No quarter shall be given. No mercy offered. Do you understand me, Nunvaret?" The Bathracht Centurion issued his final commands with a snarl the young Captain knew far better than to question. Nodding brusquely, he raised his sword in his fist and thumped the weapon against his chest in a non-verbal display of loyalty before he spun on his heel and retreated from the Centurion's black tent. Snorting the stench of those squalid quarters from his nose as he strode purposefully towards his own tent, he ducked within briefly as he sheathed his sword before he snatched a heavy cloak of black wool from its hanging place and glanced round for any sign that Ilys yet lingered. When he found none, he fastened the cloak round his broad shoulders and chose several other weapons from his personal arsenal to supplement the sword he already carried. Then he exited to hasten towards the waiting battalions of Legionnaires under his command.

The ranks allocated to him were a quandary and he did not hesitate to walk about the straggling group, critically inspecting them as he passed around their perimeter, assessing strengths and accounting for weaknesses. The number of Common Legionnaires assigned to his unit made him scowl as he muttered under his breath. They were barely recovered from the forced march they had endured in order to reach the Bathracht encampment. Many nursed fresh injuries from abuse they had received along the way and now they were expected to form the front line in the advance into enemy territory. Several even lay in semi-conscious states, ignored by their comrades in the fear that rendering any assistance would be deemed cause for punishment, but their needs could not be disregarded if he intended them to join the ranks crossing into Jyndari later that night. Cursing in resentful Dlalth, Nunvaret turned to seek the closest Lieutenant and ordered the surprised underling to bring the camp medic at once, whose attention was typically reserved for the ranks of the Demonfey, officers and the Centurion himself.

Fully aware that his actions were not only being scrutinized by the half legion of Demonfey assigned to his unit, but were also being critically measured by their own ruthless standards, he crossed the distance they kept between themselves and the filth-covered, parasite-ridden Common Legionnaires in order to confront them with unwavering confidence. Walking to within inches of the alpha Demonfey, he glared into his crimson stare and hissed in an intractable tone.

"You have a question, Drachalych?"

His peer scowled as his gaze fell to examine the crimson-clad officer challenging him, assessing his physique, as well as the number of weapons he bore upon his person, in a brief, yet thorough inspection that made his gaze narrow.

"Not at the moment, Captain."

Nunvaret's stare met the gazes of the remaining Legionnaires of the Realm boldly. He was unwilling to show any measure of weakness in such treacherous company. "Good, because I'm in no mood to offer explanations for my actions to underlings. You're here to obey my orders *without* question; understood?"

The alpha sneered and bowed to him in a brazen show of disdain. "As you wish, or should I say, as the Centurion wishes. I assume your actions reflect them?"

Nunvaret leaned closer, his glare piercing his rivals like a blade. "If you doubt it, I'd be happy to take you to him so you can pose your concerns in person?" His suggestion caused the insolent Demonfey to flinch conspicuously and immediately drop his gaze while he shook his head adamantly. Nunvaret scoffed with his own display of contempt before he stepped back. "I didn't think so. Now make yourselves useful and collect extra rations for those three before I have time to change my mind and take you before him anyway. I'm sure he'd be only too amused to hear all about your insubordination when I have no time to deal with such obstinacy."

All six Legionnaires of the Realm beat their fists upon their chests, then turned sharply and retreated towards the mess tent before their Captain could alter his plans. In spite of their rank among the elite of Reviled, none of the Demonfey wished to pay a visit the tent of the Centurion of the Bathracht encampment; not for any reason. Each one already harbored memories of previous such visits that had been harrowing enough to ensure they would do everything in their power to prevent any repetition of such a situation. What they did not realize, however, was the fact that Nunvaret was entirely aware of their memories. As they hastened as far from him as they could manage to go, he stared after them, shaking the memories he had pried from their thoughts out of his mind. He could not let any of them see that he shared their determination to avoid such a happenstance under all circumstances.

* * *

Lavender twilight faded into darkness all too quickly as childlings were gathered into several Hasparii-drawn sleighs and snuggled beneath soft lamb's wool blankets in preparation for their journey to the Temple, which was the safest place for them to be for many reasons. As the little ones were herded together, some with much difficulty as they only wished to play in the clean, fluffy snow of their home, a full unit of Fey Guard were deployed to protect them on their journey while Ayla and Nayina made good use of their experience with childfey. Turning the rushed endeavor of gathering the wee ones into a game, they were all soon in place and ready to depart; save one.

Held tightly within his father's embrace, Lorszan paid little heed to the hustle and bustle happening around them. Having never experienced a loving touch or kind word in his short life, he was unwilling to be parted from their comfort so soon after finding them and was crying bitterly. Rehstaed stood in the midst of those hastily coming and going, his strong arms encircling the small, undernourished boyfey as he spoke tender words of comfort and reassurance from his heart and not a single Fey in the vicinity dared interrupt them. Passing around the reunited pair with affectionate smiles and sharing nods of appreciation with each other for the miracle occurring in their midst, even the Captain of the Fey Guard stood idle for many moments when all the final preparations had been attended to and the group stood waiting to depart. Glancing uncertainly from the Liberators, to Rehstaed, to Veryth and then back to the fierce warrior who had transformed into an attentive father before their eyes, he found himself reluctant to interpose the evident suggestion that Rehstaed needed to part from his son so they could get underway. Clearing his throat several times with no measure of success, Captain Varka then moved toward Veryth for assistance.

"Perhaps you could?" he queried uncomfortably, receiving a silent nod of concurrence before the Healer stepped calmly to the pair holding each other closely beneath the star-strewn, winter sky. Even as he approached, Rehstaed discerned his purpose and could not keep from turning his head to glare at the Healer any more than he could contain the hiss of annoyance that slipped from his lips. At the sound, however, the youngling gasped and reared backward, struggling to escape him and it took several moments of concentrated effort on his part to calm the boyfey's fear. Only after he succeeded did Veryth speak in the sedate tone customary to all Healers.

"We must depart before retaliation finds us and steals our most precious treasure once again." Although he spoke sagaciously, his words were not necessary. Rehstaed understood the gravity of the situation. Turning to face the Fey he knew had suffered as great a loss as he, the warrior inclined his head in silent assent and then captured the Healers emeraldine gaze with his own.

"Yer r'sponsibility this night'll be unparalleled, 'ealer; yet I might dare t' impose one furt'er upon ye'?" Rehstaed's uniquely accented voice filled the quiet clearing and those gathered round them, anticipating the request to come as well as the response to his entreaty, watched curiously nevertheless.

Veryth placed his hand over his heart and bowed deeply. "I am honoured by any request you may make of me."

Unable to speak as the burden of long withheld emotion crested within him, Rehstaed gave his son over to the Healer and stared at them in poignant silence. Veryth turned to smile gently at the confused childling, assuring him with a patiently quiet tone that all would be well and he would see his father again very soon. Turning back, then, to the Fey Guard before him who stood fighting back a torrent of sentiment he could scarcely contain, he inclined his head and closed his eyes briefly. "No treasure could be more valuable and I will protect it with utmost vigilance, even unto my own life."

The malefey locked gazes, though no words were necessary to express what they both understood and after a moment, Veryth nodded once again and turned back toward the waiting sleighs that would carry the childlings away from danger.

Stepping away from the others, Gairynzvl whispered quietly to Ayla in his thoughts, drawing her by the hand from the cart into which she had clambered behind half a dozen childlings. Loathe to resist his unspoken invitation, she glanced round her several times, checking and rechecking that the little ones were secure. Leaping down then, she moved with him into the shadows and was pulled close in his embrace without another word.

Tenderly, his lips met hers, conveying the passion of his yearning and the ardor of his emotion in a touch that left her breathless. Clinging to him like the shadows into which they had concealed themselves, she longed for more moments than were at their disposal. Hasparii bugled into the night, eager to be underway and childfey squealed in delight at the sounds, but the entwined pair paid them little heed. In the few moments that remained, they held each other close, kissing, whispering, and sighing deeply; yet, all too quickly, the time of departure was at hand and Gairynzvl forced himself to release her. "Fear not for my safety, Beloved. I shall take no unnecessary risks," he attempted to reassure, but she smiled and shook her head.

"Do you think I do not know you well enough by now, Fierce One?"

He grinned at her teasing, but did not argue her insight. She knew him far better than any other had ever known him. She understood his conviction and fearlessness and knew he would do whatever was necessary, despite his reassurances. Instead of arguing, however, he guided her back to the sleigh she had momentarily abandoned and effortlessly lifted her into its bed. She brushed her hand across his cheek as their gazes locked a final time; then the driver, who had waited for them as long as he possibly could, snapped the reigns sharply.

In that moment echoes from the base of the mountain shattered the heavy silence and glaring, discordant horn calls announced the coming onslaught from the opposite side of the open portal. Where once an impassable obstacle held two factions at bay, the felled Great Gate invited free crossing and the sounds permeating the settling darkness set all into irrevocable motion.

* * *

Gathered at the base of the mountain at what they could only presume would be the easiest crossing point for the insurgence of the Reviled, the Liberators and those Legionnaires who had crossed into the Light stood uneasily behind the ranks of the Fey Guard. The male-fey waited with resolute purpose; yet as darkness settled more deeply and the light snowfall, which had been descending for the greater portion of the day, increased in intensity it became more difficult to focus their thoughts and energy. Braced against the seeking cold falling all around them, they spoke quietly about details they had not had time to previously address.

"How do we know Ilys delivered the message?" Bryth voiced what the majority of them questioned silently; his intense cobalt gaze piercing Gairynzvl's icy lavender, but the former Dark Fey shook his head.

"Until she returns, we cannot know with any certainty."

Mardan stood silent a moment, then offered the piece of information about which the remainder of them seemed ignorant. "But she did return." Surprise met his pronouncement.

"What?"

"When?"

"How do you know?"

Setting his wings defensively, he glanced around him, unwilling to share the full story while, at the same time, convinced they needed to know as much of it as possible. "She came across while Evondair was enjoying Kaylyya's welcome and Rehstaed had the rest of us diverted with his reunion. I saw a flash of light come through the portal and, although no one was physically evident, footsteps in the snow betrayed her."

Gairynzvl scowled ferociously upon hearing this and turned in several directions to peer through the darkness for her.

"Where is she, then?" Evondair interjected, coming closer from the station he had taken up in front of the Healer's tent to join the conversation.

Rehstaed echoed his suspicions. "Aye. Why shoul' she 'ide 'less she's no' done wha' she wa' sent t' do?"

They stood silent until Mardan offered a conceivable explanation with an astonishing tone of justification. "None of us have been very welcoming towards her. If she was unable to deliver the message, she might fear our reaction to such news and, thus, has chosen to remain veiled." A skeptical hush answered his atypical and notably awkward defense, but before any could pose any supplementary queries, he shook his head and continued in an attempt to redirect their mounting curiosity. "What should be more pertinent is how we should proceed assuming she was not successful?"

A sharp clangor of discordant horn calls followed this inquiry, proclaiming the intent of the Reviled without words and, for a brief instant, all gazes shifted to the swirling vortex at the base of the mountain.

"If the Reviled cross and have no knowledge of our message, then the battle will be fierce indeed." Bryth stated the obvious portentously, turning to point towards the front line of Fey Guards and the few Legionnaire guards who had crossed with the Liberators from the Goralnicht Seclusionaries. "They must be warned!"

Gairynzvl cursed in response to his pronouncement in fluent, exasperated Dlalth; hissing Ilys' name into the night sky wrathfully before he turned to face his fellow Liberators. "So many Fey will suffer needlessly because of her treachery! I should never have trusted her, but now the burden falls to me, as it should have done in the first place. *I* will go in search of Nunvaret to deliver our message personally." His avowal was met with a calamitous din of opposition, but it was Mardan who stepped forward to take him by the shoulder and gaze steadily into his crystalline-lavender eyes.

"Like it or not, *Fierce One*," he began with a familiar inflection, although he altered the term by which he had formerly addressed him, "you are our leader. You cannot disappear now, at this crucial time when all look to you for inspiration."

The former Dark One scoffed at his commendation, but when the others nodded in agreement he found there was little he could do but curse again. "Raach!"

Comprehending the Dlalth word, Mardan grinned, but would not allow his affirmation to be deflected. "As any good leader, we all know you are keen to take on the responsibility of this action yourself; to lead by fine example, but you are needed here. This endeavor must fall to someone else."

Gairynzvl shook his head in an attempt to argue, but before he could utter a single word, Bryth interposed. "I am willing to take up this cause, if you would send me? I am able to defend myself and have a strong likelihood of success."

Listening to him while shaking his head, Rehstaed also stepped forward. "Nay. You mus' remain 'ere, as you be a Cap'n and have ot'ers t' lead. I shou' go." Before he could offer any further rationale, however, Senzuur interjected with an offer of his own and then Dravahl, but when Evondair stepped forward, his offer left all staring at him in silence.

"There is not one among you who would not honor our friend and the cause he has set into motion through his fierce determination to do what is right, but each of you are warriors and that makes you essential here. There is only one logical option. *I* must go, as I neither wish to fight, nor am of any use with blade or bow. It is I who first suggested this course of action; therefore, it is only fitting that I should take the responsibility of carrying the message."

"You are presently our only Healer. You are needed here as much as Gairynzvl," Mardan pointed out, but Evondair raised a hand to forestall additional protests.

"Veryth shall return with additional Healers as soon as the childlings are delivered to the Temple and, until his return, the shefey of the village can care for any who might be wounded. I shall abide no argument to my decision."

"You, 'ealer, are as stubborn as tha' Tryngalith Mardan!" Rehstaed rebuked Evondair's determination with wit, but the underlying concern for his welfare was inescapable and his friends smilingly agreed. His humor lightened the moment, but the golden-haired Fey would not be dissuaded.

"That may be, but it shall serve me well amid the ranks of the Reviled."

In the hush that fell, Gairynzvl stepped forward to gaze deeply into his friend's eyes. Although they had known each other less than a month, his own telepathic skill and Evondair's exceptional gift of discernment had forged a connection between them he shared with few others. The young Healer understood Gairynzvl as intrinsically as he knew himself, which meant he also comprehended his pain and the similar pain shared by so many of the Legionnaires trapped in the shadows.

"It is not because you do not wish to fight any more than it is because you are unskilled with weaponry. I have seen you wield a blade and am aware of your proficiency when it is required, but I do agree; you *are* the right one to bear the message. You, Healer, *embody* Peace and if anyone among us has any chance of succeeding, it is surely you."

Chapter Eighteen

Ragged lines of exhausted Legionnaires filed through the cramped tunnels of the Braying Caverns leading to the chamber of the Great Gate. Tramping through the darkness with only the wings of the Fey in front of them for a guide, the weary Legionnaires moved together as a unit, though they were divided. The blackness was as penetrating and unavoidable as the trepidation of facing in battle well-rested, properly nourished Fey Guards and many in the forced march struggled not only to keep moving, lest they fall and be trampled underfoot, but to keep their feelings tightly constrained. Some were filled with anger and hatred for their kin, the Fey of the Light. Others recognized the opportunity facing them in the realm of Jyndari: salvation from the darkness. The prospect of fighting their kinfolk was as terrifying as it was tantalizing and the resulting havoc of emotion the situation created was more powerful than many of the Legionnaires had strength to hide. As they plodded through the heavy murk where none could see, not even with eyes accustomed to dimness, there were those who could not hold their tears at bay; yet had they been seen and required to explain their emotional display they would have been hard pressed to say with any measure of certainty whether they were frightened or overjoyed.

Flickering torchlight filtered across the languishing troops as they approached their destination, the glimmer prompting a flurry of action as hands wiped away any evidence of distress before the Legionnaires stepped out into the chamber where the prophecies of old had so recently come to fruition. Staggering to a halt in the unusual glare of more than a dozen torches, they stared through the glow in disbelief at the felled gate on the opposite side of the chamber, silently wondering at the power of The One who had single-handedly pulled it from the mountainside. Not a word was uttered, but more than a few furtive glances swept amongst the exhausted warriors as they shared their unspoken astonishment as well as the even more surreptitious expressions of hope that dawned in their wearied gazes.

Striding purposefully to the front of the ragged group and clad in immaculate crimson leather with a cape of sufficiently warming wool flowing behind him, Nunvaret glared at those under his command with as harsh an expression as he could project. His armaments sparkled in the glimmering torchlight, glinting into the eyes of his subordinates as they begrudgingly took note of his clean hair and the blush of his healthful complexion, although it was pale as all Dlalth's. Everything about him proclaimed the difference in their situations. They were meagerly equipped with over-utilized weaponry and wore uniforms that had rarely, if ever, been cleaned. Their skin and hair were covered with filth. Their cheeks were hollow and stomachs empty; yet they knew before he ever spoke a word that his expectations for them were the same as those he had for the Demonfey who stood at his right hand, whose situations were as favorable as his own. When complete silence fell among the weary legion, he issued his orders.

"We have not come here to compromise," he began with a tone that echoed around the chamber and filtered out of their realm through the spiraling vortex behind him into the blustering winter of Jyndari. "We fight by the order of the Praetor for the survival of all Dlalth. You know the Praetor Sees and Hears all. If you think you can escape by seeking the mercy of the Fey of the Light, I assure you, your punishment will be instantaneous and far more severe than anything you have ever experienced. Do not forget the Praetor is a Dream Stalker who can find you wherever you seek to hide." His chilling threat was painfully effective and he watched with an unreadable expression as the faint hope that had been kindled by the sight of the felled Gate faded in many crimson gazes.

Though, not in all.

* * *

Nunvaret's voice echoed through the slowly turning vortex of the portal into the brisk night air of Lyyshara where Fey Guards stood listening keenly as blustering snow began whipping around them, muffling the bewildering reverberations of his voice. Overhead, the barren tree tops and heavily laden evergreen boughs creaked and complained in the storm even as Captain Varka hastened to the fore of the gathered troops to hear the voice permeating the darkness more clearly. When he approached the portal however, it faded into the shadows as stealthily as any Reviled One might. Nevertheless, he did not waste time returning to the front line to bolster the courage of those under his command. Hearing the same voice riding upon the wind, the Liberators hurried to clarify the details of their strategy before Evondair set off bearing a message that could alter the course of history for all Fey.

"You will not know Nunvaret as I would," Senzuur pointed out, unaware of the Healer's exceptional gift.

"I do not, but if you are willing to share your memory of him with me I will know him as well as you do yourself." The Watcher's expression shifted to one of comprehension before Senzuur inclined his head with wordless permission and the Healer wasted no time. Without moving closer or reaching out to touch him as they all anticipated he might, Evondair focused his viridian gaze on the Dark One briefly; his attention transfixed as the image he sought filled his thoughts. Gazing at the Demonfey forming in the window of his mind, he secured his appearance in his memory, noticing his unusual crimson garments and the leather bandana he wore that held the lengths of his black hair out of his blood-hued eyes. Nodding with satisfaction after only a few seconds, the Healer released Senzuur from his delving and stepped backward, prepared to depart; yet the Watcher reached out urgently to impede his progress.

"Captain Nunvaret has as exceptional a gift as you, Healer; perhaps even more so. His telepathy is unavoidable and he will be aware of you long before you draw close. Be warned!"

Evondair inclined his head and closed his eyes briefly, indicating he understood even as he reached to remove the blade affixed to his belt, but Rehstaed immediately rebuffed this action.

"Ye' shoul' no enter th' domain of th' Reviled unarmed, 'ealer."

Bryth and Mardan agreed emphatically, but Gairynzvl shook his head and gazed with comprehension and even greater respect at his friend. "He cannot represent Peace armed."

Smiling at his friends with candid esteem, Evondair raised his hand to cover his heart as he bowed to them with closed eyes and wings furled inward in a sign of profound respect; then he turned for the mountain. Stepping briskly through the snow as he spread his wings wide, he utilized several powerful wing beats to ascend into the increasingly furious snowfall as all gazes raised to watch him disappear into the tempest.

Rising into the roiling atmosphere, his friends and fellow Fey of the Light vanished almost instantly amid the turbulence of buffeting snow. Although he realized it would obscure him from visible sight, Evondair straightaway questioned his decision to seek out the enemy while cloaked in the effects of the blinding storm where he could neither see nor hear anything other than the storm itself. The only thing he could rely upon was his in-born precise sense of direction, which all Fey possessed, and the indistinct sense of Nunvaret's presence he now Knew. The Demonfey Captain was not yet on the Jyndari side of the portal, but the moment he crossed over the Healer would become aware of him. Until he did, Evondair would wait, perched atop the mountain like a raptor poised to descend upon his prey.

Although he was aware through Senzuur's familiarity with him of the duplicity with which the Demonfey Captain protected himself, he was by no means certain of the outcome of such a treacherous encounter with a Dark One who had mastered the art of disguising his true sentiments and concealing his thoughts behind vicious emotion. He knew, however, there was no other way to communicate their plan. It was vital they did so; nothing else was as important and he was prepared to risk everything in the attempt.

Without warning, a gale of wind pummeled against him, ruffling his feathers erratically and sending the Healer tumbling downward steeply toward the rocky base of the mountain. Reflexively, his wings beat furiously to correct his momentum, but his senses were muddled by the unexpected plummet and for several moments he had no idea how close he was to his destination. Laboring to keep his place, he searched the grayish-white tempest below hoping to reorient himself with some marker of landscape, but only obscurity met his viridian gaze. The wind intensified, as if intent upon evicting him from the sky, and the effort required to remain aloft quickly became too great.

Descending cautiously, Evondair listened with dread as the sounds of tramping boots and creaking armaments became audible over the howl of the storm. A strident horn call from the direction of Lyyshara indicated the Fey of the Light were aware of the Reviled crossing into their realm and an echo of discordant bugles returned. Beating his wings powerfully in search of a landing place, Evondair's gaze pierced the blustering whiteout until he suddenly saw granite only inches below him and mere seconds before he would have crashed into the rocky outcropping. His boots slid upon the frozen, snow-covered ledge, sending a shower of rocks tumbling downward as he sought purchase; then he folded his wings and crouched down, grasping the rock beneath him with his hands to steady himself against the wind. Then he stared downward into the squall and waited.

Echoes of voices whipped round him like autumn leaves spiraling upon the wind, though they were disjointed and unintelligible. A terrifying growl of united Dlalth voices bolstering for battle ascended from the swirling vagueness below and, from the distance, the scattered sounds of a lyrical intonation broken by the ferocity of the storm drifted on the air. Evondair recognized the Celebrae petition recited by all Fey of the Light before entering into dangerous situations and, without hesitation, he repeated it inwardly.

Vrynnoth chae Luxonyth guildynn, braechanyth Luxonyth chaera vornae tywylucht. May the Light that guides vary not and cast its brightness over this darkness.

Out of the swirling shadows of snow and nighttide, a voice unexpectedly filled his mind. It was so piercing it caused him to flinch backward and shake his head. *"May it guide indeed, Healer."*

Nunvaret stepped through the slowly turning vortex of the portal into the pummeling snowstorm, grimaced fiercely at the unexpected weather; then tilted his head back as he gazed upward into the storm. Everything within his being smiled, though he curled his lips into a silent snarl while the troops under his command poured from the Uunglardan murk with the strength of enmity and forced determination on their side. Placing his gloved hand upon the hilt of his blade, the crimson-clad Demonfey hissed aloud, allowing the blizzard to claim the threatening sound and direct it upward.

Evondair shuddered involuntarily as he reached outward through his gift and became acutely aware of the unbearable dichotomy of the one with whom he connected. From the slopes of the mountain below him the clangor of blades clashing upon blades and the raucous shouts of innumerable voices shattered the monotonous howl of the storm. Even without seeing the turmoil writhing against itself; even without the use of his gift, the Healer knew the chaos of battle had begun. War and hatred had come into Jyndari and there was only one solution.

Gazing downward through the blinding snow, he concentrated on a single thought, one he felt certain the extraordinary telepathy of the Dark One would perceive.

Watcher. Freedom Awaits.

What he would do with the message, however, was far less certain.

Chapter Nineteen

Childfey huddled beneath a warming canopy of woolen blankets that Ayla and Nayina had hastily constructed when the softly descending flurries of snow transformed into a storm. Utilizing bare limbs from the forest to hold the protective cloth aloft and securing it with rope found in each of the carts, they hurriedly covered the shivering childlings. The seeking chill of the winter storm was kept at bay by the makeshift shelters and the scantily clad childlings were able to keep reasonably warm beneath the covering, nestled within a thick layer of fresh hay strewn deeply across the bed of each cart. They were much warmer, in fact, than many of them had been in countless days and, although the darkness and the howl of the blizzard were ominous, the little ones neither cried nor keened. Rather, they pressed together beneath the coverlet suspended over their heads, held together at the back of the cart by one of the adult Fey, and listened to them as they did their best to keep the wee fey calm.

Ayla hummed a soothing tune to her group of childfey squeezed close to her while she grasped the ends of the woolen tarp in her best attempt to keep it from flapping uselessly in the driving wind. Nayina sat upon the ends of the awning over which she presided, whispering a gentle rhyme often told to childlings and holding as many of her group of younglings close to her as she might successfully manage. Kaylyya sang a wordless song to those in her care, who dozed in resplendent slumber, unconcerned about the blustering storm or the fluttering blanket she held closed as successfully as she was able. Veryth sat quietly among his group, holding the ends of the blanket tightly as he closed his vivid emeraldine eyes and, through the use of his gift of reverse empathy, conveyed a sense of peace and well-being over as many of the sweet little childfey as he could reach, whether they sat cuddled close to him or amid the other groups.

Thusly reassured, the precious cargo of rescued younglings was transported to the Temple through the deepening night and the steadily increasing ferocity of the storm. Those Fey Guards assigned to protect the procession of Hasparii-drawn carts winged vigilantly close, keenly aware of their surroundings and prepared to give their lives to defend the treasure in their midst. The heavy snow was deafening to them; yet it was of little consequence to the elegant deer drawing the carts along whose strength and agility made cantering through the deep snowfall effortless and graceful.

In little more than an hour they had negotiated the many rises and bewildering turns along the obscured path between Lyyshara and Hwyndarin. As they left the deep snow and overhanging boughs of evergreen, an emissary of the Fey Guard went before them to announce their arrival and when the small caravan came to the gates of the Temple complex, they found them well lighted and opened in anticipation. Heralds of jubilant horns might have, in any other situation, proclaimed their return from the darkness; yet they remained silent in the hope of not alarming the timid younglings. Nevertheless, as the carts came to a stop before the broad doors of the Healing Wards, the Elders stood upon the snow-covered steps with arms and wings spread wide in greeting. Many Healers awaited their arrival, each holding blankets and towels of soft linen to dry and warm the travelers.

The childlings were roused from their warm nests of straw and wool to be gently offloaded and guided within the glowing interior of the Nursing Wards and many smiles of joyful relief passed between the Fey Guards, Healers and attendants as the sounds of childfey filled the serene halls. Veryth entered last, bearing in his strong arms a boyfey who was the mirror image of his father, whose curious violet gaze innocently pierced the remarkable sparkling cerulean of Zraylaunyth's. As they drew close, the youthful Elder reached out his hand to stop them.

"I have seen these uniquely hued eyes before." He spoke softly, inquiring without querying, and Veryth nodded slowly.

"Yes, indeed you have. This is Lorszan, the lost son of Rehstaed." At the Elder's enchanted smile Veryth gazed into the bejeweled glitter of violet watching them curiously. "Lorszan, this is one of the Elders of Hwyndarin. Can you say hello to him?"

The uncertain boyfey shifted in his embrace and reached out with a predominantly dirty hand to touch the Elder. Instinctively, Veryth leaned away so he would not befoul the respected leader of their people, but Zraylaunyth reached out in return, taking Lorszan's small hand between both of his own.

"I am Zray, little Lorszan, and I am overjoyed at meeting you." Saying this, the youthful Elder lowered his head to kiss the childlings hand; then leaned closer to kiss his pale and grime-smeared cheeks as well. "Oh, how overjoyed am I!"

* * *

"*Govern your thoughts, Healer! There are more here who can perceive your musings than I.*" Nunvaret's thoughts hissed as viciously as his voice ever could and Evondair did not require a gift of Discernment to sense his agitation. Clearing his mind of the entanglements of frustration and fear projected into him by the furious Demonfey, the golden-haired Healer returned a thought so piercing one might never have guessed he was not telepathic and, as a result, the Demonfey understood exactly what was necessary.

"*Lay aside your hostility and allow me to speak with you!*"

Flexing his vast dragonhide wings with exasperation, the crimson clad warrior gestured at the ground before him. "*I will speak to you in whispers no longer. Face me or be gone.*"

Evondair contemplated his less than amiable invitation with justifiable concern before answering the thoughts of the Dark One; his own betraying his trepidation. *"If I descend, will you guarantee my safety?"*

Nunvaret scoffed; then turned aside, growling audibly at the Demonfey who stood behind him, watching his actions with quizzical stares. "You see a battle raging, yet you require some employment from me?" The harshness of his tone scattered them from the close precincts they kept as they moved hastily down the flanks of the mountain to better observe the increasing violence of the conflict. Upon the snow-laden slopes, Reviled Fey and Fey of the Light clashed mercilessly while heavy snow spun in their midst, blinding eyes and coating armor. Blades rang in a terrific clangor and curses in Dlalth and Celebrae alike pierced the wintry night.

Among those on the frontline, the Legionnaires who had crossed from the Goralnicht Seclusionaries stood opposite a cluster of Dark Ones in the midst of the raging commotion. Reviled stared at Reviled with palpable confusion. Uncertain why the small band of Legionnaires had turned on their own kind, those sent to deliver retribution for the Fey of the Light's intrusion into Dlalth territory and the theft of younglings raised their weapons with confused hostility, but before they could engage their fellow Reviled two who shared the gift of telepathy spoke in whispers that could not be muffled by the noise of battle.

"Why do you oppose us?"

"Shouldn't you be standing at our side?"

They were answered with similarly piercing telepathy. *"We stand with the Liberator we have long awaited. He leads these Lighters!"* One of those who crossed from the seclusionaires turned and pointed in the direction of the Liberators who fought some distance away. Gairynzvl stood at the front of the small cluster as they engaged a group of Legionnaires armed, at best, with blunt swords and a glaringly rusted scythe.

Crimson red melded with crimson as the Legionnaires' weapons lowered, yet round them the battle raged on. Curses in harsh Dlalth and oaths in bright Celebrae pressed into the billowing storm. A contingent of Fey Guards took to the wing, raining arrows down upon the engaged Legionnaires, yet this tactic was met with bristling retribution as the Demonfey who watched the proceedings from the mountain flanks ascended into the swirling maelstrom to launch keenly sharpened spears into the attacking Guards.

* * *

"I am a Captain of the Demonfey of the Realm. I can and will guarantee nothing." The growing impatience of the Nunvaret's thoughts was unmistakable and the messenger perched above him knew, without a shred of misgiving, he would soon lose interest in their bantering and follow those he had sent towards the front.

Evondair's thoughts hissed insistently in return. *"You know as well as I do that you are more than a Demonfey Captain."*

Tilting his head upward into the storm, Nunvaret bared his teeth and cursed into the wind. "Raach, Drachalych! *Your lies will not sway my orders to destroy you!"*

Evondair grinned sidewards and pressed his advantage, fully aware of the duplicitous charade the Demonfey maintained. *"You may call them lies, but what will your comrades do if I name you a Watcher in their midst? Allow me to speak with you!"*

Considering the Lighter's threat, Nunvaret stifled a hiss of exasperation and stepped backward. *"Come down from your pedestal, pigeon. Your feathers may be ruffled, but your wings will not be broken."*

Evondair straightened from his crouched position, extending his wings as a counterbalance against the freezing gale buffeting against him seeking to drive him backward from the precipice upon which he stood. Gazing down into the blinding blizzard, he tried to focus his perception as well as his energy and purpose, acutely aware that he had no alternatives. The only option was to descend and face the certain brutality awaiting him, but the message he bore *had* to be delivered. The crucial moment, set into motion as he had watched death come to the Legionnaire who had attacked Kaylyya and himself, now stood before him and it was every bit as horrifying as the sight of that Legionnaire welcoming death. As the gales and blusters of the storm pummeled against him, he stared down into the swirling madness and readied himself for the inevitable. Everything the Fey of the Light held dear and all the Reviled had watched and waited for during bleak spans of darkness balanced upon his next actions.

If he hesitated, all could be lost.

Drawing a deep breath, he partially closed his wings and stepped from the precipice. Snow churned around him in a dizzying tumult as he plummeted downward, utilizing powerful, controlling wing beats to slow his fall, but he could not see the rocky slopes as they rose to meet him any more than he could foresee what result such a precarious decision might bring. His only choice was to follow his instincts, which had guided him thus far, and trust that, in doing the right thing, all would somehow turn out as it should. Nevertheless, as the intensifying blizzard enveloped him in whirling chaos he could not ignore the sense of impending peril that overwhelmed him any more than he could he see the Demonfey who stood staring upward, poised to deliver a punishing blow.

* * *

Bryth and Rehstaed stood back to back as a unit of growling Legionnaires closed in on them, slashing viciously with swords as well as with the glinting barbs of their powerful wings, which, in many instances, were sharper and far more deadly than the blades they bore. Dravahl and several other Watchers battled above them, seeking to protect their comrades from the Legionnaires who had taken to wing to rain death down upon them with any weapon they could hurl. Bright steal and blunt blades rang in an increasing crescendo of disorder as the fervor of conflict increased. Cries of distress and anger echoed among the writhing currents and eddies of the snowstorm that blinded all and coated the combatants in its silver-grey obscurity.

Without warning, the snow warped inward upon itself as a ripple of incandescent light streaked into the fray and howls of pain shattered the tumult. Legionnaires tumbled from the sky for no visible reason with wings severed and helmets crushed by the barely perceptible wrinkle of light as it passed. Mardan caught sight of the anomaly as he backed away from a mortally wounded Reviled and stared upward with a potent combination of delight and frustration, recognizing Ilys' distinctive glimmer of erratic light. Unimpeded by the effect the singularity had, however; the battle continued, its ferocity wreaking havoc and claiming the lives of Light and Dark Fey with equal devastation.

* * *

The Temple Healing Wards echoed with burbles of laughter and delight as giddy childfey frolicked among the ancient stonework and silently watching statues. Ecstatic beyond measure to be freed from the writhing darkness and whispering shadows that had held them captive for so long, the little ones ran among the brightly lighted halls and corridors with excited abandon, stopping often as Fey Guards, Healers and the Elders themselves invited long embraces and offered tender words of reassurance. Under the attentive gazes of every Healer residing in the Temple, who had hurried to assist with the care of the younglings and share in the joyous moments of their return whether they were presently on and off duty, the Fey laughed and cried in the presence of such innocence and the typically serene wards and corridors of the Temple resounded joyfully.

Among those watching, Kaylyya and Ayla stood quietly to one side of the Nursing Ward as Healers played like childlings and Fey Guards frolicked like wee fey; the shefey sharing contented smiles at the never-before-witnessed scene. Moving towards them after embracing at least a dozen of the scampering childfey, Zraylaunyth's bright aura blazed in the dim, candlelit corner they occupied and they inclined their heads to him respectfully, stepping back and curling their diaphanous wings inward as in indication of deference. Raising his hands in a gesture of greeting, he smiled with unreserved delight as a chorus of giggles danced upon the tranquil night air.

"By far, it is the sweetest evening vesper these halls have heard in eons," he remarked to their whole-hearted agreement; yet even as they smiled, the glimmer in his remarkable eyes faded and a far more serious expression sobered his handsome features. "I should not wish to force you from such pleasant environs or to impose my will over your own; however, my thoughts have been taken by such calamity and chaos that I feel compelled to make the request."

The shefey gazed at him with surprised curiosity, certain he sensed the battle that had not yet begun in Lyyshara when they had departed, although evidently had commenced since that time and he nodded perceptively. Closing his eyes briefly, he became aware of their thoughts as well as those of the Liberators and Fey Guards battling at the front, miles away.

"Death cries out among our brethren; the shrillness of its voice most abhorrent, but I feel certain its dissonant reverberations could be nullified in the presence of such enchanting harmonies as your own, Kaylyya Synnowyn."

* * *

Nunvaret waited just long enough for Evondair's feet to come in contact with solid ground and their eyes to meet in a succinct, intensely poignant exchange before he turned sharply sideways, delivering a kick to his opponent's chest that sent him staggering backward against the buttress of rock behind him. Pressing his advantage as Evondair gasped for breath, the Demonfey spun on his heel, stretching out one wing to slash at the disorientated Fey of the Light with a fourteen-inch wing-barb that caught the Healer beneath his ribcage, shearing open the brocade vest his wore and tearing through the black fabric of the shirt beneath to reveal the wound he had received only days before from another Legionnaire. Continuing the momentum of his spin, Nunvaret utilized his other wing to deliver a glancing blow across Evondair's cheek, then rushed inward with blinding speed to grasp him fiercely by the shoulder, spin him about and push him up against the frozen face of the mountain while pressing the cruel point of his wing against his spine.

Gasping in pain and astonishment, Evondair arched backward to escape the pressure of the seeking point of the Demonfey's wing, beating his own with powerful resistance, but Nunvaret leaned inward, hissing viperously into his ear as he pinned the Lighter against the searing cold surface of the mountain. "Resist, *Messenger*, and I shall surely impale you."

Evondair drew a ragged breath; then ceased his struggling as he extended his senses to seek the other's intentions.

"Your delving is futile and exceedingly dangerous, *pigeon*. Speak your message or feel the wrath of the Dlalth."

He did not need to delve. Evondair's gift was more extraordinary than the Dark One perceived and it told him all he needed to know with the briefest instance of connection. Laying the palms of his hands against the gnarled surface of the mountain, he lowered his wings and spoke with the distinctive, calm serenity of a Healer. Choosing his words carefully, he shared the message the Watcher disguised as a Demonfey of the Realm had waited to hear nearly his entire life.

"The Dlalth no longer control your destiny, brother. The moment of Liberation from this vile captivity is at hand."

Chapter Twenty

The Hasparii drawn cart was a far too slow and cumbersome means of conveyance. Time was of the essence and with the fate of so many strung upon the balance, there was but one option considered. A replacement contingent of Fey Guards was assembled, whose wings were not tired and who could traverse the distance to Lyyshara in a minimal amount of time, escorting the one sent to sing.

Kaylyya had not faltered, despite her astonishment at the youngest of the Elders suggestion that she could, in any way, affect the outcome of the battle. Although she had stammered her reply in a voice barely louder than a whisper, her tremulous tone was as much a result of speaking to one so highly revered as it was an indication of nervousness. After all, she had been told many, many times by the Healer of her village that her gift was singularly unique and would be put to some inconceivable use one day. Nevertheless, to have one of the Elders confirm the old shefey's musings in such a definitive way left her undeniably amazed.

While she bolstered her courage and received reassurances from her new friends Ayla and Nayina, who would be remaining with the child-fey in the Temple, the Fey Guards were assigned their sole duty: to protect the shefey they escorted from any manner of harm and return her safely to Lyyshara. Specifically, they were to guide her directly to the one named Gairynzvl who would be informed of the Elder's suggestion regarding her role in the conflict. They would then join Captain Varka's company and the battle, if necessary.

Before the small group departed, Veryth hastened to rejoin them; insistent upon returning with them to the front where his skills would be of far greater value than among the many Healers and attendants in the Temple. At his side stood several others who had volunteered to return to the battlefield in order to care for the wounded. Veryth had donned a remarkable cape fashioned from hand-spun yarn created by artisans who intertwined lamb's wool and goose down into an exceptionally warm, water-repellant fiber known as fethrall, which they then wove into exquisite garments. In his hands, he carried a second, similar mantle, though it was much smaller, which he handed to Kaylyya.

"The storm has grown intense and I have no doubt you will find the protection of another layer invaluable." Receiving it from him with notable astonishment, she bowed with her wings furled inward with respect; then hurried to wrap it round herself securely as they made their way along the corridor towards the main entryway of the Healing Wards, even now being drawn open to allow them to pass. Yet as they stepped out into the blizzard, Zraylaunyth called to them from the place where he stood surrounded by wee Fey and his recitation of a long-misunderstood prophecy echoed along the passage, carried outward into the storm and throughout the whole of the Temple complex for all to hear.

"*For the Enchantress who Sings sweet and sure shall transform discord into Harmony, brightening the path for all who long to break into the Light.*"

* * *

"Do I look like I wish to be liberated?" Nunvaret scoffed at the suggestion, spreading his arms as well as his metal-barb studded wings to display his powerful appearance robed in the finest crimson leather, but Evondair smiled. Turning boldly away from the face of the rock upon being released by the Demonfey, he gazed at him with an openly assessing stare; yet his smile only broadened.

"Not outwardly."

"I've already warned you against delving where you are not wanted, *pigeon*!" The Demonfey raised the barb of his wing to poise it threateningly beneath the Healers chin; nevertheless, the golden-haired Fey returned his glare confidently.

"I need not delve to know your true nature," he retorted. "It was shared with me before I ever drew close to you by one knows you well." Evondair's calm tone took on an indication of antagonism while his viridian eyes blazed with constrained fire and this evidence of his own true nature caused the Demonfey to look long at him, reconsidering.

"Who was it that spoke to you of me? Name him so I may exact revenge for such impudence!" His aggression had lost its former causticity and the Healer nodded. Choosing his words wisely, he provided the information he knew the Dark One, watching him like a predator, already knew.

"He resides now beyond the reach of Dlalth retaliation. He has crossed into the Light and stands with those defending these lands, welcomed and absolved."

"Absolved? Of what? Do you, who have committed the most grievous of wrongs imaginable, suggest you are in a position to grant absolution as well as liberation? You are self-righteous indeed." The bitterness of Nunvaret's accusation did not fall upon deaf ears. Crimson and viridian locked.

Across the open landscape the clash and clatter of vicious battle pierced the blunting descent of heavy snow tumbling from the sky. Cries of pain and echoes of rage faded in, then out, of the maelstrom as if crossing a vast distance of time and space rather than merely a few hundred yards. Death claimed the last breaths of Fey of the Light as well as Reviled Fey and the outpouring of so much energy charged the atmosphere with the intensity of a violent summer storm. All that existed in that moment, in that place, was hatred, fear, and suspicion; yet as the crimson smudge of war spread across the open landscape like a wound, the Healer stepped closer to his enemy and reached out with both his hands.

"We have wronged you and all those who were taken by the Dlalth. We abandoned you to the darkness. We neglected you as surely as those forcing The Integration upon you. We understand your anger and do not lay blame for those acts of violence you and your brethren have been forced to undertake against us, nor for your indignation at having been so abused, but can you not hear the result of that resentment?" He paused, turning his face into the wind and closing his eyes as he listened to the myriad disjointed voices swept to them on the blustering gale. Nunvaret stared at him, wholly uncertain; watching with viciousness and yearning building inside him with as much turbulence as the storm that raged around them. The fair Fey he fixed his glare upon stood unmoving, utterly at his mercy in that moment as the rustling wind tousled his golden hair and white feathers that seemed to gleam with a radiance of their own, even in the depth of the storm.

A horrifying wail serrated across the distance, capturing the Demonfey Captain's attention and causing the motionless Healer's eyes to snap open with dread. Instinctively, he reached outward with his senses, seeking the source of the distressing sound, desperate to discover if it came from one of his comrades.

"I hear it only too well. I have heard it for over twenty years." Nunvaret's voice faltered as he spoke the words and dropped his veil of pretense at last, opening himself to another for the first time in many years. The revelation of his torment was as excruciating to his own essence as it was to the Healer's, who turned his head to gaze back at him with dismay and anguish evident in his expressive eyes.

* * *

Arrows fell downward at the Liberators, bouncing off shields and skidding across leather fortuitously coated with a heavy rime of ice and snow. Fey Guards and Legionnaires slashed at each other with blades nearly frozen into their hands. Demonfey hurtled from the sky with spears, seeking the lifeblood of any Lighter they could catch un-awares, and the entire clearing seemed to shudder in the violence of the tumult. Screams of pain and hatred mingled with cries of lament and weariness; growls of ferocity answered viperous hisses, and the shrill clangor of metal against metal shook the snow-laden air. Beneath their boots, trampled and torn, the pristine landscape wept crimson tears while the hands of winter enwrapped the combatants in a uni-fying mantle of white.

As the uniforms of those locked in battle became masked by snow, the Fey of the Light and Reviled found it increasingly difficult to dis-tinguish Light from Dark. They looked to the wings and the shade of the eyes of the one they faced, as they alone became the means of identifying one from the other, but their similarities outweighed their differences. Red blood bled red. Fear and pain expressed itself through its own similar language and it was one they all understood.

Amid the horrors of the battle, a fresh contingent of Fey Guards joined the mêlée and two descended before Gairynzvl as the remainder went in search of Captain Varka. The former Legionnaire stood behind the vanguard, watching the unimaginable scene unfolding before him with tears freezing upon his cheeks; his wings dipped low with fa-tigue and despair. His sword rested, unutilized, against his thigh as he rubbed his hands together in an attempt to regain sensation from the cold. As they alighted, he fixed his gaze on them; then turned to look at Kaylyya who descended with them, trembling with the ferocity of a willow in a November wind.

"Why do you bring so fair a feather into such a brutal a storm to be torn asunder?" His harsh tone betrayed the frustration he could barely contain; yet to his surprise, the Guards bowed to him before answering.

"We obey the direct instructions of The Third of the Elders." Queru-lous icy-lavender pierced the speaker's gaze, but before he could in-quire further a horrifying wail serrated across the clearing. Each of them turned to seek the source of the sound while Gairynzvl cursed in fluent, abrasive Dlalth.

Halfway across the clearing, a crimson cloud of smoldering shadow and writhing darkness emerged from nothingness, turning in the midst of the storm like a maelstrom and the Fey of the Light, as well as the Legionnaires they opposed, fled from its proximity.

Gairynzvl cursed even louder. "For the love of the Ancients, why bring her here?"

"She is meant to sing." The second Fey Guard attempted to explain, but his words meant nothing to the former Legionnaire who had forgotten how she had soothed the pain and distress of his injuries with her ethereal music. Shaking his head, he watched as, only a few yards to their left, Rehstaed and Dravahl opposed a squad of six Dlalth; the fury of their distinctive Vrynnyth Ghal language rippling through the snowstorm like some discordant reverie. To their right, Mardan utilized twin blades to stave off the attack of a Demonfey Lieutenant while a blur of barely visible light circled around them, knocking unsuspecting Legionnaires unconscious as it went.

"It is the prophecy he thinks of." Kaylyya offered, repeating the words Zraylaunyth had spoken before they departed the Temple.

"*For the Enchantress who Sings sweet and sure shall transform discord into harmony, brightening the course for all who long to break into the Light.*"

Gairynzvl stared at her as if she had taken leave of her senses even as the air around them swirled with the turbulence of another alighting close by. Turning to see who it was that arrived; they watched as Veryth descended with powerful wing beats, forsaking his station at the Healer's tent to lend his assurances to the Elder's directive.

"She must Sing, Fierce One, before all are lost."

* * *

Evondair moved closer to his adversary, reaching to take him by the arm to speak in a far more discretionary tone that only the Captain of the Demonfey might hear. Nunvaret glared at him with instinctive animosity for his insolence, but his habit of tainting any of his true emotion with aggression in order to protect himself was pointless. The Discerning Healer comprehended his ruse as completely as he understood it himself and, as their gazes locked once again, a tenuous thread of trust as insubstantial as a spider's silk, stretched between them.

"We do not wish to fight," the Healer spoke in a low tone. "We fight to protect ourselves and the lives of shefey so close in the village until the message I bear is delivered."

"What message, Lighter? That you offer absolution for the wrongs you think we have committed?" He could not deny his resentment of such an offer any more than he could disguise the anger and loss of twenty-two years that churned within him with more turmoil than the calamity raging around them.

Unexpectedly, Evondair hissed at him with unconcealed exasperation. "Can you lay aside your anger long enough to *Listen* to me?"

Habitually, Nunvaret glared back at him, baring his teeth to hiss in response, but he did not. Stifling the rage mounting within him, insistent upon expression, his gaze narrowed as he pulled the fair Fey closer. "I would listen if you said anything worth hearing."

Evondair's viridian glare stabbed into crimson, but he smiled wryly. "Then hear this, for I shall not repeat it. We shall lay down our weapons and welcome you back into the Light IF you will lay down your own."

Nunvaret stared at him, plagued by distrust; then scoffed and shook his head. "Is that it? Is that your all-important message?"

* * *

Zraylaunyth stood upon the bulwark of one of the Temple walls, winter whipping around him as if hysterical, whispering to him in voices only he could understand.

It spoke of wrath and loathing in wailing tones. It articulated enmity and mistrust through its icy hands. It shrieked in anguish as the life-force of countless Fey suffused into its inexorable embrace.

Sparkling cerulean lifted to the starless sky, seeking release from the torturous song of the storm. Cobalt, emeraldine, amber and violet glistened in the azurine sea of his gaze amid crystalline tears; yet the howl of the tempest did not relent. Beside him, his brother Elders stood in silent contemplation; Seeking to Know what the winds of the tempest conveyed.

Listening keenly, they held their silence and waited; watching with growing dread as a crimson cloud of smoldering shadow and writhing darkness began turning in the midst of the storm.

* * *

"Sing?" Gairynzvl's incredulity was matched only by his surprised stare, but Veryth nodded resolutely. "Here? Amid this commotion?" The Healer continued to nod. "How will anyone hear her?"

"Her song is an enchantment. All shall hear."

"But why? What purpose could it possibly serve? We have failed in our endeavor and this is the result." Despair filled his every word and Gairynzvl could not hide his anguish any more than he could disguise the overwhelming guilt he felt at having set such a tempest of death into motion, but Veryth moved closer swiftly, taking him by the arm to turn him round so they might look out across the bleak landscape.

"You have not failed. You only await the messenger's success. It *is* coming, I have no doubt, but until evidence of his success becomes apparent, the Song of the Enchantress may save lives!"

He had never heard Veryth speak so vehemently, but the conviction of his hope transferred to Gairynzvl, as well as to those who stood with him, through the wonder of the Healer's unique gift of Empathic Transference. Icy-lavender fused with gleaming emerald and the Fierce One nodded, looking past his friend to the delicate shefey who stood watching them with snow melding into her jade aura. The winter wind buffeted against her, swirling around her in tempestuous fury, but she smiled at its touch and looked up into the sky at the falling, tumbling, swirling rhythm of its dance as if into the gaze of a lover.

"As she sings, extending the magic of her gift as far as she is able, I shall reach across this expanse with an assurance of hope," Veryth explained. "Together, we may give pause to the violence so the message can be shared."

Gairynzvl agreed. "It may be enough."

Yet before they could take further action, from the heart of the burgeoning crimson-black cloud swelling in their midst a second hideous shriek pierced the atmosphere. Rippling outward across the combatants like waves across a shore, it communicated through its penetrating shrillness a sensation of fear and fury none could ignore.

* * *

Evondair glared at Nunvaret, his entire being awash with cynicism and suspicion as the essence of his adversary wrought havoc with his own. Hatred and anger infused itself into the harmonious inclination of his own temperament. Fear and loneliness that could not be assuaged leached into him like a poison that dimmed his vision and made his heart hammer with dread. "This is the message," he stammered with sudden irresolution. "We want to help you." Uncertainty spun his thoughts and the clarity of his purpose wavered.

"Why?"

The Healer closed his eyes as if under a spell, his senses reeling as the full weight of the Dark One's harrowing life pressed into him like a blade. Memories of brutality far beyond his comprehension burned into his mind so forcefully that he groaned in pain. Images of sadistic cruelty, blood and wine, laughter and horror, twisted in his thoughts. Shaking his head, he tried desperately to retain his focus against the increasingly frenzied pull of more memories of unthinkable atrocities than he could count. They writhed in his consciousness like demons conspiring to unravel him as the Dark One from whom they poured watched him without blinking.

"Because of the Legionnaire," he answered, half to the Demonfey before him, half to himself.

Nunvaret shook his head impatiently. "What Legionnaire?"

Again, Evondair shook his head, recalling his struggle with the Legionnaire in the Hasparii drawn cart. The ferocity of their interaction; the violence he had unleashed upon the Dark One; the blood that poured over his hands combined with the memories wrenching at his sanity until he could barely breathe. "The one who smiled.... I killed him... and he *smiled.*"

Nunvaret stared with dawning understanding at the golden-haired Healer while he wavered in a muddle fugue; then he hissed with frustration as the faltering Fey leaned precariously backward as his eyes closed. Yanking him back into a standing position, Nunvaret cursed in viperous Dlalth. "Hyythachragh! No one has time for your fragility." Closing himself off from the overwrought Healer so the torment of his past would no longer engulf him, he pressed into his swirling thoughts and forced his telepathy into Evondair's mind regardless of his lack of consent. *"Clear your head, Healer!"*

The potent shock of his transferred thoughts was like a bolt of lightning. Evondair's viridian eyes snapped open, refocusing on the Dark One before him, although he could not restrain the tears that forced their way beyond his opposition. "I am sorry," he offered sincerely.

Nunvaret hissed once again, fully cognizant of the fact that he was not apologizing for his actions, but for all the young Captain had suffered. "I don't require your sympathy, Healer. Right now, I only require your stability. We have a message to deliver before none remain to hear it."

Chapter Twenty-One

Whirling winds encircled the battling Fey; a swirling white cyclone of chaos enwrapping chaos. As the blustering gales increased, the biting cold grew inescapable and the enshrouding mantle grasped everything it encountered with a numbing clasp. Even Legionnaires who were accustomed to discomfort found themselves shivering violently as the remorseless cold robbed the struggling Fey of their innate agility and dexterity in its compassionless embrace. The battle waned, leaving weary, shivering, snow-encrusted Fey staring at each other with exhausted hostility.

In the stillness that resulted an understated intonation became perceptible; replacing the clash of metal upon metal and the wail of the howling tempest. A sound not unlike the distant echoes of melodic birdsong blending with sweet fluted tones danced among the pirouetting snowflakes, reaching out from the heart of the battlefield to claim the combatant's attention. Exhausted Fey Guards gazed uncomprehendingly into blank crimson stares while the same Legionnaires lowered their blunted weapons to look round them wonderingly and in the growing hush the volume of the delicate song increased. Soothing reverberations of stringed lutes infused the ethereal refrain, repeating and enchanting, while the peals of birds not physically present echoed into the snow-laden evergreens.

The vortex of shadow and crimson swirling in the center of the battlefield swelled outward against the quietness it met hissing like a pit of furious vipers in the hush. Yet, in spite of the discord and violence of the battleground and the maelstrom of angry sound congesting in it's midst, an inexorable sense of calm spread outward from the source of the song and those mesmerized by the captivating music turned to stare with fatigued, unified gazes upon the one who Sang.

She stood upon an outcropping of granite above them, her mitten-protected hands clasped before her while snowflakes settled delicately over her wrappings of wool. Beneath the hood she had pulled up to cover her bright blond hair, her snowy-jade eyes stared out across those to whom she sang, watching as her incomparable gift permeated hatred and conveyed harmony. Beside her, a Healer with piercing emeraldine eyes looked over the shivering horde as well, sharing a sense of reassurance and hope that belied the horror of death that lay unmoving at their feet. Wings of brightest white feathers, as well as crimson dragonhide, lowered from defensive and aggressive postures and hands that had gripped leather-wrapped steel relaxed. A breathless hush settled over the clearing so that only the yowling moan of the storm and sweetly enthralling music prevailed.

* * *

Standing in defiance of the gales blustering against him with his broad white wings stretched out brazenly, Zraylaunyth listened with a growing intimation of hope as the wails of the wind and its shrieks of death were replaced by the most beautiful music he had ever heard. Far beyond the skill of any accomplished musician, the serenade lilted into his consciousness like the balm of a summer morning. Even he, the Third of the Elders, could not force himself to keep his eyes open and those two who stood quietly beside him paused as well, breathing deep and slow in the peaceful tranquility transposed in music.

Kaylyya sang and he smiled, but even as the sparkling sea of his eyes, a mosaic of shades and hues, closed to a dream of the sweetest harmony his essence had ever touched, a tendril of darkness snaked into the void.

* * *

"How can we possibly share our message with so many?" Evondair asked, standing shoulder to shoulder and wing to wing with Nunvaret as they gazed across the snow-spun landscape. Unable to see through the blizzard, they listened to the clatter of swords against swords and the discordant cries of distress carried on the wind. Glancing hesitantly at each other with the thinnest filament of trust stretched taut between them, they sought a solution to their mutual problem.

"Neither of us can achieve this without the other," Nunvaret boldly proposed and the Healer turned to listen more attentively.

"Go on."

"I have the ability to direct my thoughts into the minds of others."

Evondair scoffed with a sideways smirk. "So I have discovered."

"Even many others, but I can't be certain if they'll believe the message I share with them."

"You will not order them to decimate us the moment we disarm?" Years of mistrust forced the question to cross the Fey of the Light's lips before he could contain it and the Demonfey growled.

"If you, who can know me as well as I know myself won't trust me, how will anyone else?" Beating his wings forcefully against the tempest of snow and wind battering against them, Nunvaret considered turning away, but the Healer raised his hands in a mollifying gesture, curling his wings inward respectfully.

"Forgive me," he drew a deep breath. "Please, continue."

Glaring at the golden-haired Fey with barely contained exasperation, the Dark One contemplated his plan in brooding silence for many tense moments before shaking his head. "I can tell them; yet, only you, Discerner, will know with certainty if they believe me."

"Believe *us*," Evondair corrected. "We should be within their sight when we make the attempt. Certainly, none shall be inclined to believe whispers riding upon the wind. Yet, if we are seen together, side by side and unarmed, it may, perhaps, lend credence to our assertion."

Nunvaret glared at him with undisguised doubt and, although he had closed off his essence from the perceptive Fey of the Light, Evondair could easily sense his skepticism. Taking him by the arm and pulled him closer, the Healer returned the DemonFey's crimson glare with all the intensity his own viridian gaze could deliver, assuring him of his veracity in the only manner he could. "I have come to you without weapons or treachery to relay a message of hope. If you desire freedom from the accursed domination of the one from whom you shield yourself every moment of the day and night; the dream-stalker who forced you to slaughter your comrades for his own perverse pleasure and who took from you that which you could not refuse to give, then you must trust me."

Tears blurred the crimson stare of hatred and anguish that pierced him, but Evondair continued, undeterred. "Trust is most certainly earned, not simply given. I understand that, and if we had time, if countless Fey were not, at this very moment, suffering, bleeding and dying, I would not hesitate to do whatever you might ask of me to prove my honest intent, but we do not have the luxury of that much time." He watched the eyes of the Demonfey, moved to his core as suspicion and fear collided turbulently with the most agonizing desperation he had ever seen. "Can you dare to hope, Legionnaire?"

Nunvaret's features twisted in torment, but he shook his head. "I long to, Healer, but we are too late. The one about whom you speak is coming."

* * *

Upon the battlefield, all eyes, whether crimson or colorful, were transfixed upon the enchantress who sang the sweetest music any had ever heard. Even as the tranquil, melodic music filled them with a sense of well-being and hope; even as the calming, joyful echoes of birdsong lifted spirits and caused some, who had not heard such blissful sounds in far too long to smile as if in a dream, the writhing crimson shadow staining the center of the clearing with its hideousness expanded and began to twist. Standing in its core, his shape indistinct and blurred in rotating shadows, the greatest evil any of them could ever encounter spread his wings in a display of strength before he stepped through the slowing spiraling portal.

Clad in black leather pants and boots with a silken black shirt that belied the frigid temperature and wind swirling around him, with gauntlets upon his hands that extended upwards to his elbows and which bore cruel metal spikes that flared outward, the darkest of all darkness appeared. Wearing a cape of exquisitely worked leather that billowed out behind him, Uxvagchtr stepped onto the blood-stained snow of Lyyshara and hissed like an enraged dragon, the sound permeating the serene music filling the clearing and echoing through the snow-burdened evergreens. Turning his head, which was crowned by an elaborate headdress made from intricately worked silver fitted around his massive triple set of horns and completely obscured his eyes, he took in the scene unhurriedly. Licking his lips like a salivating predator inspecting its prey; he looked down at a Fey Guard lying in the snow at his feet.

Terrified beyond measure, the sweet music of Kaylyya's song faded into the howl of the wind as she stared at him, frozen in fear. Veryth and Gairynzvl took up position at her sides, the Healer gently laying his hands upon her in an attempt to assuage the trepidation pouring like contagion from the vile monster in their midst. Quietly he whispered reassurance into her ear.

"Do not look at him, sweet snowflake. Close your eyes and Sing or we are all surely lost." Filling her with the strength of his own unfailing confidence, he turned her slowly round to face him; embraced her with his arms as well as his broad wings, and listened to the tremulous hints of music emanating from her essence as they strengthened through his intervention. Beside him, Gairynzvl also benefited from his outpouring of positive energy; the potent transference of optimism and courage surging within him with revitalizing vigor. Turning to glare boldly at the Master of all Reviled, he stifled a defiant hiss seeking to escape him as a sweet intercession of music whispered once more into his being.

Kaylyya's song intensified and her captivated audience did not turn away from her to watch as Uxvagchtr stooped to collect the Fey Guard at his feet, drawing him into his arms. Yet breathing, the unfortunate Fey wailed in distress as the Imperial Praetor looked at him ruthlessly, running his gloved hand across the other's cheek with terrifying tenderness before he lowered his head to kiss him. Only Gairynzvl and Veryth stood beyond the trance of Kaylyya's music. Only they witnessed the Dark One's kiss turn horrifyingly vicious; then run crimson as the agonized cries of the Fey Guard were muffled by his deepening passion. Drinking in the Fey of the Light's blood with unflinching composure, Uxvagchtr did not release his victim until his wings and limbs ceased to flail against him. When they did, he dropped him back to the earth and stepped over him with callous disregard as blood ran in bright rivulets down his pallid skin.

He walked only several yards before he came upon another who sought in vain to escape when he paused to look down, smiled wickedly, and stooped to draw him into his gruesome embrace.

"Hush, little dove," the vile monster whispered in his gentlest voice as his victim strained against him. "Such sweet resistance. Do you know how it makes your death even more deliciously vitalizing?"

* * *

"*We cannot leave them to face him alone.*" The First spoke without words into the thoughts of his companions as they stood upon the Temple walls listening to the placid music of Kaylyya's song and the dichotic agony of the Fey Guards upon whom Uxvagchtr prayed. Zraylaunyth turned away from the unbearable brutality of the scene, growling with such ferocity he shocked his brother Elders from their silence and they turned in unison to stare at him.

"No, we cannot and I would hasten at this very moment to impale him where he stands!" The young Elder hissed with vengeful emotion;

the hideousness of all he had Seen through his remarkable gift of Discernment twisting in his thoughts and transferring to the others with such potency that they groaned in horror. Through his extraordinary gift of pure Empathy, the First could Feel the full range of emotions surging like a turbulent tide among the evergreens of Lyyshara. The Second, through his gift of Telepathy unlike any others, could Know all that happened upon that battlefield. He sensed the tempestuous maelstrom of anger, hatred, fear and doubt that spun among the Fey of the Light and the Legionnaires with blinding intensity. Sharing all they could individually experience with each other, they felt the horrors of the battlefield as keenly as those who stood upon it and the triumvirate was moved to their very essence to take action.

"Our presence on the field of battle must hold greater significance than retribution alone; although, young Zraylaunyth, even I confess, little else might satisfy more completely." The Second spoke with poignant emotion stirred in his voice and his bright aura glowed red with the intensity of the violent emotion pummeling through them.

"Retribution shall be delivered in a most unexpected manner," the First said with absolute confidence; fully aware of the audacious endeavor undertaken by the Liberators and in complete agreement with their initiative. In a brief moment of silent communion, he shared this awareness with his brothers and they nodded in concurrence; yet it was young Zraylaunyth who spoke out for further action.

"He will take the lives of all who cannot resist him and gain inestimable strength through the vile plunder. We must go at once and stand with our brothers in opposition of his malevolence or I shall never be able to look any of them in the eye again."

The Second said nothing, only nodded; turning to gaze at The First, who was the oldest and wisest of them. He stood impassive for many moments, his eyes closed as he sought to Know more fully what occurred at that moment so many miles away from them. The others waited as patiently as they could while he sought what he needed; then his eyes opened wide in absolute dread.

* * *

"Remove your armaments and fly out with me above the battlefield," Evondair urged his companion even as he stepped away from him to peer through the intensity of the blizzard in the direction of Lyyshara. Silence fell heavily on the gales of the wind and the darkness suddenly betrayed no secrets.

"Remove my armaments?" Nunvaret repeated in disbelief, but Evondair only nodded.

"Something has happened. The fighting has ceased."

"It is he," Nunvaret offered with certainty.

Twisting round to gaze back at him with miscomprehension, Evondair shook his head. "He?"

The Demonfey hissed sharply at his obtuseness. "Yes, He, *pigeon!* The Imperial Praetor, Uxvagchtr. He has opened a portal and seeks to satisfy his lusts among the fallen."

Horror paled Evondair's handsome features and his mouth fell agape as he sought to understand precisely what the Dark One was telling him, but he could not force such appalling notions into his mind. The Demonfey at his side, however, could do so easily. Grasping the Healer roughly by his arm, he glared into the deep viridian of his gaze and pressed the vision of what he saw happening on the battlefield into his mind. The unexpected, sadistic brutality of what he saw caused the Fey of the Light to groan as a sickening wave of revulsion dug into him like a blade, but Nunvaret pulled him closer and spoke in a tone he could not ignore. "He'll do far worse to them if we fail to intercede. Yet be certain of this; if we aren't successful, you'll know firsthand the horrors you discerned from me. The Praetor fancies pretty ones like you and will enjoy tormenting you immensely."

Hissing at him angrily, Evondair yanked his arm from the Dark One's clasp and glared at him.

"Don't like that thought?" Nunvaret's answer was the narrowing of the Healers eyes and a deep growl that made the Dark Fey nod. "Good. Now keep that hatred and anger foremost in your thoughts.

It's the only thing that can block him. Don't let any other thoughts enter your mind."

The Healer grimaced as his mind spun with horrifying possibilities; then he shook his head. "How can we possibly convey a message of hope through hatred and anger?"

Nunvaret smiled. "*You* cannot."

Chapter Twenty-Two

The Elders of Hwyndarin hastened from the parapet upon which they had stood, watching, listening to and feeling the battle raging in Lyyshara. Issuing commands through direct telepathic links with the Fey Guards who remained in defense of the Temple, they were met within moments in the main hall of the massive complex and provided warming cloaks of fethrall, wool-lined boots and gloves fashioned from supple leather. Everything the Elders wore was in shades of white, which reflected their conjoined auras into a shimmer of radiant light that ever encircled them; yet now this unique glimmering seemed to hold a far more relevant significance. They were the Light preparing to face the darkest of the Dark.

The First was handed a single blade of glistening gold and the finest wrought steel, which he accepted and then gazed down upon with a scowl. The Second was offered a lithe bow fashioned from willow wood and a quiver filled with gold-tipped arrows while the Third was provided a spear similarly wrought of gold and glimmering steel, but they refused these weapons. Handing the exquisite sword back to the Fey Guard who stood staring at him in confused silence, The First shook his head. "Our bravest of friends, Evondair, is most correct. We cannot represent Peace while bearing weaponry."

"We shall rely upon our gifts of magic to protect us," the Second continued.

"And the power of a magic unknown is the most compelling magic of all," Zraylaunyth added, completing their unified thought so that the Fey Guard smiled, lowered his head and wings in an indication of respect, and stepped back from them.

"It is unlikely, however, in the event that we are unable to return from the place of battle, the wise and youthful Liberators shall be named leaders of Hwyndarin until Elders from the Gvynnalyth Temples of Dyyrzon Luul can travel here." The First spoke with authority and all those who heard his voice lowered their heads with acceptance of his decree. Then, without further preparation of any kind, the Elders turned and made their way towards the vast main portal of the Temple, which was opened by two stationed Guards who bowed as they passed. The dark night swept into the interior; snow and howling winds encircling them as they stepped onto the portico and turned in the direction of Lyyshara.

"Nyyrvanyth Lax Instrabylnaeum," the First said into the wind. His brothers nodded singularly and answered.

"To the courage of fools!"

* * *

Dropping the lifeless Fey of the Light from his callous embrace, the Imperial Praetor looked up from his feast and gazed round him once again. The battle had ceased. Legionnaires and Fey Guards stood side by side, coated in a unifying rime of snow frozen to the leather and metal of their uniforms as they listened in breathless silence to something he could not hear. The blizzard raged, howling angrily through similarly encrusted evergreens that formed a natural border around the clearing. Unconcerned about the blood running down his chin and neck, Uxvagchtr stretched forth his senses into the vast expanse of woodland and, utilizing the magic of the headdress he wore that intensified his perceptions, he sought an advantage.

He did not require sight in order to See or Know. The headpiece of silver, platinum, and crystal augmented his senses and gifts to such a degree that his telepathy and discernment were nearly inescapable. With them, he explored his surroundings extensively, familiarizing himself with the village and villagers of Lyyshara in moments and discovering among its bountiful forest the resource he sought.

"What is he doing?" Gairynzvl queried in a low tone, but Veryth only shook his head, unable to venture a guess and unwilling to disengage his outpouring of positivity in order to answer more fully. Turning aside, the former Legionnaire scanned the battlefield for his fellow Liberators, finding Mardan, as well as Rehstaed, staring up at them with blank expressions only a few yards away. Shaking his head in an attempt to clear away the captivating sound of Kaylyya's song, he moved closer and took the Celebrant-Fey Guard by his broad shoulders. "*Celebrant.*" He spoke with the familiar inflection of feigned disdain they had come to accept from each other, but Mardan only blinked slowly, utterly entranced. Hissing impatiently, he raised his hand to cover his friend's brilliant cerulean eyes as he shook him insistently. "Clear your head, Celebrant!"

The urgency of his tone pierced the veil of intoxicating tranquility that had descended upon him and Mardan blinked repeatedly, shaking his head and stepping backward from Gairynzvl as the vestiges of the peaceful song filling his essence scattered into the storm. Focusing his piercing gaze on Gairynzvl, his expression of confusion conveyed what he could not articulate.

"There is no time to explain, except to say that Kaylyya is an enchantress of extraordinary influence. We must act in the reprieve her song has created before the Praetor overpowers her." As he spoke, Gairynzvl moved to Rehstaed, covering his eyes as he had done with Mardan and shaking him resolutely. "Return to us, Rehstaed."

"The Praetor?" Mardan's muddled response intermingled with his fellow Liberator's exclamation of bewildering Vrynnyth Ghal. Twisting about, the former Legionnaire pointed towards the towering figure of Uxvagchtr who stood in the midst of the battlefield, turning his head this way, then that, as he sought something inexplicable.

"The leader of all Reviled. He will consume all with his evil if we do not act." The bright streaks of blood upon the Praetor's pale skin lent terrifying poignancy to Gairynzvl's words and his friends grimaced in unison.

"Wha' d' ye suggest, Fierce One?" Rehstaed asked even as he turned to seek his countryman. He located Dravahl several yards away kneeling over a fallen Legionnaire as both stared blankly towards the enchantress.

Gairynzvl replied resolutely. "We need to rouse the others before we can move against him."

Anticipating his suggestion, Rehstaed had already crossed the distance between himself and his comrade, reaching to restore Dravahl to consciousness in the same manner Gairynzvl had employed.

"Where is Bryth?" Mardan's question filled the heavy quiet of the formerly chaotic battlefield as the Liberators turned in opposing directions to scan the field in search of their friend. He lay upon the ground fifty or more yards away with a Demonfey poised menacingly over him, a spear of crimson and black steel raised high, but both had turned their faces in the direction of the singing enchantress and had ceased to struggle.

Tilting his head back into the turbulence of the storm, Uxvagchtr drew a profound breath; then howled into the tempest with such piercing volubility that those standing round him, staring with empty gazes, were shaken from the dazed spell under which they had fallen. Kaylyya immediately stopped singing and shrank from the dreadful sound, covering her ears and burying her face in Veryth's embrace even as he turned towards the Liberators, his bright emeraldine eyes conveying their shared astonishment and horror.

From the depths of the Lyysharan woodland, a chorus of howls answered the demanding call.

* * *

"We must go now or all will be lost." Evondair prepared to depart, flexing his wings forcefully to shake off the snow that had begun to cling to them, but Nunvaret hesitated.

"We can't defy the Imperial Praetor right in front of him. Such an act of defiance will cost us our lives."

Striding back to the visibly uncertain Captain of Demonfey, the golden-haired Healer set his wings assertively as he pointed into the distance. "Many have already lost their lives! I am done arguing with you, *Demonfey*. The message must be delivered and I would rather die trying to share it than live with the guilt of failure because I shrank in fear." The accusation in his tone was as infuriating as it was compelling and Nunvaret snarled in response.

"I am no coward, *pigeon*."

Evondair hissed at him with uncharacteristic belligerence, "and I am no pigeon." The Fey of the Light retorted crossly as he stretched his brilliant white wings to their fullest, utilizing formidable wing beats to ascend into the turbulence of the storm without the use of precursory running steps. His strength and resolve irrefutably displayed, he looked down at the Demonfey and gestured towards the battlefield.

"Will you join me or will you cower amidst the snow?"

* * *

Howls echoed from all directions as the Imperial Praetor lowered his head and listened to the chorus with a deceptively charming smile curving his lips. Striding forward, he looked down on an unmoving Legionnaire who lay face down in the snow and reached down to haul him up from the ground with one hand. The lifeless Dark One hung in a limp, morbid display as Uxvagchtr took pleasure in breaking off his wings for no apparent reason. Turning the Legionnaire over then, he ripped open his clothing, licking his lips in anticipation as he took hold of the warrior's unutilized dagger and used it to open his chest. Lowering his head slowly, he drank the blood that barely flowed; yet even as he did, the dark crimson of his visible aura deepened.

"We must stop him. He is gaining strength from the fallen!" Gairynzvl's imperative urging was met with enraged concurrence.

"But how? What can we do against such evil?" Mardan's uncertainty was mirrored by the Watchers, who spoke in a rush of anxious fear.

"I've seen him do far worse."

"We can't hope to overpower him."

"If he gets his hands on you, you'll wish for death long before he kills you."

"I canno' bear t' see 'im feast'n on th' blood o' our brothers. I'd impale 'im where 'e stands wit' me' own wingbarbs 'fore I watch an'more," Dravahl spat in fury and stretched out his scarred wings in preparation of ascending, but the others held him back.

"Self-sacrifice will not win the day," Gairynzvl began, but Mardan reached out suddenly, placing his hand upon his fellow Liberator's shoulder to interrupt him.

"Self-sacrifice might, indeed, be the *only* weapon at our disposal."

The others scowled at him irresolutely, but waited for him to elaborate on the plan forming in his thoughts. As they debated their course, piercing howls of unnumbered wolves rang from the close precincts of the forest. Turning to watch their advancement as blood poured from his open mouth, Uxvagchtr lifted his head and howled to them in reply; the sound rising to a strident note before falling back into a guttural growl and the bewitched animals fully comprehended his directive. Breaking from the protection of their woodland home, the seldom seen and often harmonious beasts closed upon the surrounded battlefield, converging on Fey Guards and Legionnaires alike with glinting bared teeth and vicious snarls.

Mardan elaborated on his idea hastily even as he strode to the nearest fallen warrior and took his spear from his lifeless hand, "Take any spear you can find and follow me. We will encircle him in a single, unified attack. With luck, he will not be able to defend against all of us."

* * *

Buffeted and blustered by the twisting gales of the storm, Evondair and Nunvaret traversed the short distance to the battlefield in moments. Blinded by the mayhem of snow and wind, they were forced closer to the ground than they might have preferred, but as the clearing came into view, so too did the Imperial Praetor. Upon seeing him, the Fey of the Light who had never looked upon pure evil before could not keep from arresting his forward progress. Hovering amid the swirling rage of the storm as he surveyed the horror unfolding below them, Evondair could not compel himself to move closer. Nunvaret sped by him, then turned to gaze back even as their arrival caused Uxvagchtr to lift his head from the neck of a struggling Legionnaire he held in a crushing embrace. Focusing the perception of his unseen eyes on them, he pressed his thoughts forcefully into their minds.

"Ah, Nunvaret, where have you been?"

The Demonfey closed his eyes, attempting to shield himself with duplicitous hatred and rage even as he reached outward to those standing with blank gazes and pressing an unwavering message into their fortuitously quieted minds.

"Such a beautiful gift you've brought. Come and share his splendor with me." Blinded by sudden lust, the Dlalth Master's gaze drank in the vision of the golden-haired, stunningly-dressed, brilliantly-winged Fey of the Light who hesitated in evident fear behind the Captain of Demonfey. Hurling the Legionnaire to the ground whom he had been devouring the moment before, Uxvagchtr stepped on and over him as he sought to close the distance between himself and the object of his brazen desire. Stretching out his massive wings, he gave the impression he would launch himself upward into the churning storm.

Around him, wolves attacked Light and Dark Fey indiscriminately, entranced by the inescapable dark magic radiating from the intricate headdress that crowned the Dlalth Master's head. They ripped feathers and dragonhide, tore pale and blushing flesh alike and rent life with hideous fury as the former combatants sought to defend themselves, as well as each other, from the onslaught. From the depths of the woodland where the homes and stables of Lyyshara lay undefended, screams echoed vicious snarls and communicative howls, betraying the unthinkable fact that the wolves had set upon villagers and warriors alike.

Hurrying to gather spears from the ground where they had fallen from lifeless hands, the Liberators scattered in several directions, heedless to the curious gazes of the Legionnaires who stood nearby. In the absence of Kaylyya's song, reality once again encroached upon the tranquility that had briefly descended upon them, but they did not return to the violence of their former attack even as snarling wolves closed in around them. As the Imperial Praetor focused his attention on the beauty of the Fey of the Light the Demonfey Captain had brought to him, an urgent whisper of hope transposed the howling of wolves and the winter wind. Many Legionnaires turned from the bewitching serenity of the Enchantress to gaze upward at an unlikely pair of Fey hovering above the battlefield from whom emanated the wholly unexpected and traitorous suggestion.

"Liberation is at hand!"

"Bring him to me, Nunvaret, so I can taste his exquisiteness and you shall earn unrivaled favor." Uxvagchtr prodded with his thoughts impatiently, beating his wings with anticipation, but the Captain of Demonfey did not even acknowledge hearing him. Staring with an expression of intense concentration across the battlefield, he communicated an imperative command that left his legion staring at him as if he had taken full leave of his senses.

"Lay down your weapons!"

Although he was not telepathic, Evondair could easily sense the merciless evil and despicable intent focused upon him as he hovered with powerful, circular wing beats above the Master of all Reviled who was staring up at him, licking his lips in a shameless display of lust. Without warning, Uxvagchtr raised a blood-stained hand toward the Healer, directing a potent surge of magic towards him that filled his entire being with a sudden and inexplicable need to move closer. In spite of the Praetor's terrifying appearance, the seductive coercion forced upon him was more than Evondair could resist. Redirecting the circular motion of his wings in order to move closer, he did not notice Nunvaret turn sharply to glare at him with unconcealed impatience.

"Keep your place, *pigeon*. Remember what I told you." Growling at the fair Fey in a tone that was not to be ignored, he caused the Healer to pause while he tore his gaze from the bewitching beauty Uxvagchtr forced into his mind and looked once again at the Demonfey Captain who reminded him of what had been stolen from his mind. "He will devour you in every way imaginable." His warning stopped Evondair's forward progress, but had the unanticipated repercussion of turning Uxvagchtr's eyeless glare onto himself.

"Nunvaret!" He hissed out loud, the tempting allure of his tone engulfed by rage.

From the opposite direction, a unified outcry of motivating bravado pierced the fury of the winter tempest as the reunited Liberators and those of the Watchers who yet breathed, as well as the remaining Goralnicht Legionnaires took to wing. Aiming the spears they each carried at the Master of all Dark Fey, they moved towards him with rapid haste, contriving to overwhelm him through the force of an unanticipated attack.

Those Legionnaires who still stood unmoving, listening to the repeated, urgent demand from their Captain to lay down their weapons, turned to gaze at each other and then at the Liberators with a roiling combination of misunderstanding and distrust. Dare they disarm in the presence of the Imperial Praetor whose power of magic and intense malevolence could not possibly be eluded? Dare they act so impetuously when surrounded by armed Fey of the Light and bewitched wolf kind? Dare they risk to hope so riotously?

Before any could act, Uxvagchtr growled. "Hudvathrich paachlenum ghraal!" The words issued from the mouth of the Imperial Praetor even as he bared his teeth at Nunvaret viciously. With anger seething visibly in his crimson aura, he raised both hands towards the Demonfey hovering over his head and directed a bolt of scarlet magic into the center of his body. The Demonfey shrieked in agony as the blazing current stretched from the Dark One's hands through his body and into the fury of the blizzard beyond. Arching backward in violent distress, Nunvaret's wings curled inward protectively, but the current of brutalizing energy held him in place. He did not fall, nor could he escape the excruciating serration of the Praetor's magic by fleeing on the wing. He was held captive to the agonizing penetration of merciless magic severing through his body as long as the Praetor directed the current of energy at him.

Shaking his head to clear away the lingering dismay of Uxvagchtr's alluring thoughts, Evondair moved to render aide to his companion, but the potent negative influence of the crimson energy radiating from the Dlalth Master held him at bay while Uxvagchtr laughed with cruel pleasure. Looking down at the beguiling beauty and abysmal evil of that Dark Fey with a sudden rush of hatred mounting inside him unlike anything he had ever felt before, Evondair hissed viperously and cursed in fluent Celebrae.

His extraordinary gift of Discernment helped him to realize the consuming negativity pummeling through him radiated directly from the dark magic issuing from the Dlalth Master, but the same force overpowered his rationale. In that moment, the only thought in Evondair's mind was violence; yet, before he could determine the best course of action to counter the wrathful energy consuming him, he caught sight of the contingent of Liberators and Watchers hurtling towards the Praetor with glinting spears seeking pale flesh and he could not conceal the smile that turned his lips at the discovery.

Although he did not turn, the Praetor saw them as well. Unwilling to be distracted from the punishment he had unleashed upon Nunvaret, he gestured in a circle around himself with his free hand and muttered a spell, creating a sphere of shimmering crimson that encircled him. It reached outward as well, seeking those standing in close proximity with tendrils of unbearable pain. Legionnaires, Fey of the Light, and entranced wolf-kind scattered away from this vile radiance in confused haste while he turned with leisurely patience to gaze upward at the beautiful malefey above him.

The magic he had unleashed effectively protected him and forced the unit of attackers seeking to overwhelm him to veer away, thwarted by his glimmering supernatural armor. Regrouping several yards away, Rehstaed, Bryth, Mardan and Dravahl attempted to direct their spears through his shield, but, although the weapons pierced the circle, as they crossed the threshold of raging energy two were instantly shattered. They fell in pieces at the Praetor's feet while the remaining two were misdirected outward once again. One pierced an unsuspecting shewolf while the other plunged into the closest Legionnaire.

"He protects himself with dark magic," Gairynzvl shouted above the howling of the storm and the cries echoing from the village. His fellow Liberators gathered around him, ready to re-strategize, but the Watchers and Legionnaires from the Goralnicht Seclusionaries turned to stare at a Demonfey they knew only too well who was being held in the air above them by that same dark magic.

"It's Nunvaret," Dravahl shouted.

"He's finally getting what he deserves!"several others snarled in reply, but Dravahl shook his head.

"Can you no' hear 'im?"

Nunvaret's cries were scattered amid the blustering snow and carried upon the shoulders of the wind into the Lyysharan woodland. They shattered into the sky above as his torment persisted with merciless cruelty, but the wails of his distress were not consumed by the storm. Nor was the determined repetition of his telepathic voice pressing into the consciousness of any with the ability to hear.

"*Lay...down...your weapons. Liberation...is...at hand.*" The determination and expectation conveyed through his thoughts was as inescapable as the pain he endured and those who heard him stared at each other with confusion. Dare they believe him?

Screaming in unrelenting distress, what he Saw, Felt and Knew transferred from his essence outward with all the potency his remarkable telepathy could unleash and more than those upon the battlefield listened. The Three who flew into the fury of the storm received the transference of his torture with unmatched horror.

The triumvirate hissed resoundingly in unified rage.

Chapter Twenty-Three

Raising his free hand, Uxvagchtr directed a second stream of crimson energy toward the beautiful, golden-haired Fey he greedily desired, encompassing him in a similar radiance as that which held the Demonfey suspended beside him, but this dark magic did not inflict pain. Rather, it filled the Healer with an irrepressible yearning unlike anything he had ever felt before. Even stronger in influence than the telepathic seduction the Dlalth Master had forced upon him previously, Evondair found himself drawn toward the Imperial Praetor and he could not inhibit his own actions. Unable to oppose the physical compulsion to move as close to him as possible, Evondair suffered a torment of longing unlike any he had ever experienced. The dark magic imposed an inescapable, shocking hunger and a turbulent conflict of thunderous desire and revulsion within him that surged with unbearable intensity.

"What is he doing?" Kaylyya cried out in dismay, unable to comprehend his actions as she watched Evondair descending towards the Dark One, but the perceptive Healer standing close beside her needed no explanations.

"He is under the control of the Praetor's vile magic," Veryth clarified with a grim tone. Easily able to interpret the evil of the Dlalth Master, he refocused the outpouring of his uplifting positivity and encouragement with fixed determination; directing it solely at his fellow Healer to aide him in any manner possible while Kaylyya stepped away from his side towards the towering figure in the midst of the battlefield. Her unexpected actions placed her directly into the path of the Healers focused energy and it filled her with a boldness she had never experienced before. Though she watched in mute silence, a tempest of frantic rage swelled within her, congesting into a fuming ire as she watched her sweet love dragged against his will into the waiting, deadly embrace of the darkest of all Fey.

From his much closer vantage point, Gairynzvl watched as well and his essence screamed in desperation, but whether it was his own emotion or that of his friend he could not be certain. It did not matter. Spurred into action by a sight he had witnessed too many times before and fully cognizant of what the outcome would be, he clenched the spear he held in an iron grasp. Reaching out to snatch the weapon Mardan held at his side, he turned to the Liberators and spoke hastily. "The message is being delivered! Spread the word to the Guard to give quarter to any Legionnaire who lays down his weapons."

"What are you doing?" Mardan recognized the wrathful, unruly glint in the Fierce One's eyes and briefly refused to give over his spear, pulling him back as they wrestled for ownership over it.

"I will do what I must to protect my friend." Pointing in the direction of the vile Overlord, Gairynzvl brought their attention to Evondair's plight.

"*Our* friend, Fierce One," Mardan argued. "You will not go alone. Allow us to help you by sharing your strategy."

"I have but one plan; to destroy that vile monster before he harms another living soul." Gairynzvl growled, physically shaking with the effort required to restrain his fury.

"Aye, Fierce One. I too!" Dravahl hissed from behind him.

"But how d'we pen'trate 'is defensive magic?" Rehstaed queried, even as several Legionnaires standing round them turned to listen.

"It's that cursed headdress," one volunteered unexpectedly while another nodded in agreement.

"It intensifies and focuses his magic."

"Without it, he'd be vulnerable," the third continued their group thought and the Liberators stared with evident uncertainty at those who had, only moments earlier, been trying to kill them, but Gairynzvl did not hesitate. Reaching out to lay his hand upon the first's shoulder, he agreed with a broad smile.

"I agree, brother. How do we remove it?"

Glancing at each other indecisively, his friends listened with astonishment to several suggestions the Legionnaires offered. "We could pierce the abhorrent contraption with our spears."

"No, shear his head from his shoulders!"

"Pierce him through the heart."

"He hasn't got one!"

"How do you suggest we get close enough?" As they hastily debated and several other Legionnaires turned from staring at Nunvaret to join in the discussion, the Liberators could not deny the fact that the message had, indeed, been delivered and the result was proving far more incredible than any of them might ever have anticipated.

Looking across the wide clearing that made up the Lyysharan battlefield, they watched as Legionnaires gazed at each other skeptically, but their expressions were marked with undeniable hope. Though some growled in anger, shook their heads and cursed in incensed Dlalth, most turned in search of the closest Fey Guard to hand over their weapons. Those Guards stood in utter disbelief, unsure of the appropriate action to take, but the Guards followed the orders given to them the evening before and the surrendering Dark Fey were not harmed.

Those Legionnaires and Demonfey who chose not to believe the implausible suggestion that liberation was at hand or could not force themselves to accept such a preposterous suggestion, regrouped and hastened to defend their Praetor. They were a mere handful, however, in comparison to the multitude of eager Legionnaires that willingly disarmed. In their acquiescence, Fey Guards turned to defend those who had been their enemy only moments before from bewitched wolves.

Struggling against the torturous desire hammering through him, Evondair drew closer to Uxvagchtr, penetrating his shield of magic with no resistance as he was drawn downward from the tumult of snow and wind. The Imperial Praetor smiled with depraved delight and reached out for the handsome young malefey, his thoughts focusing on acts that flooded Evondair's mind with unparalleled horror. Grimacing with painful effort, the Healer folded his wings and alighted before the Dlalth Master, tears welling in his viridian eyes as the darkest of all Fey drank in the sight of him.

"Seldom have I seen such masculine beauty," Uxvagchtr slurred with undisguised hunger. Raising his hand, he reached to touch Evondair's golden hair and stroked his cheek with appalling tenderness while his victim shuddered. His exceptional gift of Discernment, which at other times was a source of strength, now betrayed him as it allowed Evondair to know with certainty everything the Vile One intended to do. Slowly tracing the contours of his high cheekbones and the line of his jaw, Uxvagchtr focused his attention on Evondair's mouth. Bending closer to him, he spoke in a soft, lust-filled tone."Do not fear me. I shall inflict no harm upon you."

The Healer's stomach lurched as the full potency of the dark magic compelling him took hold and, in spite of his natural inclination to resist, he closed his eyes and tilted his head upward to receive the Praetors kiss. Tears slipped from his gaze as he was drawn closer and all the chaos of the howling wind seemed to enter his mind. Lust of unmatched intensity thundered through his body and spun his thoughts as Uxvagchtr's kiss lingered and deepened. Desperate to escape in any manner possible, Evondair tried focusing on the repeated cries from the nearby village that pierced his thoughts like frozen shards. He listened to Nunvaret's screams of unrelenting distress that drove into the core of him like the biting, frozen gales, but none of these sounds could severe the influence of evil over-ruling him. His body shook violently as he struggled against the embrace of the Praetor with every measure of strength he possessed, but he could not escape and his shaking only served to please the Vile One.

Cutting through the madness, the loathing and the infuriating desire pounding through him, one sound suddenly captured his full attention. Wresting his mind from the passionate attention of the Praetor and the betraying responses of his own body, a single sound pressed into his essence. It touched him like the soft coo of a dove in the tender light of morning, delicate and ethereal. Like the light of day that increases with each passing moment, so too did the insubstantial sound of harped strings and soft birdsong intensify. It filled his mind like the radiance of daytide, invigorating and inspiring his spirit in spite of the slow descent of psychosis forcing its way into his being. It touched him far more tenderly than the hands caressing his body and filled him with serene tranquility that surpassed any hour of blissful sleep he had ever enjoyed. Sweet, melodic, and utterly captivating music pressed back the nightmare forcing its darkness into him, transcending his torment and imparting peace beyond understanding.

Veryth watched with an unblinking stare as the outpouring of his energy filled Kaylyya with courage and purpose; then rushed over her like a torrential flood that streamed onward to encompass his fellow Healer and friend. Though tears blurred his typically bright, emeraldine gaze and the focused conveyance of energy rapidly depleted his own, he did not waver for an instant. His aura diminished; his stance gave way beneath him and he fell to his knees; still, he delivered every ounce of strength he embodied towards his friend. As the sweet sound of melodic birdsong filled his mind, Veryth fought to keep himself conscious, leaning forward onto his hands as he struggled to concentrate his thoughts and his effort was not in vain. Even as his eyes closed and his head bowed, he caught sight of Evondair's wings opening.

While several Legionnaires argued the best method for removing the Praetors head from his body in order to relieve him of his magic-enhancing coronet, Gairynzvl watched his friend with an unbroken glare. Powerless to intercede, though every ounce of anger and hatred within him screamed with resentment, he stood frozen by the sight. Beside him, Mardan hissed with a similar vehemence and then spoke with a tone of finality. "Though I would not wish to cause injury to

Evondair, I say we come at the Beast from all directions and pierce his layer of magic with every weapon at our disposal. He cannot deflect all of us at once."

Weary of debate, his companions nodded with wordless agreement and immediately turned to collect as many spears, arrows and swords as they could carry with more than a few Legionnaires collecting weapons at their side.

"She sings to comfort him," Gairynzvl muttered, half to himself, half to the Celebrant-Warrior glaring at his side.

"I doubt he can be comforted." They did not look at each other, fully aware that Mardan spoke the truth, but then he offered a suggestion that raised their spirits from the dark pit into which they were sinking.

"Though I have never attempted it because of the level of danger it presents, I *have* read of a spell that may counter dark magic."

Turning to pierce the cerulean fire of Mardan's gaze with the icy intensity of his own, Gairynzvl did not need to ask him to proceed and Mardan smiled with grim determination. "I would fight at your side, Fierce One, and at the side of my friends, but I will remain behind you and seek to unbalance his merciless advantage."

Nodding once, Gairynzvl turned to receive an armful of spears from a Legionnaire so scarred from abuse his features appeared blurred. Raising his hand to the Dark One's shoulder, he spoke with a tone of authority he seldom utilized. "You have suffered enough, brother. Find shelter until the struggle is over; then your wounds shall be tended."

The Legionnaire shook his head, speaking in a rasping voice that betrayed a past filled with much screaming. "I would rather risk death defending the freedom you bring, Liberator."

Blazing lavender locked with darkest crimson before Gairynzvl spread his nebulous wings to ascend into the storm with a weapon-laden contingent behind him. Stationary upon the trampled snow of the battlefield, Mardan bowed his head briefly, then fixed the wrath of his burning cerulean gaze upon the Vile One while raising both his hands. "*Maenal infernum chlyya Luxonyth, braechanivandra vornae tywylucht!*"

Provide a blazing inferno of Light whose brightness consumes this darkness!

From his hands, a blaze of radiant Light shot outward seeking the glowing incendiary of hatred and violence enveloping Uxvagchtr, Nunvaret and Evondair. The potency of the formidable spell he cast caused Mardan to stumble backward, but he concentrated on maintaining control, braced himself and unleashed the full vigor of his defiant nature into the spell he created. It blazed even brighter and stronger, but even as it did, the clearing was rent by an enraged scream.

Raising his head from the pleasure of the kiss he had forced upon the golden-haired Fey he held like a treasure, Uxvagchtr shrieked in anger and unexpected pain as a jagged bolt of clear, bright Light penetrated the glimmering crimson of his dark magic. Like an energetic discharge of lightening, the streak of brilliant light was drawn to the powerful headdress he wore and danced across its metal and crystalline intricacies, arcing between his six horns and sending out a shower of sparkling effervescence. Infuriated, he flung Evondair to the ground, pressing him into the snow beneath one foot as he turned to seek out the impertinent wielder of the bright magic assailing him.

As he turned, a vicious onslaught of weapons rained down at him.

Hurtling at him from every conceivable direction, spears and arrows pierced the shield he had generated around himself, which was now weakened by the neutralizing magic of Light. It took all the Dark Lord's focus to deflect the death-seeking barrage. Completely occupied with defending himself, he released Nunvaret without warning and the exhausted Demonfey plummeted to the earth, unconscious before he hit the ground. Beneath the boot of the Vile Master, Evondair was also released from the overpowering lust forced upon him and as weapons fell around him, his mind filled with only one thought.

Ejecting a current of scarlet energy toward the source of clarifying magic, Uxvagchtr growled an incantation of dreadful purpose. Unwilling to risk another strike by the brilliant illumination that sent agonizing jolts through him like the shock of lightning itself, he spoke a derivation of an all-too-familiar spell, directing it back onto the Spell Caster attacking him. "Cruciavaeryn Hvaulcht!"

Mardan's scream echoed across the battlefield as he fell beneath the agonizing Spell of Inflicted Pain cast onto him. Upon hearing the sound, Gairynzvl turned in the air to find the one who suffered such distress and when he saw the Celebrant he had once hated, yet now called friend, writhing in the snow he hissed with rage. Pivoting on the wing, he raced upward into the fury of the storm, momentarily leaving the battle behind as he sought greater altitude. In his arms, he carried a dozen spears, bundled together and primed for purpose with dark grime emblazoning each bristling point; a sure sign of poison upon the blade. The storm buffeted against him and sought to hurl him from the sky, but he struggled upward, desiring greater height until he reached the pinnacle of the blizzard where the gales tore at his feathers and stole his breath. Unable to continue, he turned and glared downward into swirling white nothingness.

Struggling to free himself from the pressure of the Praetors boot pressed down upon his chest, Evondair sought to push himself up from the snow. Temporarily distracted by wave after wave of seeking arrows, hurtling spears, and swords turning end over end, Uxvagchtr shifted his stance and the Healer found his opportunity. Grasping the Vile One's leg across his knee, Evondair raised his wings in a single, vigorous wing beat, twisting as he forcefully drove himself forward to throw off the Praetor's balance.

Cursing balefully, Uxvagchtr stumbled sideways and spread his wings wide to maintain his footing. As he did, the membranes of his dragonhide wings were punctured by seven arrows and a sword lodged itself into one of the central wing-joints. Growling in pain and anger, the Praetor flung his arms wide, scattering inflicting, brutal magic in a random dispersal onto any Fey within reach, but even as he did a sound penetrated his consciousness unlike anything he had ever heard before. Hissing in rage, he looked round him for the source of the noise, its delicacy and subtlety strangely beguiling….and entrancing.

Folding his wings, Gairynzvl embraced the collection of spears he carried and allowed the ferocity of the storm to drive him downward, increasing the speed of his stoop to a perilous velocity. Unable to see the ground below through the turbulence of the storm, he pointed the spears he held in his strong arms as far in front of himself as he could manage and prayed for the blessing of the Ancients that he was still on course, but it was all he could do to keep from spiraling out of control. The rate of his descent was so rapid he dared not open his wings to correct his direction lest they break backwards from the force of the wind. As he cleared the heavy cloud cover and the battlefield became visible once again, he realized to his dismay that Uxvagchtr had moved.

The towering Dark Fey was stronger than the Healer had anticipated. Even wounded, the Imperial Praetor could not be thrown to the ground as he had hoped and Evondair hastily sought another alternative. Pushing up from the ground with another forceful wing beat, he impelled himself into his enemy, wrapping his arms round his middle as he continued to use the influence of his powerful wings, as well as the strength of his legs, to drive him backward.

"Raach!" The Praetor's curse preempted his unexpected reaction. Grasping the unpredictable malefey by the lengths of his golden hair, Uxvagchtr yanked his head backward violently and turned Evondair's face towards his seeking bite. "I did not want to hurt you, Golden One. Remember that," he snarled as he sunk his teeth into Evondair's neck just below his jaw. The force of his bite caused Evondair to shout and lurch backward in surprise, but his resistance was exactly what the Vile One delighted in most. Wrapping his free arm around his victim, Uxvagchtr pulled him closer, lifting his head briefly to smile while he watched the beautiful malefey bleed.

The sight was more than Kaylyya could bear.

Hissing wrathfully for the first time in her life, she spread her graceful wings and raced towards the vile monster attempting to drain the life from her beloved. Without a thought to her own safety or the perilous danger she faced, she hurtled headlong into the crimson shadow encircling the Praetor. Ignoring the cries from her friends to desist, she launched herself with riotous anger at the only target the Dlalth Master presented: his horns. Grasping hold of them with strength intensified by a furious rush of adrenaline, she beat her wings tenaciously, forcing his head backward and compelling him to release his victim as he sought to escape the violence of her attack. Even as her beloved fell to the Praetors feet and rolled away from him, his hands pressing down on the puncture wounds in his throat, Kaylyya was tossed like a child riding an enraged Tryngalith.

Shaking his head angrily, Uxvagchtr reached to capture the insolent shefey harassing him and launch her into the closest evergreen, but she eluded his grasp. In an attempt to keep her grip upon him, she shifted her hands, inadvertently taking hold of the magical headdress he wore. He cursed in obscene Dlalth, thrashing his head violently and tossing the delicate shefey like a leaf upon the fury of a storm, but she clung onto him with a persistence he did not expect.

Under the duress of his thrashing and the weight of Kaylyya holding to it for dear life, the headdress and source of all his magnified magic suddenly cracked with an atrocious sound. Heedless, Uxvagchtr bent deeply, drew a sharp breath, then straightened violently while throwing back his head in a final attempt to free himself from the bothersome shefey;, but this action only succeeded in separating the magical diadem he wore from the crown of his head. Broken into several pieces, it slipped over his triplet of horns and was sent tumbling away from him, with Kaylyya still clinging onto it. Staggering backward at the unanticipated emancipation, he grasped wildly after it; yet when he realized what had happened, that such an inconsequential mite of a shefey had forced him to unwittingly relinquish his most treasured possession, he went wild with rage.

Cursing unintelligibly, he spun in the direction she had been cast, raised his hands with his fingertips curled like claws, and hissed a hideous spell of lethal magic. *"Mordanglicht invarnaeum glaast!"*

At the sound of his voice, Kaylyya arched backward abruptly, screaming.

"NO!" Evondair echoed her scream, watching with paralyzing horror from his sprawled position on the frozen ground as his beloved was captured mid-flight and flung to the earth with ruthless brutality. The headpiece crashed beside her, shattering into fragments. The sight of its destruction caused Uxvagchtr to stand immobilized, forced to reassess his capabilities. At his feet, Evondair struggled to keep enough pressure on his wound to control the bleeding while he stared in shock and disbelief at Kaylyya. Attempting to straighten in order to rise and hasten to her side, he was unprepared when Uxvagchtr snarled ferociously and kicked his legs out from under him.

"You can do nothing, worthless Healer. She is dead! As you shall wish to be long before I'm through with you," he hissed with sadistic pleasure, watching his victim curl into a ball as grief and pain wracked his body.

From the roiling clouds above them, a streak of nebulous hues and barbed death hurtled downward. Without the magic of the headdress he had grown so accustomed to, Uxvagchtr failed to foresee Gairynzvl's decent. Standing utterly engrossed by the sight of the suffering he had inflicted, he did not notice the impending attack until the shrill noise of wind whistling across feathers and the sound of growling filled his hearing. Then, the Praetor looked up to see a wholly unanticipated sight: a Fey of the Light plummeting from the sky holding an armful of death.

Death meant for him!

Opening his wings at the last possible moment in order to correct his trajectory in spite of the rash speed of his decent, Gairynzvl screamed as feathers were ripped from his body and his powerful wings bent backward perilously. Aiming for the Praetor's chest, he thrust the bundle of spears he carried outward, hurling them away even as Uxvagchtr raised his hands to deflect the deadly onslaught with frenzied magic. He was only partially successful. Though he managed to scatter five of the hurtling spears, one found its mark and buried itself deep in his shoulder while another impaled him through his thigh. Raising his head to the sky, the livid Dlalth Master rent the storm with his fury.

Curling his wings inward with every ounce of strength he possessed, Gairynzvl spiraled beyond the Vile One and the outpouring of vicious magic he unleashed. Careening in an uncontrolled plunge, he struck the ground hard and tumbled in a disarray of wings and limbs numerous times before he finally came to a halt. Lying senseless upon the frozen battlefield, his fellow Liberators and the newly emancipated Legionnaires watched his unmoving form with mute foreboding.

Rallying to Uxvagchtr's protection, the Demonfey who were unwilling or unable to believe the message they had heard from Nunvaret formed a circular perimeter around their leader. Growling in rage at their enemy, they were prepared to defend him at any cost. Several closest to the Liberators immediately engaged them, delivering vengeance against the unarmed group without mercy. Dravahl and Rehstaed fought barehanded with admirable ferocity while Bryth and three of the Goralnicht Legionnaires searched frantically for abandoned weapons, but without armaments they stood little chance. Pierced through the side, Dravahl fell first and Rehstaed was rendered senseless seconds later as a shield crashed over his head. Fey Guards and Legionnaires alike converged on the Demonfey, cursing in bright Celebrae and grisly Dlalth as the moment of hope and peace they had all experienced slipped from their grasp.

Curled upon the blood-stained snow at the Praetors feet with his hands locked over the wound he had sustained, Evondair listened to the renewed fighting, mourning all that had been lost in the attempt of freedom as anger, despair and persistent hope grappled within him for supremacy. Yet, in spite of the wrathful emotions surging within him, a solitary thought plagued his mind.

How else might we attain peace if we do not become peace?

Chapter Twenty-Four

Plummeting into the clearing that glowed red from hatred, evil and the blood of many, the Temple Elders streaked from the darkness of the storm in a brilliant blaze of Light that emanated from their combined auras. As they gained momentum in the force of their joined stoop, they uttered an incantation that curved the Light they bore with them into a concentrated beam. Directing this gleaming shaft of illumination at the crimson sphere glowing below them, they fought the Darkness with pure, bright Light and it exploded on contact with the crimson shield of the Vile One. The cacophony of sound resulting from the clashing of these opposing forces sent all close by reeling backward and even the darkness shrank from the unanticipated assault.

Bending to cover his ears and glare with hatred at the Golden One lying at his feet, Uxvagchtr hissed viciously as the Temple Elders alighted before him. Only once before had they ever faced each other and the outcome of that conflict had set the stage for the events that now unraveled around them. As soon as his feet met the ground, Zraylaunyth sought to hurl himself at the beast before him, but his brothers held him back. The First grasped him by one shoulder while the Second managed to take hold of one wing. Restrained, the youthful Elder hissed ferociously at the pallid, crimson-eyed Dlalth Master towering over him and watched with undisguised antagonism as Uxvagchtr snarled like an enraged dragon, raised his foot menacingly; then stomped ruthlessly down upon Evondair, pressing his weight into his wounded throat before he managed to roll out of the way. "Be gone from here, *Mercazenandrach*, or I'll crush the life from him!"

Looking down into the glassy, viridian gaze of his long-time friend, Zraylaunyth reached out with his senses and understood Evondair's pain in an instant. It did not stem from the injury to his neck, but the inescapable agony of his broken heart and the youthful Elder hissed again with even greater rage.

"It would seem you have already done that, *Drynalynvagcht*." The First answered with a carefully moderated tone, looking beyond the depraved monster in their midst, across the blood-stained battlefield. His bright gaze took in the scene in a brief moment; yet he already Knew the anguish the conflict had created. His gaze swept across the clearing, seeking those faces with whom he was personally familiar, as well as the bright colors of Kaylyya's distinctive wings and when he found them the sight of her crumpled form lying untended in the snow pulled a growl from his throat before he could contain it.

Uxvagchtr smiled spitefully. "So, you are not as impassive as you pretend to be, Maergalyys." He spoke provocatively, using the Elder's name when no others dared. "Now that I know what angers you, I'll work harder to make it happen more often." Taunting the greatest of the Elders, the Praetor turned in the direction of the Lyysharan village. Raising his hands, he muttered in guttural Dlalth to create a spell of lethal potency that sprayed outward from his hands like fiery sparks. The scarlet-hued dark magic stretched outward, seeking unsuspecting victims and everywhere it reached screams echoed from the shadowy woodland. Wails of distress tugged at the heart and pierced the spirit while screams of rage serrated across nerves like blades skirling against blades.

Without waiting to listen, the Elders raised their hands together in a single, unified action and spoke a counter-spell of containment, seeking to nullify the evil outpouring, but before they could complete the incantation, a triplet of Demonfey lunged towards them from behind the Praetor with spears raised.

The Second foresaw the ambush and turned in a preemptive, protective motion like a blinding winter squall, shoving his brothers away from his sides and bearing the full force of the attack alone. Deflecting one spear with a bolt of light expelled from his hand, he was unable to defend himself against the other two, which lodged themselves deep in his chest. The shock of pain that penetrated his body caused his brethren to cry out, though no sound escaped his own mouth as he stared down at the fatal wound in astonishment. Falling onto his knees, he took hold of the weapons as his brothers recovered their balance and turned to render any aid possible, but the appalling spectacle that met their joined gaze left both immobilized.

"Jynaravrahn!" They exclaimed in desperation, staring at their fellow Elder and eternal brother as tears slipped from his eyes, even as they closed. Left momentarily powerless by the severity of the unforeseen loss, it was as if the other two had also been struck and, in truth, they had; so conjoined were the Three. As the Second lapsed into endless sleep, Zraylaunyth raised his head and keened into the blustering wind with an emotion beyond comparison.

Uxvagchtr raised his head as well, laughing with pitiless glee as the pain and anguish he embodied spread outward from his heartless core. Crimson glitters scattered into the wintry night like fire and flame cascading through the darkness. The quiet environs of forest echoed with sounds of fighting, screams of horror and crashes of unknown violence while those standing upon the battlefield listened in torment. They could not race to render assistance and leave their friends undefended, nor could they bear to hear the evidence of such ruthless magic. The peaceful village would never be the same; not after the Vile One shook his hatred outward like showers of sparks from a blazing flame and wrought so much destruction.

Everything those sparks touched was pierced with jagged shards of negativity that instantly festered into wounds of distrust, abhorrence and cruelty whether they fell upon Legionnaires or Fey of the Light, the young or elderly, shefey, malefey or animals that abided in harmony. The embers of dark magic provoked rage and mindless violence. Many stood in mute horror, watching the conflagration as it stretched outward from his hands, the crimson glitters of malevolence reaching into their tranquility, seeking only devastation. Others, who had been scorched by that inferno, hurled themselves into friend and foe, awash with inescapable wrath that demanded release in the most vicious form imaginable.

Comprehending the magnitude of the spell the Vile One cast, Zraylaunyth and Maergalyys stood shoulder to shoulder as they raised their hands in opposition. Speaking as one, they lifted an arc of Light over the battlefield that glimmered into and against the darkness. Where the radiance of the Light fell like a bright shadow, the potency of the Praetors contemptible magic was contradicted; yet even more amazingly was the impact the arc had upon the storm. As it pressed upward into the tumult, it penetrated the ferocity of the blizzard and reversed the effects of its wrath, creating bright openings in the winter squall and quieting the moaning gales. As the intensity of the storm diminished and the blanketing snow transformed into fluttering flurries, Uxvagchtr turned to face them balefully.

Without his headdress of magic, the spell he had cast held him at the limits of his abilities, but his cruelty and hatred knew no bounds. He had other means of shifting the advantage back to his side. Looking down onto his golden toy, he pressed the heel of his boot into Evondair's throat and glared at the pair of Light-wielding Fey, daring them to risk his life by continuing.

"Desist, *Mercazenandrach,* or I'll inflict such pain upon him your immortal memory will forever be harrowed by the slightest thought of it!" As he spoke, he lowered one hand to direct the crimson sparks of his malicious magic onto the Healer, his lips twisting into a sneer when Evondair screamed in unbearable misery. The Elders turned to look deeply into each other's eyes, wordlessly communicating between themselves before they reached outward to press their resolve into the tortured thoughts of their friend.

"Forgive us, brave Evondair. There are so many in danger. We cannot submit to his evil."

Although the tormenting flood of dark magic was more than he could bear, Evondair understood. Around him, cries of pain melded with screams of terror. Friends lay in ominous silence among similarly quiet enemies while those who remained pushed themselves beyond the limits of their strength in a futile attempt to persevere. His beloved lay slain and beyond his reach. Veryth, his brother in spirit if not in blood, lay face down in the snow, drained of his strength through his selfless outpouring to those he supported. Mardan writhed under the relentless torment of the Spell of Inflicted Pain. Gairynzvl had not stirred since his self-sacrificing plummet from the skies, nor had Nunvaret who lay in a crumpled heap not far from the Liberator he had chosen to trust. From the distant woodland, Evondair could hear the noise of conflict and the wails of the bereft. The anguish of hatred was carried upon the currents of the quieting blizzard, reaching in every direction to settle upon all of them like frozen tears.

It was in that moment, as unyielding agony, riotous loathing and seething discontent pierced his body like daggers again and again; as cries made the wind wail and his fellow Fey clashed in interminable violence that Evondair understood to the fullest extent the poignancy of the thought that had plagued him for so very long.

How do we attain peace if we do not become peace?

Fear produced fear. Anger created anger. Hatred bred contempt and cruelty prompted retaliation. What force could possibly stand against the infiltration of mind-numbing negativity that plunged them all into a deep well of darkness?

Tears filled his eyes as he stared upward into the scarlet haze stifling his life from him. Uxvagchtr sneered contemptuously as the energy he had stolen from his victims in the form of their own life-blood filled him with power that he used to strengthen the spell of wrath and fury he cast outward. Glaring down at the golden-haired, beautiful Fey he desired and despised with equal passion, he concentrated the dark magic he poured over him and smiled callously when Evondair's screams doubled in intensity.

Silence shifted in his mind like a tidal wave. Darkness swirled thickly at the corners of his essence and Evondair knew they would be eternally lasting if he submitted to them. Gritting his teeth against the ruthless magic brutalizing every inch of body and the deepest recesses of his mind, he returned the Vile One's stare. Upon his back with his wings curled inward in an irrefutable display of pain, he drew a shuddering breath. Uxvagchtr stooped to brush his hand over the Healers cheek and to allow it to wander across his body with sadistic tenderness; the dark magic he controlled twisting into thunderous desire that made Evondair cringe away from him and groan prodigiously.

"You endure so deliciously, Golden One. Pity you have forced me to treat you so harshly. I'd have enjoyed lavishing you with sensations you've never experienced before, and for untold spans of time, just to watch you suffer." Such a declaration was more than Evondair could bear. Swallowing hard against the rising sickness that sought to escape him, he stared up at the pure evil staring lustfully upon him. In spite of the Vile One's depravity, he knew the only course available to him.

Wielding a magic Evil could never comprehend, Evondair turned his head against the weight of the Imperial Praetors boot and spoke in a rasping tone the Dark One could hear, but could never understand.

"I Forgive you."

Chapter Twenty-Five

Blood crimson stared unblinking into gemlike viridian. As the Darkest of the Dark sought to comprehend what he had just heard, his full attention was draw away from the hostility he was generating and the callous magic he had created sputtered like a torch guttering into darkness. "You *forgive* me?" He repeated incredulously, unable to fathom such a preposterous overture. Glaring down at the Healer, he shook his head, thoroughly confounded, but his confusion only served to enrage him further. Snatching Evondair viciously by his hair, Uxvagchtr bared his teeth in a rancorous threat.

"Insolent *Drachalych*! You *forgive me?*" he hissed venomously. Straining to lean forward and sink his teeth into the beauty that tempted and vexed him, he was even more perplexed when he discovered he could not. Although he snarled furiously and strained against the unseen force holding him back, he was incapable of inflicting any further harm.

At Evondair's benevolent offer, the glimmering Light spreading all around them reached downward to oppose Uxvagchtr's darkness. Recoiling from his unwelcome touch, Evondair sought once again to escape the Dark One, but when he realized how the Light had incapacitated him, he closed his eyes and breathed a deep sigh. The torturous waves of pain, hatred, and intolerable desire lashing his mind and body slowly ebbed. Then, he opened his eyes and returned the Praetors venomous glare with tears filling his eyes. "Yes, I Forgive you."

Uxvagchtr growled savagely at him, laboring to bend closer and impale him with his teeth once again, but, in spite of his vindictive intent, he could not move. Cautiously, Evondair raised one hand and wrenched himself free from the Vile One's grasp. Uxvagchtr hissed at him with furious ire, but could not force him to stop. Without removing his other hand from covering his still bleeding wound, Evondair pulled himself away from the Leader of the Reviled and struggled to his feet. "I shall not return your violence, Praetor. Neither shall your ranks of victimized Legionnaires who are, even now, breaking from your domination to stand in the Light." Evondair looked past Uxvagchtr at those upon the battlefield.

All around them the wintry tempest calmed at the touch of the radiant Light melting into its core. The arc created by the Elders revealed bright blue skies where there had been roiling gray storm clouds and its seeking cold was replaced by a soothingly warm caress from the winter sun. Legionnaires and Demonfey paused to gaze up into the clearing sky with protected gazes while Fey of the Light breathed cautiously with a renewed sense of hope. They stood beneath the growing radiance of the Light as it spread, penetrating the weakening storm and filling the clearing with a life-giving, revitalizing luster. As this took place, the Elders continued their powerful incantation, speaking in a monotone, droning Celebrae that empowered the arc of illumination stretching across the sky and everywhere that brilliant Light touch, inconceivable magic was conveyed.

Where its glittering radiance fell, the dark magic of the Praetor was scattered. The Spell of Inflicted Pain he had cast with ruthless determination dwindled, leaving Mardan lying face down in the snow, gasping and moaning in euphoric release while Veryth slowly gathered his feet beneath him and stood. Bewitched wolfkind no longer craved Fey blood and raced, crying and whimpering, into the sheltering embrace of their forest home and the screams from the Lyysharan village hushed.

Uxvagchtr straightened and gazed about as well, shrinking from the sparkling morning sunshine while he took in the unimaginable scene.

Legionnaires stood in scattered groups breathing freely for the first time in far too many years and, although the brilliance of bright, clear Light had been fatal to them previously, they were now somehow able to withstand its shimmering unharmed. Some shrank in haste towards the mountain, terrified, but they were pursued by Fey Guards who impeded their retreat. They did not pose any additional violence. Instead, they invited the Legionnaires to remain in the Light, accepted and reunited with their brethren, and many willingly flung their armaments away with loathing.

"*Gaar lvanath chrisyndven hrall!*" Uxvagchtr growled at those Demonfey standing close at hand, causing several to thump their weapons against their chests in habitually loyal service to their leader. Others glared back at the Praetor with barely contained hatred burning in their crimson eyes, throwing down their weapons vehemently and turning to offer themselves to the mercy of the nearest Fey of the Light. Such defiance was more than the Imperial Praetor could tolerate and he hissed with violent rage.

In any other situation, he would have struck them down with any number of cruel spells designed to inflict vast quantities of pain and suffering, but, despite how infuriating their defiance was, he found the brilliance of lustrous Light streaming across the battlefield even less tolerable. Cursing in viperous Dlalth, he stalked towards the place where Kaylyya had fallen and snatched up the pieces of his magical diadem before he growled an incantation that instantly reopened the dark, spiraling portal through which he had originally crossed.

"He seeks to escape!" Bryth shouted to a group of Fey Guards who stood closer to the Dlalth Overlord than he, but the Elders instantly lowered their hands and spoke in a unified voice that echoed across the vale in spite of the fact that there were just two of them.

"Do not oppose his return into the darkness!"

Unwilling to disobey so compelling a command from their leaders, the Fey Guards lowered their weapons and watched as the seething portal swirled faster, then faster, sucking at the brightness filling the clearing. Pointing into the slurking gateway, the Praetor ordered his few remaining followers to cross and then growled at the Elders vindictively. "Your impertinent magic won't hold sway, *Mercazenandrach.*"

Shaking their heads in unison, the Elders turned to look purposely at Evondair. "It was not our magic, *Drynalynvagcht*, that opposed your darkness."

The Praetors blood-hued glare fell once again upon the Healer as he sought to comprehend what the Elders implied, but he could not. "My darkness will ever be present, just as it's always been. Your insolence can't contain it."

Zraylaunyth took a menacing step forward, raising his hands in a brazen threat. "Perhaps not, but the forgiveness he offered has nullified the potency of your darkness. There is no magic within the realms of Light or Dark that holds greater power."

Uxvagchtr glared at Evondair with seething hatred, growling as he took a single step into the portal and his voice faded into the remote distance even as he spoke an intractable warning. "Keep the Light close, Golden One, and dare not forget lest, in that moment when your wariness falters, this Darkness consumes you."

Evondair watched as evil faded from view, the chill bite of winter seeming to diminish with his departure and the full radiance of the sun, freed at last from the winter tempest, smiled warmly on all of them. The luminous sunlight, however, could scarcely soothe the pain that lay scattered so close at hand and a poignant hush fell upon the vale as those who remained to breathe stood in remorseful observance of those who did not. Legionnaires and Fey of the Light had fallen in equal numbers, their blood uniformly staining the snow and the loss was felt grievously by those who knew them. Tendrils of the breeze reached to caress the cheeks of those who mourned in silence even as tentative birdsong lifted from the embrace of evergreen boughs heavy-laden with snow. The soft sound wrenched at Evondair's heart and he turned, stumbling towards the place where his love lay as hushed as the cerulean sky.

She lay in subdued stillness, silent of all the music that had ever lilted from her essence. Falling to his knees, he doubled over to place his cheek next to hers, embracing her with his free arm and spreading his wings wide upon the snow as a grief he had never known consumed his being.

"*Jshynjshar ovaerydd,*" he whispered to her softly, rocking in distress as his mind emptied of cognizant thought and heart-wrenching emotion overwhelmed him.

Yet, in the chaos of his agony a persistent thought repeated in his mind.

Do you truly forgive him? Even for this?

Even for this?

Lifting his head to gaze down at the pale cheeks and closed eyes of his Beloved, his heart hammered as if he had just flown from the distant shores of Lundoon.

"Even for this?" he asked himself aloud, wholly uncertain.

As he gazed upon her, he became aware of many watchful stares and raised his head to search the battlefield, half annoyed and half desperate for the comfort of a friend. His searching viridian gaze met bright cerulean before Mardan closed his eyes and lowered his head as he folded his wings forward in lamentation for his friend's loss. Clear, sparkling emeraldine penetrated the anguish in his stare as his gaze met Veryth's as the Healer moved closer to offer aid and comfort. Then, the scrutiny of his tear-filled viridian locked with dappled, crystal-cerulean as bright and clear as the winter sky.

Zraylaunyth's voice filled his mind. "*Even for this?*"

He looked down once again upon his love. He missed her so painfully. He felt incapable of drawing his next breath. Anger pitched in his essence like a violent sea crashing against the rocks of his soul's foundation and wreaking havoc with his harmonious nature. Even as his tears fell, he nodded.

"Even for this," he whispered apologetically, moving his hand to caress the silken blond hair that had first captured his attention. "Forgive *me,* Beloved, though I shall miss you with each breath until my very last. Even for this."

The End

Epilogue

He did not see the brilliant glimmer of radiant Light that fell from the sky.

In his desperate grief, he saw nothing and felt only unbearable anguish as a roaring emptiness engulfed him. He was not aware of the Power his pure act of Forgiveness had unleashed, neither was he conscious of the magic that sparkled around him like glittering snowflakes dancing upon the sunny breeze.

His heart seemed to split in two; then in twain once again, and yet again, shattering into pieces too infinitesimal to number as a wail of absolute dejectedness burgeoned in his core. Baring his teeth at the pain, he struggled to contain his misery and shook his head against the soft touch of a hand upon his shoulder. "Leave me in peace, Veryth," he growled with irritation, unwilling to allow the Healer to tend his injuries. Silence answered him, but the touch persisted. Annoyed beyond rationale, he flexed his wings in a furious backward motion, attempting to fling the Healer away in anger, but his wings met no resistance. Undeterred, he hissed petulantly. "I said leave me be, Veryth!"

"Veryth?" The soft sound, though less than a whisper, infused his agony with a grace he had only experienced once before and his eyes snapped open with utter astonishment.

Water-blurred viridian melted into snowy jade and everything he understood dissolved into sweet, ethereal music as he wrapped himself around his Beloved, heart, body, and soul. For that moment, the only thing that mattered was the touch of their hands, the warm press of their lips, and the soul-infusing embrace they shared.

* * *

Amid the quiet environs of the Temple Healing Wards, Evondair finally came back to himself. Lying beside the shefey he loved and in the company of many of his friends who, like he, were recovering from their injuries, he looked up into the dappled crystal-cerulean gaze of Zraylaunyth with profound confusion.

He didn't need to ask. The answer came, before he ever spoke it. *"Sacrifice will Liberate when Hope falls into Shadow."*

Evondair shook his head. "I sacrificed nothing."

Zraylaunyth turned to look at Gairynzvl who stood beside him with one wing fully bandaged to repair its brokenness. Several other bindings adorned his pale complexion. "You sacrificed more than any of us, Healer. More than I ever could have done."

Turning to gaze beside him at Kaylyya who lay quietly sleeping, nestled into his embrace and covered by his wing furled round her tenderly, he blinked slowly.

"No magic within the Light or the Darkness holds Dominion when Love Forgives." Mardan recited a passage of Ancient Texts they all had been taught since they were childlings, yet none had fully comprehended.

Until that moment.

Zraylaunyth nodded. "You, my brother, are a True Healer, for you healed wounds with a magic beyond the skills of any."

He had no answer, but needed none. They all knew the youngest of the Elders spoke the truth. Around them was all the evidence that ever could be required. Dark Ones filled the Healing Wards, their many wounds being tended, whether physical or emotional. So many had chosen to return into the Light that their numbers overwhelmed the capacity of the Wards. Cots stretched into neighboring rooms that were typically reserved for study and across the corridor into the library. Pallets of blankets and pillows were even laid upon the marble floors. Several Demonfey spoke quietly with Captain Varka and Dravahl, lingering near the rapturous warmth of the massive Healing Ward hearth while discussing plans to return into the darkness of the Uunglarda to rescue as many as they could reach.

In the corridor, giggles and squeals of younglings played among the shadowy candlelight. Bright laughter and the distinctive, beguiling language of Vrynnyth Ghal rang into the quiet precincts of the Temple as Rehstaed caught Lorszan in his arms and swept him up into the air above his head before drawing him close to kiss the boyfey repeatedly in a lavish rain of fatherly affection. Across the chamber in guarded silence, the crimson gazes of several less certain Demonfey and Legionnaires watched those around them hesitantly.

"Will they, too, find healing through this magic?" Evondair asked no one in particular, unprepared when Nunvaret stepped from behind Mardan and nodded. Dressed no longer in blood-crimson, but soft fabrics and silks he had long been forced to relinquish, he smiled knowingly.

"They already have. They simply don't understand it yet."

Gairynzvl turned to look at the Demonfey he remembered only too well and smiled from one corner of his mouth. "They will." He might have elaborated, but at that moment Ayla alighted by the doorway and gazed into the dimly lighted interior, the soft touch of her thoughts mingling with his and his attention was immediately distracted.

"You have been sorely missed, Fierce One. If I were you, I would linger in the Wards no longer." Bryth, who bore more bandages upon his person than the former Dark One whom he addressed, prompted his friend to action, pushing him away from the group surrounding Evondair's bed. Not loath to go, Gairynzvl inclined his head respectfully to his friends and strode purposefully towards the shefey waiting for him.

Their thoughts touched in tenderness, then their hands, the contact soothing the loneliness both had felt in the other's absence. "*Jshyn-jshar ovaerydd,*" he whispered softly to her in the drawn-out hush of his thoughts and she smiled, embracing him passionately. Wrapping his arms about her, he touched her lightly with the delicate caress of his wings, lowered his head to kiss her, and lost himself in her golden aura.

* * *

Deep in the murky gloom of Vrasduuhl, the fortress of Hvyyr-bachvra glowed with sulfurous torchlight as screams echoed from its heartless core. The shadows cringed in response to the sounds as a re-fraction of silvery light glimmered briefly in the eerie glow. No other sounds announced its presence, but the wrinkle of light moved with purpose towards the towering gates of the fortress, lingering at the base of the monstrous edifice before gliding upward along its black-ened walls. At one of the side streets, a shadowy figure wearing crim-son goggles followed its progress along the wall until it reached the pinnacle of its passage. When it did, a horrifying wail serrated through the darkness and the goggled figure looked towards the tower of the fortress even as the undulation of silver and shadow paused before dipping towards the inner portal, following a unit of Demonfey into the interior before it slipped silently into the gloom. Unheeded, the noiseless apparition glided along the dim corridors lighted by sputter-ing torches of sulfur that filled the entire stronghold with a stomach-churning reek until it came to a chamber guarded by twelve monstrous Fey clothed in black leather. They bore weapons unique to the Prae-tor's ranks: long spears with curved, serrated blades on one side and heavily barbed bludgeons on the other.

At one end of this chamber, a massive chair of silver-inlaid obsid-ian stood upon a raised dais. Upon it, Uxvagchtr lounged in brooding silence, watching as a lifeless body was dragged from before him and a fresh victim was shoved from the shadows and flung to the floor to await the Praetor's sadistic pleasure. Before he spoke, however, the silvery wrinkle of light darted from the shadowy corridor and disap-peared behind him.

Raising his head sharply, Uxvagchtr stared with astonishment as, from out of nowhere, a gentle hand caressed his ink-embellished cheek. Without Uulyyaegrahl, his ornate, magic-enhancing headdress, he had not been aware of the silvery apparition's approach and sat in enthralled silence as the unseen being touched him teasingly and whispered softly in his pointed ear.

"Wouldn't you rather be plotting your revenge, Mighty Praetor?"

Dear reader,

We hope you enjoyed reading *Breaking Into The Light*. Please take a moment to leave a review, even if it's a short one. Your opinion is important to us.

Discover more books by Cynthia A. Morgan at
https://www.nextchapter.pub/authors/cynthia-morgan-fantasy-author

Want to know when one of our books is free or discounted? Join the newsletter at http://eepurl.com/bqqB3H

Best regards,
Cynthia A. Morgan and the Next Chapter Team

You could also like:

The Eternals by Richard M. Ankers

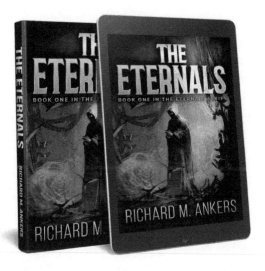

To read the first chapter for free, please head to:
https://www.nextchapter.pub/books/the-eternals-gothic-fantasy

About the Author

Cynthia A. Morgan is the creator of the mythical realm of Jyndari and author of the epic fantasy "Dark Fey Trilogy", which draws the reader into a mystical realm of primordial forests, magic and the lives of Light-loving and Darkness-revering Feykind. Compared to a fantasy version of a play by Shakespeare, "Dark Fey" is a brutally beautiful story of Love, Hope, and finding Purpose and Peace in the Darkness. It is a tale of Perseverance and Sacrifice with an intense dark fantasy edge.

Morgan is also the author of the popular poetry blog "Booknvolume" where her rapidly increasing following is regularly treated to Morgan's own brand of poetry, English Sonnets, and musings about life. She is a current member of the Poetry Society of America, Independent Author Network, has had poetry published on numerous websites and is rapidly becoming an author to keep your eye on.

Some of her other interests include a deep love of animals and the environment. She is inspired by music and art, as well as fine acting; is frequently heard laughing; finds the mysteries of ancient times, the paranormal and the possibilities of life elsewhere in the cosmos intriguing, and Believes in the power of Love, Hope, Peace and Joy; all of which is reflected in her lyrically elegant writing style.

You can find Morgan through social media in the following places:

Blog: http://www.booknvolume.com/
Website: http://allthingsdarkfey.wix.com/feyandmusings
Facebook: https://www.facebook.com/booknvolume
Twitter: https://twitter.com/MorganBC728
& https://twitter.com/DarkFeyMorgan29
Pinterest: https://www.pinterest.com/cynthey728

Breaking Into The Light
ISBN: 978-4-86750-592-2

Published by
Next Chapter
1-60-20 Minami-Otsuka
170-0005 Toshima-Ku, Tokyo
+818035793528
10th June 2021

Lightning Source UK Ltd.
Milton Keynes UK
UKHW010638060721
386714UK00001B/263